George's
Hurricanes

K.W. Garlick

SR
Stillwater
River

Visit our website at **www.StillwaterPress.com** for more information.

First Stillwater River Publications Edition

ISBN-10: 1-946-30033-0
ISBN-13: 978-1-946-30033-1

Library of Congress Control Number: 2017958046

1 2 3 4 5 6 7 8 9 10
Written by K.W. Garlick
Published by Stillwater River Publications, Glocester, RI, USA.

Dedication

This book is dedicated to people of Prudence Island,
a very special, caring and supportive community.

Narragansett Bay

Prudence

Stone dock

Sa

T Wharf

US Navy

Park

School House

Bristol Colony

Coffee Shop

Chalmers Store

← Sand Point

Po

← Ho

PRUDENCE IS

Pine
Hill

Beach

Potter's Cove

Providence Point

Nag
creek

Old Grave yard

ffice

Warnerville

W

S — N

E

stead

"Prudence" Ferry

Bristol →

AND

R.I.

People said he was crazy. They even had their own special name for him, Crazy George. Anyone would have to be crazy after what he had experienced. But George wasn't crazy; in fact, he was quite smart, maybe not educated but highly intelligent. And he would devise, with a little help, an elaborate plan to exact revenge on those who had contributed to the death of his entire family. Oh, he was crazy all right, crazy like a fox.

Prologue

The winds had started to pick up in the midafternoon hours, and by early evening they were near hurricane strength. She sat in her living room and watched the progression of the storm. Sunset had come and gone and the sky was turning gray.

Then she saw the movement.

It was a figure, a man she thought. He was drenched, soaking wet, and struggling against the winds that were pushing at him. Had he come from the beach? She thought so, but wasn't sure. He was walking straight to her house.

As he got closer – she was sure it was a man now – his hair and clothing appeared to be that of someone who had spent the last eight hours in the bay. He seemed to be in distress: one foot dragged oddly behind him, his hands fluttered like birds. He stumbled up onto her side porch and to her door.

Carolyn moved quickly to help the troubled man. As she rose, the door flew violently open and in lashed the rain and the wind. There, on the threshold, loomed the figure framed by the storm-lit night. She screamed — and then she recognized him. Oh, my god!

Those would be her last words and the dripping, disheveled figure the last person she would ever see. Then he was on her,

1

knocking her back into the kitchen and onto the floor, as furniture and dishes tumbled. She sprang to her feet. Fear clouded every conscious thought except the need to escape. Quickly standing, she threw herself at her attacker, but a powerful left hand found the right side of her face. A brilliant flash of light, then a sudden complete darkness were attached to that human appendage.

The creature from the turbulent bay stood above her, his clothes ragged and waterlogged, his eyes cold and his expression empty. When he spoke, the words echoed dully, like hailstones on a tin roof.

"You can thank your husband for this. You will be seeing him very shortly."

And then he was gone, out the shattered kitchen door, across the deck and down the stairs, back to where he came from.

BOOK I

Chapter 1

The storm had pushed the body up onto the shore.

It was lying face down on a small stretch of sandy beach in Bristol Colony, a close-knit island community facing southeast into Narragansett Bay. The island, named *Prudence* by its founder, the Puritan outcast Roger Williams, had since the early 1900s been home to generations of families who enjoyed the no-frills getaway the island offered: no restaurants, no bars, and a limited summertime ferry schedule. It drew a special breed: only those comfortable with sharing their tools, time, and lives with their neighbors seemed to thrive, and it was often said, among themselves and to outsiders both, that there was no in-between. You either loved Prudence or you hated it.

Matt Sears discovered the body after walking down to check on his sailboat, a twenty-four-foot Indian, his pride and joy for the last Thirty years. Gale-force winds had been predicted as Hurricane Carol struck a glancing blow to lower Narragansett Bay and southern Rhode Island, but the storm had tracked farther north than expected and now stronger winds, hurricane force, battered the local shoreline. It was the summer of 1954 and the tide had just come in.

Matt hoped that he had secured his boat sufficiently. To minimize the violent pitching it would likely suffer, he had attached a stern drag and added an extra seventy-five feet of hemp to his mooring line. But as he came down the beach he saw immediately that it had not been enough. The boat had torn free of its mooring and lay pushed up on the beach. The winds had died down to near gale-force, but large breakers still pounded on the shattered hull.

Trying to get a closer look at his vessel, Matt pushed himself against the blowing wind and rain and awkwardly tiptoed his way through a beach strewn with debris. A blue swatch of cloth and a long tangle of brown hair half-entombed in beach sand galvanized him as he glimpsed it. His heart pounded in his chest at the thought that it might be a body. Several tentative steps brought him closer to the prone form, partially buried by sand the wind had pushed up against it. He dropped to his knees. Reaching out with his right hand, he stripped away the beach from the elevated mound. A sickly bluish foot emerged, weathered and badly scraped. Matt abruptly ceased his uncovering. The hope he had harbored — that it was something else, a dead seal, a mass of fisherman's leads and seaweed — vanished. Blinking rapidly, his vision faded for a moment. When it returned, he took in the foot again, and with sudden awful clarity noticed the toes, curled in upon themselves like cocktail shrimp, still sporting spots of bright crimson nail polish. With a scramble, sand flying, he pushed himself up, trying mightily to retain his early morning breakfast.

Shaking, his face a wan grey, he pulled his short frame to standing and slowly got control of himself. He looked out onto the bay, out where the body had obviously come from, and the wind and rain stung his face. He wondered how the poor woman had found her way to this body of water and to this beach. His hands shook and his mouth was suddenly dry, despite the rain-soaked scene.

Matt's gruesome discovery changed his focus entirely. At once his sailboat became secondary. Bracing himself against the buffeting winds, with his yellow rain hood flapping, he reached into his yellow rain slicker and removed his handkerchief and wiped his rain-splattered glasses. He quickly searched the shoreline and found a thick stick within the debris. With a silent plea of forgiveness, he tenderly poked the back ribs of the poor soul.

There was no movement. He hadn't really expected any, but it was amazing how quickly his concern had changed into simple objectivity. Matt could have been poking a hundred-pound sack of flour. The person was dead, and the dead are not concerned with indignity or pain. They only serve to lessen the awkwardness the living must suffer when dealing with them.

He hurried back to his Jeep. The bulky waders, the rain suit he wore, and the bursitis in his right hip hindered his movements. He drove his '45 Willys Jeep as quickly as he could, up Aldrich Hill and down Broadway. Along the long sloping roadway, large elms, maples, and oaks that normally provided haven from a piercing summer's sun pitched violently back and forth. Hundreds of their tiny green sun shades were torn free with each powerful gust and moved sporadically, like a swarm of migrating sparrows in early fall. Finally arriving at Brad Wheeler's house, Matt pulled into the narrow, extended dirt driveway. He hurried from his parked Jeep, making no attempt to avoid the deep puddles that seemed to be everywhere. He knocked as hard as he could on the door and nervously shifted his weight back and forth on his feet. Brad, the only police officer on the island, finally opened the door.

"Hey Matt, what brings you here on a day like this?" Brad said, the curiosity and concern clear on his face. "Come on in," he urged, but Matt shook his head fervently. Brad's wife Milly came in from the kitchen, a dishtowel in her hands. She regarded Matt with the same curiosity as her husband.

"You gotta come quick, there's a body, a dead body on the Colony Beach." He stumbled over his words, out of breath and very agitated. "Found it near my boat, didn't make it through the storm. Not much left of it. The boat I mean."

"Okay Matt, try and relax. Do you know who it is? Is it a man or a woman? How long do you think it's been there?"

"I-I don't know who it is. Pretty sure it's a woman, short but a little heavy. I got no idea how long it's been there. Wasn't the best day for walking the beach, if you know what I mean. You gotta come quick."

"All right Matt, I'll be right there," Brad said, taking a step back, scratching the back of his head, trying to think it through. "I need to call my brother, and we'll need to get something to put the body in. I'll also need to call Portsmouth and get them involved. You get back to the beach and stay by the body. Don't let anybody near it. Give me about forty-five minutes. Sorry about your boat. Thanks, Matt, thanks a lot."

Matt turned and trudged back to his Willys. He had delivered the message — now it was someone else's problem. "Hope he gets there in forty-five like he said, don't want to stand next to that thing all day," he said to nobody.

* * *

Brad watched Matt Sears as he navigated his Jeep through the wind and rain. His wife, by his side, held his arm. She searched his face for his thoughts.

"Better call Morris," Brad said to her, and they walked together to the wall phone in the kitchen. "Hope he hasn't been hitting the jug."

"Probably has, you know he drinks when he has down time," Milly said. "Always does."

Brad's brow furrowed, but he knew she was right. He picked up the receiver and dialed Morris's number by heart. "Hey Morris, you up for playing detective and coroner?" Brad said into the shiny black phone when the line connected at the other end.

"What the hell are you talking about?" said an impatient, almost angry voice.

He didn't sound too bad. It was still early, Brad observed; another couple of hours and Morris would have been a lost cause.

"Body washed up down at the Colony. We need to get the panel truck."

"What?" Morris said, suddenly startled by the news. "Again? This is the third time since '44. What the hell is going on? This is getting to be a little nuts, Don't you think? Who found the body?"

"Yeah, something is amiss, that's for sure. Matt Sears found the body when he went to check on his boat. Bring that old canvas tarp we used for the others."

"I know the routine. I'll head on down there in bit. Won't touch the body until you get there. You gonna call Portsmouth now or after we get back?"

"I'm going to call Chief Anthony right now, let him know what's in the works. Don't know how soon they can get over here. Still blowing pretty good. See you in a bit. Thanks, Moe."

"Yeah, yeah. I'll send you the bill." With a click the line went dead.

Brad donned his rain slicker, kissed Milly goodbye, and hustled to his Chevy pickup truck. Wanting to know if the island's two ferry landings had survived the storm, Brad took the long route to Bristol Colony beach. The docks' condition would determine just how much help they might receive from mainland Portsmouth. Homestead Dock was severely damaged and would need significant repair work, but the Sand Point pier was still in working order. The ferry could still make its scheduled runs to the island, if only to Sand Point. Chief Anthony and the state coroner would be out first thing tomorrow morning to examine the body and move it to the state medical examiner's lab.

The thoughts swirled in his head as he drove, another body, another murder? It was almost too much to take in. How could this many murders occur on such a sleepy little island?

Brad Wheeler had moved to Prudence Island with his wife Milly in May of 1930. They had lived in Seekonk, Massachusetts, prior to that. Born in October of 1905, he was the youngest of two boys. He and his wife Milly had seen the ad in the *Sunday Providence Journal* that farm acreage was for sale on Prudence. They had been looking for a quiet place to start their homestead, a place away from the turmoil of an encroaching humanity. A safe place free of distractions, where they could raise a family and instill in them the traditions and values they held so dear. They wanted, also, to place their passions into farming, harvest from the soil what their sweat and toil were meant to yield. The young couple were not intimidated by hard work; they had both been raised in families that stressed it.

Something about the ad and its description of the property struck a chord with them. When they saw on a map the island nestled in Narragansett Bay, intimately close to its neighbors but far enough removed that any unplanned intrusions would be a remote possibility, it pulled them in like iron to a lodestone. They made arrangements to meet with the seller's agent on the island and scheduled their visit. Brad's older brother Morris and his wife Mary also expressed a keen interest in this potential pilgrimage. A fresh start might be good for them, too. Morris had returned from a war in Europe that had eternally injured his emotional well-being. The idea of escaping to a new locale, where his social shortcomings would not be magnified, intrigued him. Mary quietly hoped the relocation might save their marriage, which had grown increasingly rocky in the years after the war.

They made the trip to the island one frosty morning in late March. A ride in the intimate passenger cabin of the *Prudence,* the small ferry that serviced the island, provided a glimpse of the island's character and the people who lived there. Friendly, warm, simply-dressed people engaged them in sincere conversation without probing while the ferry slowly chugged its way south, farther into Narragansett Bay. The four hajjis felt welcomed.

Margaret Church met them at the ferry when it docked at the Homestead landing. A tall, thin woman in her early sixties, she represented a family that in some convoluted way had connections in New York City. Those contacts had suffered disastrous financial repercussions during the market crash of 1929. In between puffs on her cigarette, she told the foursome that her client was very motivated to sell — any reasonable offer would probably seal the deal.

* * *

They squeezed into Margaret's tarnished old Ford and with Coco, her brown standard poodle, perched between Margaret and Brad in the front seat, they bounced along hard-packed dirt roads, never once encountering another car in the two-mile trip to their destination. Entering the property through rugged flat stone pillars, they coasted to a stop in front of a plain-looking garrison with two separate entrances at either end. Three brick chimneys poked through an asphalt-shingled roof, and the farmhouse was painted white with black shutters. A stretch of outbuildings with a lofted barn in the middle was only a few steps off to their left.

"It sure looks like people recently lived here," commented Brad.

"Sure did," Mrs. Church affirmed Brad's observation. "The Guertins lived here, Francis and Irene, with their daughter and son-in-law. Quiet people, kept to themselves, but then again that describes just about anybody on this island. We all thought they owned the property and found out the hard way that they were renting. They were devastated when they learned they had to vacate the property. Had to leave in a hurry, too." Her cigarette bounced on her lower lip as she told her tale, smoke curling around her short gray hair.

Brad and his brother walked through the barn and outbuildings; all the farming equipment and tools of just about every discipline had remained on the property and were included in the sale price. The brothers then walked the property while their wives and Margaret inspected the farmhouse. Only about a third of the homestead's twenty-two acres were actually being worked.

After completing their walkabout, they met up with their wives in the big living room, which held an impressive stone hearth against the west wall. Margaret had built a strong warming fire that chased the chillness from the chamber.

"Think I'll leave you folks here for a bit," she said, "the next ferry is not until three-thirty this afternoon. My husband turned the water on a couple of days ago, so you ladies can use the bathroom. I left some ham sandwiches and a thermos of coffee on the kitchen counter, so help yourselves. This will give you a chance to look at things a little closer and talk it over. Remember, no reasonable offer will be declined. See you at three." With that, she turned and walked out the front door, a trail of cigarette smoke following her.

The four travelers felt immediately at peace; there seemed to be an unspoken but clear and collective consensus that this would be their new home. The women saw no issues with the house and the men soon saw themselves as farmers. No obstacle could or would be entertained to prevent their relocation. They had arrived in Shangri-La.

Margaret Church returned at three and they made a discounted offer, which to their surprise was quickly accepted. They had purchased paradise for a song. They began living in their house and working their farm two short months later.

* * *

Now, wearing his police chief's hat, Brad Wheeler, with the wheels of his truck digging ruts into the gray sand of Bristol Colony Beach, found himself with yet another body on his hand. After yet another hurricane.

Morris was there, as was Matt Sears, plus four other men, all with their own unique foul weather gear on, and they huddled close together with their backs to the wind and rain, like emperor penguins on a frozen wasteland. Morris had backed the panel truck as close as he could get to the body.

Brad leaned into the gale and secured his cap before the winds took possession of it. He yelled to be heard above the fray. "Hey folks, anybody got an idea who this might be?"

"Earl Platt here is pretty sure it's Carolyn Waters," shouted Morris. "Seems she wears this dress a lot."

"She's a little heavy, too," added Earl.

Brad walked around the body. "A little strange the way her arms are folded under her. Let's have a look. Give me a hand rolling her over. We'll do it slow and easy, don't want to damage any potential evidence."

They turned the body over slowly.

"It's Carolyn Waters alright!" said Earl. "My Mary is going to be real upset by this. How the hell did she end up here? Why are her hands bound together?"

Brad looked at Earl, his spirit immediately wounded. "I have no idea," he said. "This is just awful. My lord, why would anyone do such a thing?"

* * *

The Wheelers worked their farm for the next two years. More equipment was purchased and livestock brought in. Their senses resonated daily with the sounds, smells, and images of the farm they had only previously imagined. The sisters-in-law rose to the challenge of maintaining a productive garden of carrots, green and yellow beans, broccoli, tomatoes. and other vegetables. Plentiful and fresh produce soon began to grace their kitchen's table. Glass preserving jars were the completing step in the horticultural process. The soft, tender hands of the fairer sex soon turned rough and chapped. Engagement rings that could not tolerate the demands of working Mother Earth were soon removed and placed in a teacup in the back of the dining room hutch, only rarely retrieved for special events. Brad and Morris planted and worked the large fields of corn, both golden and silver queen. Smaller fields of potatoes, cabbage, and cauliflower were seeded and tended to.

But their happy life slowly began to unravel. Moe Wheeler's drinking began its slow thievery of hopeful and happy days. Life can't be built on a foundation woven with a million tiny fractures. A crippling anxiety from a horrific European war had Morris seeking the calming effects of alcohol as a daily regimen. Its continuous use had sealed his fate years ago, and he was oblivious to the self-destructive path he was on. But it was soon clear that a small rift had begun to force itself between the couples. Morris's drinking had escalated to the point where he became insulting toward his wife. Brad's wife Milly could no longer live in the same house with her brother-in-law; she would not be a witness to the mistreatment of her sister-in-law.

Brad also gradually found himself shouldering more and more of the farming responsibilities. His brother began to sleep late, usually after a night of drinking, and would be irritable for most of the remaining day. Simple farm decisions turned into involved and draining, sometimes heated, discussions. Morris's participation was no longer an equitable trade-off. It became too much. It was time to leave Shangri-La.

Brad and Milly built their new home about a half-mile north of the farm and moved before the damage to the family equilibrium became irreparable. But Brad knew he would need to travel a different path, a trail separate from his brother.

Prudence Island is part of the township of Portsmouth, Rhode Island, and Brad noticed that the town was struggling with a number of its responsibilities on the island. There was spotty road maintenance, no police presence, and a volunteer fire department and ambulance service hampered by old, poorly maintained equipment and conveyances. Town vehicles had to be barged over to the island and stored in a remote area, where a small work and storage shack was built. There the vehicles sat outside in the elements year-round, until town workers came for scheduled maintenance visits. These municipal trucks, when brought to the island, had long outlived their usefulness in Portsmouth. Now on the island, the vehicles all suffered from neglect and lack of use. Town workers, when they came to the island, often found them difficult to start, and they were always breaking down. Routinely they would report back to their supervisor that their job could not be completed — or sometimes not even started.

There were grumblings among the residents of the island and soon a collective accord, that an equitable return on their tax dollar was not forthcoming. Brad saw his opportunity and quickly pointed out the inequities to the Portsmouth town administrator and town council. Before the officials could offer their well-rehearsed response and excuses, Brad provided an intriguing solution to the developing dilemma. It seemed to Brad that one man with the right collection of

14

skills could fill a role long needed on Prudence, and he was convinced it could be done frugally. When the job responsibilities were clearly defined and it was certain that the town budget could support this new path, the town aldermen quickly accepted Brad Wheeler's proposal.

Brad became the man with many hats and was soon the island's police chief, fire chief, road foreman, and was responsible for all safety and rescue efforts. Town officials were comfortable with him. He was personable, competent, and the multi-role position was a welcome new change for him. There would be resentment, pushback — his brother would no doubt feel abandoned. But Brad had witnessed his brother's slow withdrawal from his farming obligations and could no longer be a passenger on that sinking ship.

* * *

Brad and Morris wrapped Carolyn Waters' body in the canvas tarp and placed it in the big chest freezer they kept in the barn. The freezer hadn't worked in years but it was airtight. They scattered plenty of ice over the corpse and closed the cover.

"Thanks for the help, Moe. I'm gonna take a ride up to the Waters place and check it out."

"You want me to go with you?"

"No, I'm all set for now. But you can call a few people along Narragansett, see if anybody saw anything. No sense in trying to keep this thing under wraps. The whole island knows all about it by now, especially considering the way Earl's wife loves to gossip."

"Suits me fine. I'll make some calls just as soon as I spend a few minutes with my jug. I'll let you know if I hear anything. But this ain't no coincidence. Although Carolyn's hands were tied up and I don't think the other ones were. I'll bet she was alive when she ended up in the bay. This one don't smell right. We got some pervert running around this island. Some bastard with a lot of patience. Ted Esau washed up on the beach back in '44 and Tom Tuttle in '48. That's a long time to wait. So be careful."

15

"You might be onto something, Moe," Brad replied grimly. "Looks like I'm going to be playing detective for a while. I hope Chief Anthony can lend me some assistance." He gave his brother a serious look. "Little early to be hittin' the jug, ain't it?"

"Don't start with that. I'm on my own time now. That shit gets old real fast."

Chapter 2

Brad made his way up to the Waters home, taking the back road along Bay Avenue. It was the less-traveled road. Another bizarre death, he thought, this time a decent woman who only sought the good in others. Why would anyone want to do this, to her of all people? Bound, bludgeoned, and probably drowned like the others. Tragic was the only label for this. What the hell is going on?

Driving north on well-acquainted roads, roads driven a thousand times before, brought to him familiar memories. He remembered attending Carolyn and Freddie Waters' marriage with his Milly. They had witnessed her and Freddie grow up, fall in love, and get married. Never had they seen a happier couple — they appeared flawless in their friendship and love for each other. Carolyn and Freddie wanted to share their special day with their island friends; all and any were welcome.

Brad knew it took a certain type of person to live in a closed community like Prudence. You had to be prepared to share a lot of your life with the islanders, and you had to have an outer layer that could deflect without reflection. There were grumpy, miserable old bachelors who lived year-round on the island. They wanted nothing but to be left alone, and when they were obliged to interact with others, they only wanted to complain about those same people. Carolyn and Freddie were different. They genuinely liked the people of Prudence and made every effort to demonstrate it. Carolyn hand-crafted Christmas wreaths every year and distributed them freely at the Union Church Christmas Social on Pier Road. They had their closer circle of friends and were well-liked by just about everyone.

"Well, I guess not everyone," Brad shared with his bouncing pickup.

* * *

Carolyn Waters had heard all the warnings about the approaching hurricane. The whole island was talking about it. She didn't see the reason for all the hysteria. It was only supposed to be a glancing strike, a good blow, but nothing like the Hurricane of '38. That was a storm she would never forget. She had witnessed its destruction and seen the bodies washed ashore in its aftermath. No hurricane would ever frighten her again.

Carolyn's little cottage was in the Smith Farm section of the island and faced southeast onto Narragansett Bay. It would be the direction the winds would be coming from, a bad place to be. She had prepared as much as she could, bottling extra drinking water, making as much ice as her little freezer could handle and filling her Coleman cooler with it. She topped off her kerosene lamps.

Carolyn had grown up in Attleboro, Massachusetts in the twenties and thirties. During the summers, she visited her Aunt Liz, who owned a cottage on Prudence Island. Carolyn was an only child and her aunt always found room for her. It was where she met her husband, Fred Waters, when they were teenagers. His family had a small cottage just a short distance from her aunt, and Fred and Carolyn grew up spending carefree summers together. It seemed then as though the island was comprised of one large, happy family. Everyone knew each other. Sometimes it was annoying when it felt as if people knew too much, but those times were rare. It was the perfect way to form a beautiful and lasting relationship.

And so they became comfortable with each other. They swam and walked the sandy beaches during the day and sneaked away in the evenings for their lovemaking rendezvous. Carolyn and Freddie were in love and everyone they knew could see it. They were married in July of 1936 at the Union Church on the island. The reception was held on her aunt's front lawn overlooking Narragansett Bay. It was a perfect day.

Carolyn and Fred began their friendship on the island. All their happy memories were of their times on Prudence and all their close friends were on the island. It made sense to start their lives together there. Purchasing a small lot near the shoreline on Beach Road, they built their home in the spring of 1937. Fred became an apprentice carpenter to Peter Marrow, the resident general contractor, and when business was slow he fished the bay for scallops, quahogs, and lobsters. Their home was completed just a few months before the Hurricane of 1938 ravaged the whole area. Their little cottage somehow survived the tempest, although they did lose fifteen feet of shoreline to the storm. Carolyn remembered huddling in her small half-cellar with Fred, convinced their new home would be torn away from its foundation, but they had somehow survived. They were fortunate. There were many who did not fare as well.

Carolyn and Fred came together with the rest of Prudence Island to mourn the loss of the Caswell family. Bernard Caswell, his wife Connie, their daughter LouAnn, and their son Trevor were killed in that same deadly storm. Bernie was the lighthouse keeper at the Sand Point station and his family lived with him. A towering storm surge destroyed the rugged lighthouse in just a matter of minutes. The only family member to survive was their oldest son, George.

What made the loss especially painful was that most of the island had gone out of their way to welcome the Caswell family less than two years previous. Bernie had secured the position of lighthouse keeper and had brought his family with him. He and his wife thought the lighthouse location on the sandy strip of land that protruded out into the bay was a little precarious. But the islanders were unanimous in their belief that the lighthouse was indestructible. Peter Marrow, the contractor, and his island crew, working under federal guidelines, had labored through some very hot and humid August days to construct the navigation aid. Most of the island had witnessed its tedious progression. It seemed that they were mixing and pouring concrete for days on end. The Caswell family, lulled into a sense of security by Peter Marrow's voice of confidence, perished in a sea so violent that it destroyed their rugged home as if it were made of straw.

* * *

Brad turned off Bay Avenue and onto Beach Road. The Waters place was at the end on the left. He turned off the single lane dirt road onto a short, gravel-packed driveway. He got out of his truck and stood facing the cottage. Gale-force winds pushed at him and a loud banging noise made Brad look up at the side deck; the door on to the deck hung at a steep angle, held in place by only its bottom hinge. It swung wildly in the forceful wind and repeatedly bashed against the porch rail. Someone or something with a lot of strength or mass had to have done that. Brad knew he had to start paying attention to everything he saw; in all likelihood, this was a crime scene.

A loud crash from within the house froze him where he stood. His heart suddenly racing, he impulsively reached for his sidearm but his hand found only an empty belt. He was furious with himself. Someone was in the house and he was without his .38. Carolyn Waters had been murdered and this was now a homicide investigation. What the hell was he thinking? "Need to carry your sidearm all the time," he said to himself. "Time to get your head out of your ass."

Frustrated with himself, he reached behind the front seat and grabbed an old ball peen hammer and quietly climbed the porch stairs. He shouted into the house, "You need to come out with your hands up and come out real slow!"

From inside came a naïve, questioning voice. "Who's that, is that you, Chuck?"

Flustered, Brad answered. "Never mind who it is, just come out real slow with your hands up!"

A short elderly man with long gray hair tucked under a weathered Red Sox cap emerged from the house with his hands held shoulder high. It was Steve Gilchrist, a distant neighbor of Carolyn Waters. Bewildered, he looked at Brad.

"Hey, Brad, what are you doing here? Thought you were Chuck Selhammer. Knocked over a glass vase, real sorry about that." He grinned sheepishly.

Brad felt suddenly foolish brandishing the hammer. His ire flashed. "Never mind what I'm doing here, what the hell are you doing here? It's a good thing I didn't have my gun. You could have been shot. And put your damn hands down."

"Shot! What the hell for?"

"Carolyn Waters has been murdered, you dumb bastard, and this is a crime scene. Do you know what that means? What are you doing in her home?"

"Oh, I heard she had died. Didn't know she had been murdered. What an awful pity. Mary Platt gave my wife a call a little while ago. I let Carolyn borrow my spare radio for the storm updates. Hers was busted. It was just until she got a new one. I wanted to get it back before people started traipsing through the house. Is that a problem?"

All Brad could think of was an expression his brother Morris used all the time: *Life is hard. And it's real hard when you're fucking stupid.* He didn't know where to start.

"Steve, Carolyn Waters has just been murdered. She's only been dead a few hours and you're strolling around her home like you own it. Not only is it a dumb thing to do, it's pretty insensitive, too. Now get your ass out of here before I arrest you for compromising a crime scene." He paused as if considering. "I still might do that."

This seemed to light a fire under the gray-haired man. "Really sorry, guess I didn't think," he said, coming down the porch steps. Suddenly he stopped, an expression of pain spreading across his face. He made as if to speak, then thought better of it. Then thought again. "Can I take my radio with me?"

Brad sighed, his anger dissipating. "No, the radio stays here for now. I'll make sure it gets returned to you when things are all wrapped up here. Do me a favor, though, and put the radio back where you found it."

Steve Gilchrist walked back into the house and placed it on the kitchen counter near the sink. He returned to the side porch and slowly walked down the porch stairs, strolling off toward his home.

Brad stood there for a few seconds, shaking his head in disbelief. Then he began to look at things. The door had been shattered at the upper panel. Someone tall with a big shoulder had paid a visit to Carolyn. The wooden jamb near the latch and deadbolt had also been shattered.

"She had the door locked," Brad thought out loud, and stepped inside.

* * *

Carolyn and Freddy were happy and comfortable in their simple living. Then came the events of December 7, 1941, when Japan launched a sneak attack on the U.S. Naval base in Hawaii. Freddie enlisted in the Marines. Carolyn begged him not to go, or at least wait until he was drafted. Maybe the draft board would not find him out on their little island in the middle of Narragansett Bay. Freddie would not hear of it. Japan had attacked American soil and a lot of Americans had been killed. Freddie did not want to be sent to Europe. He felt the real enemy was Japan. He did not want some sergeant at the draft board determining his fate. Enlistment offered some options.

Carolyn saw him off at the six o'clock ferry on a cold morning in February of 1942. Brad and Milly were there too, along with what seemed like half the island. Carolyn had cried for days before his departure, and the women in her circle had offered words of encouragement and succor. Freddie was just as sad and had shed his own tears, a morose figure who had once been so jovial. Separating from his soulmate was tragically painful. Everyone wished Freddie well, shook his hand or hugged and kissed him. They hugged Carolyn, too, and told her that her Freddy would be home before she knew it. Then they all left for their homes. The young couple needed their last minutes alone. Carolyn stayed strong for Freddy. She walked him to the end of the pier and to the boarding plank. A solitary dock light barely illuminated the sad couple. Freddy turned to his love and they embraced one last time. Carolyn squeezed him, never wanting to let go until he finally said he had to go. He gave her one last kiss and then walked onto the ferry. She watched until the ferry was just a speck in the distance, and cried the whole ride home.

Freddie died on Okinawa in May of 1945. Carolyn never took another husband, never wanted one. The memory of their joy and time together, brief as it was, would be enough to sustain her. All her life, since that cold winter day at Homestead dock, she longed to see her husband again. On the day of the hurricane, when a stranger tore her porch door from its hinges and snuffed the life from her, she was granted that reunion.

* * *

The kitchen table had been pushed up against the wall and two of the chairs had been knocked over. A couple of drinking glasses lay shattered on the floor along with some scattered dinnerware.

"She fought back a little, too. It was over pretty quick."

Brad walked through the rest of the house. Nothing seemed out of place. He walked back out onto the porch and into the squall. He surveyed the area around the deck and then saw the footprints. They were large prints, bigger than the others in the same area and set deeper into the wet soil. They led out to a set of tire tracks.

"This is where he carried the body. Why did he need to move her?"

The ground was still wet from the storm; Brad couldn't make out any identifying marks from the footprints or tire tracks. *This wouldn't be easy*, he thought.

"Hope somebody saw something." Brad did his best thinking when he did it out loud. He righted the side door and put it back in its place. Amazingly, it still fit. He had some light line in the pickup that he used to secure the doorknob to the porch railing. That would keep the wind and rain out until Chief Anthony could take a look himself.

Brad thought back to his conversation with the rocket scientist Steve Gilchrist. *Thought you were Chuck Sellhammer*, he had said.

"Time for a talk with Chuck. He's got some big feet." The wind snatched away his words.

Chapter 3

Buck Taylor sat in his tiny living room and waited for the shocking news to break. He looked out over the east passage of Narragansett Bay and it was a sea of churning whitecaps. The winds still rattled his south-facing windows like it was a high school drumline. But the gusts were slowing down and the rattle would soon be a hum.

The wait began to wear on him. *Might as well have a drink,* he thought.

Besides, nothing would be going on today. Everyone was hunkered down in their homes, riding out the storm. His cheap bourbon sat on an old inverted milk crate next to his weathered stuffed chair. He took a long drink.

"Ahhh!" The ecstasy escaped his lips. The smell, the taste of whiskey and the warming. numbing feeling from his first drink of the day was almost divine. The wait would be easier now.

Several drinks and about an hour later, he saw the neighbors begin to venture out. They scurried to each other's homes. Only Drew Robinson and Annie Boyes had phones in their neighborhood, and it seemed as if they were the town criers. Doors were knocked on and looks of shock and disbelief were soon on the faces of those who had opened their portals. Some of his neighbors braved the blustery winds and gathered outside in their yards to talk about Carolyn Waters' sudden death. Some stood with hands to their cheeks, shaking their heads in incredulity as they listened to the details.

Brad Wheeler's truck went by heading south, its roof light flashing, and the collection of neighbors stopped their chatter and watched. Some pointed at the truck, almost confirming what they were discussing. There was another brief exchange and they turned and looked up at Buck's cottage.

"They're deciding who has to come and tell me the news," he said to himself, and he had another drink from his bottle. "Have to pretend to be surprised and real sad," his voice dripping with sarcasm. Then he saw Drew Robinson stoically make his way to his cottage. Buck took a long drink from his bottle. "Show time."

* * *

Buck started working for Peter Marrow when he was sixteen. High school had not gone well. There were some social issues. He had trouble staying attentive in class and his grades reflected that lack of focus. If they could have let him have a beer or two before class, he would have done fine. The good-looking young gals were a big distraction, too.

Peter had decided to give Buck Taylor a chance and take him on in his work crew. He had picked up a government job and needed the additional help. Buck had always been a troubled kid. Maybe a tough luck kid would be a better way to describe him. Never malicious, always a good kid, he just seemed to make the wrong choices. Peter had known his parents. Buck's father, Warren, was a good man and a hard worker. His mother, on the other hand, had not been the most nurturing woman. Darlene liked her hard liquor a little too much. Most people believed she was physically and emotionally abusive to her two children, Buck and his younger sister Linda. She seemed, however, to relish in her mistreatment of Buck. It was believed that it was her unwanted pregnancy with Buck that brought about her forced marriage to Warren Taylor. They had dated for just a short while when she found herself pregnant. Warren Taylor was the last man she would ever want to marry. He was wishy-washy, kind of wimpy, not the real man that she wanted in her life. But the sex had been good and he could stay hard forever. Sex wasn't a complicated issue for Darlene. She loved it and it didn't take her long to figure out that there were a lot of obliging men out there. She had been lucky for some time. Rubbers and pulling out had worked up until she had her fling with Warren. She had been drinking that night, maybe too much, and Warren was really giving it hard. It felt too damn good to stop him. Then she was pregnant. And Warren Taylor was such a bumbling fool. She did not want him or his baby.

Darlene was more than five months pregnant when she decided to marry Warren. She had put it off as long as she could. Her friends had started to ask questions. Her father was dead and her mother was indifferent about the whole thing. Darlene's belly was swollen and it was obvious she was pregnant, but her mother had never said anything. Darlene finally told her mother that she was pregnant and would have to get married. Her mother asked her who the father of her baby was and Darlene said that she thought it was Warren Taylor.

Her mother sighed. "Well, I guess he ain't too bad. You could have done worse."

It was so typical of her mother. "Well, I suppose you'll be a big help, Grandma," she said, clearly frustrated.

"Don't start any crap with me, you're the one that got yourself knocked up," was her mother's toxic and blunt reply.

Darlene and Warren got married before the justice of the peace at the town hall in Portsmouth. Warren had borrowed his father's car and they sat in the rear seat for a few minutes before their one o'clock time slot. Darlene reached under her dress, removed a small bottle of bourbon, and had two long drinks. Warren watched as the bubbles made their rapid, short-lived rise to the bottom of the bottle. He asked her not to drink right before they got married. Darlene felt it was time to set him straight, establish some ground rules, so to speak. Actually, there was only one.

"You don't tell me what to do, anytime, anywhere. You got that?"

Warren could only nod his head, somberly. He hoped that things would get better.

Their reception on the island was small, just her mother and her uncle from Fall River, Warren's immediate family, and some of their friends. It was, however, very raucous, and Darlene got very drunk. Later that night she insisted that Warren make love to her, although she didn't exactly say it that way.

"Let's do it," she demanded.

"Don't we need to be careful, with you being so pregnant?"

"Being careful was something we should have done months ago. If you're so worried about it, you can do it from behind. Just do it hard and do it as long as you can. It's about the only thing you're good for."

Warren could only nod his head again, just like all the other times. They were in the living room of their little cottage. Darlene dropped to the floor and got on her hands and knees. She pulled her dress up over her loins and arched her back. She wasn't wearing any underwear, she rarely did. He dropped his pants and entered her from behind. She felt so good. Darlene gave a soft, deep and primal moan. Warren wondered why he loved her so much. She met his hard, deep thrusts with her own heated stabs and then he knew why.

Darlene and Warren had their baby boy three months later. They had argued over their son's name. Warren wanted to name him Francis, after his father. Darlene had insisted on calling her new son Buck. She thought it was a manly name.

"You can't put that kind of name on a birth certificate. What are people going to say?"

"I don't give a shit what people think or say, you oughta know that by know. You go ahead and put Francis on the paperwork if you want. But I'm gonna call him Buck and I'll make damn sure everybody else does, too."

Just over a year later Buck's younger sister Linda was born. Kit DiPrete, the island midwife, delivered her. She was a beautiful little girl with a thick head of curly platinum blonde hair and sturdy little legs.

Warren tried his best to be a good father. He knew he had to be, especially with Darlene being such a poor mother. Keeping the children fed and in clean diapers was always a struggle. Darlene never saw that as her responsibility; as a matter of fact, she never saw much of anything as her responsibility. His children were often dirty and unkempt. Warren knew the whole island talked about his wife's lack of mothering skills, and it hurt deeply. He was away at work during the day and it worried him. As the children got older, Warren began to see signs of physical abuse, especially when Darlene had been drinking. He would come home from work to find fresh welts and bruises on his kids, especially on Buck. He would confront Darlene. The thought of his children being in danger, their safety compromised, had given him the backbone he needed when dealing with his disappointing wife.

Arriving home after work, never knowing what new bruise or welt he would find on his kids, tore at him. Then one day it turned truly horrifying.

Buck was huddled on the kitchen floor, knees drawn up to his chest, his eyes red and swollen from crying. He cradled his right hand, which was wrapped in a dirty, wet dish towel.

Warren was instantly to his little boy's side. He placed his lunchbox and heavy jacket on the floor and began stroking Buck's hair. "What happened, pal?" he asked, afraid of the answer he knew would receive. Young Buck's eyes immediately darted to his mother and then back to his father, but fear had stolen his voice, leaving only his lower lip to quiver in terror.

Warren gently lifted his son's right hand and removed the soggy, tarnished dish towel. A lobster-red and abraded hand emerged. Warren was enraged and stood to confront his wife.

"What the hell happened to Buck's hand? It's all red and blistered!"

With a wooden ladle in her left hand, Darlene stood by the kitchen stove, tending to a festering pot of boiling water and spaghetti. She wore a tired, rust-brown bathrobe, open at the front, revealing patchy underwear and a food-stained tee shirt. Her hair was oily and hung flat against her flushed cheeks. Her right hand held a lit cigarette and a juice glass half-full of vodka.

She stared straight ahead, took a long pull on her cigarette and blew the smoke up at a kitchen ceiling already discolored from years of accumulated cooking grease and smoke.

"Damn kid put his hand in a pot a boiling water," she said, completely void of any pathos. "Had to start a new batch all over again. I think he's got your brains."

"What kind of monster are you?!" Warren hollered and took a challenging step towards his wife. "Don't let me ever catch you doing stuff like that to the kids. I'll do something. I don't know what, but I'll do something."

Her right eye squinted from the smoke of the cigarette tucked into the corner of her mouth, and Darlene slowly turned her head toward Warren. "I didn't do nothing. Besides, *you* ain't gonna do nothin'. Not you," she snarled.

"Yes, I will. You just leave them alone." And he scooped up Buck and headed for his bedroom, hoping he might console and rebuild his little boy.

Three years later, Darlene ran off with a sailor from the south end of Prudence. The U.S. Navy had a small ammunition storage area there and it was manned by about forty sailors and officers. There was a deep water T-wharf where destroyers and destroyer escorts berthed for loading and off-loading of required munitions. They were far from the navy's finest and they were all female-starved. It was an environment that Darlene thrived in. Some young kid from Mississippi with his brains in his pants went AWOL with her. Warren never found out if the kid was apprehended. It didn't matter. He knew Darlene was gone and was never coming back. At least his kids would be safe. Buck was ten and Linda eight. Warren hoped he could repair the damage.

Chapter 4

The Caswell family moved into the lighthouse at Sand Point in the late summer of 1937, and they were quick to participate in all of the island's social functions. The oldest son, George, was only a year younger than Buck and they became friends with little effort. George also had a sixteen-year-old sister LouAnn who was very attractive, with one heck of a figure. Buck was drawn to her and made several attempts to elevate their relationship. They were often together in the social settings of the island, part of the same crowd. LouAnn was friendly in the beginning, but soon began to rebuff his advances. Buck's drinking quickly became an issue for her. He didn't think his drinking was a problem and neither did her brother George, but she soon started to date Jeff Baxter. Jeff was one of those phonies that Buck simply could not tolerate. LouAnn would figure it out sooner or later, and then Buck would be there to hold her hand. It was just a matter of time. In the meantime, George and Buck had their friendship. George liked his beer, too.

Buck appreciated George's focused mindset, and understood it completely. George Caswell was the only one in his family to survive the powerful Hurricane of 1938. It was a very heavy burden to pay for someone else's ineptness. He had witnessed the drowning deaths of his mother, father, brother and sister, and all of it had left a very deep scar. He would never be whole again. George would always be timid, withdrawn and aimless, a lost soul. But the island population had been cruel and thoughtless in their treatment of George. They should have let him deal with his loss in his own way. His life was full of lonely days filled with sad reflection and feelings of abandonment. His nights consisted of restless sleep, punctuated by nightmares of his family being swept away in a turbulent sea. But time dulled the pain and healed the wound. George persevered. He had a deep inner strength.

Only days after the hurricane, George had been brought to a temporary morgue to identify the remains of some of his missing family. It was obviously a very trying and anxious moment for George and he had muttered some strange and confusing comments. It only reinforced everyone's belief that the emotional damage was severe and permanent. He had to be psychologically damaged after what he had endured. How could he not be?

George had been quiet and shy before the hurricane. People knew it, too, but they didn't want to remember that. It made them feel better if they could pity him. It was just the way he was. They began to refer to him behind his back as Crazy George, and other than the strange observations at the mortuary, when he identified his family, he had done nothing to encourage that label. But they had labeled Buck, too, the whole self-righteous bunch of them. First, they pity you and then they label you. It's just a natural progression. It never restricted Buck and George's friendship. Funny how they judge you based on their own set of standards. Many of those self-righteous bastards were the ones that really needed the pity. Buck could never see himself sitting down and having a cold beer with most of them. He wanted nothing to do with those hypocrites. He enjoyed a drink every now and then, and all of a sudden, he was being pitied. How they talked to him and treated him changed dramatically. He could only imagine what they said behind his back. It reminded Buck of a story he once read about Winston Churchill. Apparently, a woman in Parliament was criticizing him: "Winston, the way you drink is shameful. If I were your wife I would put poison in your tea," to which Winston replied, "Madam, if you were my wife I would drink that tea." He always liked that story and he would've liked to have had a beer with Winston Churchill. Buck thought Winston Churchill was a lot like him; they were both smart and they understood just how good alcohol was for the soul.

Chapter 5

Overnight, Hurricane Carol moved farther out to sea and away from the coast. The winds died down and it became a sunny, crystal-clear day. Although it could only tie up at the Sand Point wharf, the ferry resumed its usual schedule. The dock at Homestead was moderately damaged and it would take several weeks to be made serviceable again.

Arriving on the eight a.m. ferry, Brad met Chief William Anthony and the state medical examiner at the Sand Point wharf. Chief Anthony was a stocky, barrel-chested man of average height. He looked tired. No doubt he had stretched himself and his department thin overnight with all the storm-related calamities. His uniform looked like he had slept in it and his five o'clock shadow resembled a shallow birthmark.

Brad extended his hand as the chief stepped off the ferry gangplank. "Hey Bill, good to see you. Looks like you've had a long night." His voice and handshake were grim with the task that lay ahead.

"I have, Brad. Looks like you didn't sleep too well, either. Good to see you, too. Brad, this is Dr. Capone. Doc, this is Brad Wheeler. But I think you gentlemen have already met."

Brad had indeed met the tall, thin M.E. His services were twice before required on the island with the drowning deaths of Ted Esau and Tom Tuttle. Brad remembered the doctor as a quiet and withdrawn man but committed to his craft. The examiner's work would be thorough and his report very detailed. The dark curly hair that Brad recalled had thinned and turned gray around the temples.

"Hey, Doc," said Brad in an almost apologetic voice. "Not sure I want to keep meeting this way. But good to see you."

"My lot in life," Dr. Capone replied dryly. and they shook hands.

"Gentlemen, we're gonna have to squeeze into the front seat of my truck," Brad announced

It was about a fifteen-minute drive to the Wheeler farm. They arrived there with little conversation on the way. Morris Wheeler was waiting for the trio at the farm and he assisted Brad and Chief Anthony with getting Carolyn's body out of the big ice cooler and onto a plywood table. Morris had covered the table with a couple of white sheets. A big light with a brass turn switch hung down from a rafter collar tie above.

They stared at the pale and battered body before them. Carolyn had been a warm, caring woman only hours ago, and now this would be the only image the men would have of her whenever her name was mentioned.

Finally, Chief Anthony invaded their silence. "Brad, do you think she was sexually assaulted?"

Brad was stunned by the question. He looked at his brother Morris for an answer. Morris only shrugged his shoulders.

"We didn't see any marks or bruises in that area. She had her underwear on. I wouldn't know what to look for. I just don't like getting that close to a dead woman's body."

"Well you need to look for that kind of trauma, Brad," Chief Anthony said, now in his abstract professional voice. "Doc, that's part of your procedure, right?"

"Yes, of course," and the examiner began searching the tangled hair on Carolyn's scalp.

"The doctor is going to need about an hour or so with the body. You got a place where we can sit down and talk? I grabbed some files on the two previous drownings, although I understand it's your theory now that they may not have been accidents. I could use some coffee, too."

"I don't think they were accidents, Bill," said Brad.

"No goddamn way they drowned, not on their own, that is," chirped in Morris. "I'll get some coffee from the house. Just made a fresh batch about an hour ago. You gents can get comfortable in the office."

Brad led the way to the office at the opposite end of the barn. He settled in behind an old oak desk that had numerous scratches, names, phone numbers, and business calculations all over it. In the middle was a calendar pad from 1936 with a hundred coffee stains on it. A big double-hung window on the north wall was to Brad's right. It hadn't been cleaned in many years and had spider webs in all four corners. The room had a musty odor from years of dust and smoke from the Parodi cigars that he and his brother Morris smoked. There were a couple of oak Windsor chairs in front of the window.

Brad pointed to them. "Grab a chair and have a seat, Bill. Where do you want to start with this?"

"Like I said, Brad, I brought the files from the other cases, but I just haven't had any time to look at them. They were handled by Don Driscol, the chief before me. Why don't you give me a recap on those and with what just happened yesterday?"

Brad first told him about Ted Esau in the hurricane of 1944. "We found his body up on Sandy Beach. It's a south-facing beach near the north end of the island. It was a drowning, or maybe a forced drowning now. Ted was just thirty-eight. Married, two little girls. His wife said he went to check on his work skiff that was moored in a little cove on the west side. No signs of foul play, said our doc here."

"Anything at the time make you suspicious?"

"No, not really. Ted's wife said he had been keeping an eye on the waves in the bay and the direction of the wind and thought it was time to check on his boat. Tom Tuttle and Crazy George gave him a hand moving it and setting it up in the cove. He should have hauled it, but his trailer had snapped an axle in the spring when he put the boat back in the water. He just hadn't gotten around to repairing it. No one else had a trailer big enough. It was a good size work boat."

"Who's this Crazy George?" the chief asked, his curiosity suddenly piqued.

"He's a guy who helps with odd jobs around the island. Lost his family in the '38 hurricane. He was just an eighteen-year-old kid at the time and was never quite the same after that. His name is George Caswell. I need to stop calling him 'Crazy George.' Not real professional. He's just a simple, good-natured guy."

"Wasn't he part of that lighthouse family that died in the hurricane? He was the only one to survive."

"Yeah, that's him. Anyway, the weather bureau had predicted the hurricane and Ted moved his boat over to the cove on the west side so he would be in the lee of the island, away from the southeast winds. People do that sometimes in the really bad weather. Apparently, something happened to Ted when he went to check on his boat. He wasn't a very good swimmer, according to his wife. That didn't help. It was early evening."

"Okay, what happened in '48?" asked Chief Anthony

"That was Tom Tuttle. They found his body washed up on the beach not far from the navy T-wharf on the south end. He sort of kept to himself. He liked to fish. We think he went fishing off the T-wharf during the storm. Why he did that is anybody's guess. It's a good place to fish in normal weather. The navy commander at the base allows folks to fish there when there's no activity at the pier. A lot of people do that. Tom had a bunch of fishing line wrapped around his feet and lower legs when they found him. We think he fell in with his pole and everything just got tangled up. The pole and all the line were still attached to him when they found him on the shore. He had a lot of bumps and contusions on his body, a of lot scrapes, too. We think he got slammed up against the pilings at the T-wharf, before he broke free and washed up on the beach."

"You didn't think that was a little odd, fishing during a hurricane?"

"No, not really. He had been telling people he was going to do that. Always wanted to experience the thrill of it. If you knew Tom, you'd understand. He was a bachelor, lived by himself. No one to question his stupidity."

"I suppose you're right, Brad. That brings us to yesterday. Mrs. Waters."

"Carolyn was murdered, that's a certainty. I'm confident of that and I'm sure her bound wrists had a lot to do with that conclusion. I'll bet she was alive when she went in the water. The doc will confirm that."

Brad and Chief Anthony talked more about Brad's findings and his plan moving forward. The coroner walked into the room and let them know he had completed his work. It had taken less time than anticipated. Carolyn Waters had definitely drowned and the right side of her face had been caved in, he informed them.

"My guess? This was done by a rather large man, and he was left-handed," said Dr. Capone. "I'm confident the X-rays will confirm that her right cheekbone was shattered. She got hit pretty hard."

The chief shook his head in disgust. "Let's take a quick ride up to the Waters place and take a look around. I want to take some pictures, too. We need to be on the next ferry leaving the island," he said. "The doc will need to get the body back to the morgue. But I gotta tell you, Brad, you're on your own with this one. Two of my men were hurt last night trying to help a family from their flooded home and I already have a man recovering from appendicitis. Plus, I've got some road damage from the storm that I am going to have to deal with. I just can't spare anyone right now. I'll help you when I can. I'll send you a copy of the coroner's report. Keep me in the loop."

They rewrapped Carolyn's body in the canvas tarp, put her back in the makeshift coffin, sprinkled fresh ice chips and, like loyal soldiers honoring a fallen comrade, they carried her to Brad's pickup.

Packed again into the front seat of the truck, they drove up to the Waters place.

"Listen, Chief, I'm gonna let you guys do your thing while I pay a visit to a neighbor of Mrs. Waters. Chuck Selhammer is his name and the cottage is just a short walk from here. Don't think there's much there, but I want to follow up on it," Brad said.

"No problem, do what you gotta do," Chief Anthony replied.

When Brad returned from his visit to the Selhammer place, he found the chief and Doctor Capone waiting by his truck.

"How'd you gents make out?" he asked them.

"We took a bunch of pictures and walked the crime scene pretty good, made some notes," the chief told Brad, as he had done hundreds of times in his career. "Wasn't a big crime scene, don't think it moved beyond the kitchen. How did you make out with the neighbor?"

"Wasn't much of a visit. He's been sick as a dog the last few days with the flu or something. His wife's been feeding him chicken broth and toast for a while now. He looked awful. Nothing he could offer, and I didn't want to hang around."

Cramming themselves for the last time into the pickup, Brad took his charges to the 10:30 ferry and they loaded the big cooler that contained Carolyn Waters' body. Paying their respects, islanders stood in silence as a good friend and a beautiful woman left them to begin her own distinct journey.

Standing alone, purposely separating himself from the gathering, was Peter Marrow. He struggled with the significance of the senseless act and knew there was a message being sent. Soberly, he knew the message was meant for him.

* * *

Several days had gone by since Carolyn's body had been removed from the island. Brad was still waiting for the coroner's report. There was talk and speculation everywhere, as he expected; Mrs. Waters was a huge part of the collective soul of the island.

Holding a half-inch breaker bar and socket, Brad walked out of the tool shed at the Wheeler farm to find Peter Marrow standing by the red town pickup truck, its hood up.

"Hey, Brad, what the hell are you and Chief Anthony going to do about this?" challenged Peter.

"Oh, Christ," Brad mumbled to himself. He had just begun the process of replacing the fuel pump in the municipal truck and briefly fantasized about using the tool in his hand on the side of Peter's head. He finished his walk to the truck, put the tool on the large fender, and turned to Peter.

"Do about what?"

Peter leaned in closer to Brad and spoke in a muffled voice, as if someone might overhear their conversation. There was no one else around. Brad could smell that Peter had been drinking.

"You know, all these murders, especially now with Carolyn Waters. It all sounds very suspicious to me. Making me real nervous. You know we talked about this before at Tom Tuttle's funeral. You thought I was reaching then. You still think I'm reaching?"

"Yeah, I still think you're reaching. What the heck is making you so nervous? And no one is saying they're murders yet. We're still getting information."

"What the hell are you talking about, Brad? You know they were murdered. All three of them, and they all worked for me. Well, not Carolyn Waters, but her husband did. It's that Caswell family from the lighthouse. They're coming back for revenge. I got the willies over this. I can't sleep at night. They're gonna come after me next."

Brad could see that Peter was truly in an agitated state. "Peter, try and relax. Officially, nobody has said anything."

"Don't screw with me, Brad. We've been friends for too long, so don't treat me like I'm some nosy reporter. You had two or three people with you on the beach when you rolled Carolyn Waters' body over. They all saw that her hands were tied with tape. That's murder to me."

"Okay, Peter, I'll grant you that it looks like foul play. But to go from that to Ted and Tom were murdered too is little rash. And now you're talking about some family that died sixteen years ago is now out for revenge? Come on, Pete. Revenge for what?"

"I don't know, Brad," Peter said, his hands suddenly shoulder high in exasperation. "But it's got me scared! You need to start looking real deep into this. Maybe it's the son, Crazy George, or his fool friend Buck Taylor. Those two are as thick as thieves."

"Try and relax, Peter. I'll be looking into everything. We haven't scratched the surface yet. I'll be in touch. Go on home. Keep yourself busy. And Peter? Stay away from the liquor. I can smell it on your breath. That ain't ever gonna help."

"Oh, I'll be in touch; you can count on that," and Peter stormed off toward his truck, scuffing the dirt several times with his boots. Opening the driver's side door, he turned back to Brad. "Do something, Brad. Because if you don't, I will."

"Peter, you don't want to say things like that," Brad replied, frustrated that it had gotten to this point. "As your friend, I'll let that go, but as a police officer, I could take it as a threat. Sober up, let it go."

Peter got in his truck, slammed the door, backed out into the dirt driveway and drove away, his back tires briefly throwing dirt and gravel back towards Brad. Looking at the soil and dust that settled around his work boots, he shook his head again in frustration. "This is only gonna get uglier," he whispered to a quiet landscape.

* * *

The report from the coroner came in the mail the next day. Brad retrieved the letter from his mailbox at the post office. There was a small knot of people at the general store next door. It was the island gathering point, especially around ferry time. There was a wide wooden walkway with a sturdy roof overhead that connected the post office and general store. At midpoint, an oversized wooden phone booth had been constructed, and it protruded out from the porch like a tiny peninsula. The three sides had glass windows, but the entrance on the porch side had no door; too many nor'easters had taken their toll, and it had been permanently removed years earlier. Private, intimate phone calls were difficult, but it was the only public phone on the island. There were a number of names and heart-shaped true loves carved onto the inside walls of the booth and the handrails that ran the length of the walkway. Two-by-ten flat benches were to either side of the booth, but most people preferred to sit on the handrails and rest their feet on the benches below.

The whole island was buzzing about Carolyn Waters' death. Brad had to listen to a number of theories and a couple of "I'm-sure-he-did-it" scenarios. Chip Creighton, a tall, thin man from just up Pier Road who nervously chain-smoked Lucky Strikes, had his theory that he was dying to share with Brad.

"You know, Brad, you need to look at that big fat guy that helped Carolyn Waters with her water pump a couple of years ago. You should have seen the way they were hugging and holding hands when he left on the ferry."

"I'm pretty sure that was her brother, Chip."

"You sure about that?"

"Yes, I am, his name is Arthur. He's her older brother."

"Well, my sister never hugged me like that."

"Ain't nobody ever hugged you like that," Hank Tropoli added, and everybody laughed.

Brad chuckled, tipped his hat, and turned to leave.

"See you been packing the last few days." It was Buck Taylor; he emerged from the tattered phone booth. "You ain't gonna shoot nobody, are you?" He laughed — *hee hee!* — a snickering laugh. He'd been drinking.

Brad had been uncomfortably wearing his holstered .38 Smith & Wesson the last couple of days. It had become a talking point on the island. Even Milly questioned his wearing it.

"Only if I have to, Buck. Listen, I need to ask you a few questions."

"Sure, what do you wanna know?"

Brad had learned a while ago not to have a conversation with a drunk. He had spent almost a lifetime learning that lesson with his brother Morris, and more recently with Buck Taylor.

"Can't talk right now, can we talk tomorrow morning? You're helping Joe Bearse with his foundation, right? I'll stop by in the morning. We can talk then. See you tomorrow." Brad rattled it all off in a hurry — this was not a debate and he wasn't asking for permission. He nodded to Buck and was on his way.

Buck stood in his alcohol haze with his mouth hanging open. "Uh, uh, sure thing, Brad. See you then," he said in a small, bewildered voice.

Brad knew he'd have to time his trips to the post office a little better.

* * *

Driving directly home, Brad parked in his usual spot next to his chestnut trees. Spotted chickadees and goldfinches fluttered about the bird feeder that Milly had hung there and then quickly settled back to their sunflower seeds and suet. His curiosity overwhelmed him and Brad turned his truck off and quickly opened the large envelope from the coroner. Dinner and Milly's company would have to wait.

The autopsy revealed that Carolyn Waters had drowned and her right cheekbone had indeed been broken. Some minor cuts and bruises on her neck and shoulders, but nothing that would have contributed to her death. No signs of sexual assault. A small note from Chief Anthony was attached; apparently the Chief had reviewed the report and would call him in a few days.

Brad looked up from his paperwork and stared out his front windshield. Blue jays had just arrived at Milly's feeder and were beginning their aggressive behavior. Who and why would anyone want to drown Carolyn Waters? He could not think of a single soul. Finding this criminal and understanding his motive would be Brad's single challenge. He felt overwhelmed. He was really just a backwoods cop, more like a shepherd keeping a watchful eye over his small flock. Hell, it wasn't even a full-time position. Prudence didn't even have a jail. But this was the hand he had been dealt. Maybe Chief Anthony could free up a detective in a while. Brad left the coroner's report on the seat and headed for his front door. Tonight Milly was making his favorite, fried chicken and biscuits. He had a feeling it might not be well received by the knot in his stomach.

Later that night, lying in bed, the events of the last few days began to press in on him. A good night's sleep would be fleeting this evening. His world had suddenly been turned upside down. Two events, years apart and years in the past had potentially been redefined and now the deliberate drowning of a special woman had only added credence to those other assumed drownings.

But three deaths taken separately would never lead to a motive. He knew he had to examine the three separate drownings as a whole. Even taken together, the events still did not define motive. It's not like he had walked into a home, found the place ransacked and bereft of valuables, and then discovered a body. He had to listen to his gut, and as much as he didn't want to buy into it, his gut told him that Peter Marrow was onto something. Eerily, it was the only thing that made any sense. The common thread here was that they all did work for Peter except Carolyn. But her husband had, and they had all worked extensively on the Sand Point lighthouse project. However, so had Dave Brooks and Buck Taylor, although only for a portion of the schedule, and they were both still upright, although Buck wasn't the clearest definition of upright. Dave Brooks would be his first visit tomorrow morning. He was the only surviving member of Peter's work crew that could provide any reliable and objective insight into the weeks leading up to completion of the Sand Point lighthouse and the drownings of his workmates years later. Now he would begin a long night of his tossing and turning.

* * *

Parking his pickup in Dave Brooks' front yard, Brad discovered Dave in the toolshed behind his home. He was in the process of loading up his workbelt for a trip up on his roof. He had lost several roofing shingles during the storm and his ladder was already propped up against the side of the house.

"Hey, Brad," offered Dave, a bit taken aback by Brad's unannounced visit. "What can I do for you?"

"Hey, Dave. Wonder if you can help me. I'm trying to rethink Ted Esau and Tom Tuttle's drownings. What do you remember about them? Can you shed any light on Carolyn Waters' death? You all worked together during the island lighthouse project. Anything out of the ordinary then?"

Putting his tool belt back on his workbench, Dave wiped the sweat from his now-furrowed brow. "That's a lot of questions all at once." He paused again, curled his lips inward, stared at the calendar on the shed wall, and subtly nodded his head several times. "You know, Brad, we're talking about six and ten years ago. Ted and Tom were both good friends of mine. We had worked together for quite a few years. It was a tough loss. I thought they were both accidental drownings. Now it seems you're not so sure?"

"I guess not. Like I said, just kinda rethinking things a bit. What else can you tell me?"

"Tom's drowning seemed a little crazy. We all told him he was nuts for thinking about fishing off the T-Wharf during a nasty storm. I can remember Buck Taylor telling him he thought it was crazy, too, and nothing is crazy to that loony tune. Buck even wanted to watch him from the shoreline. Wanted Tom to let him know when he was going so he could go with him."

"Never heard that detail. Did Buck go up to the T-Wharf with Tom?"

"Don't think he did. Said he never did go. We talked about it a few days after Tom drowned."

"Did you believe him?" Brad questioned.

"I guess. You never know with Buck. What's real and what's fantasy with him is always up for debate. You know what I'm talking about, Brad. But if you're thinking Buck had something to do with Tom's death, I don't think so. I mean, Buck might be a freaking loser, but he's a harmless loser. I don't think he's got that much brain power."

"Dave, how come you never mentioned this before?" Brad responded, irritated by this new information.

"It was just idle conversation, none of us ever thought he'd really go fishing in the middle of a hurricane. Plus, he told me that he'd never ask Buck to go along with him. That would be the last thing he would ever do."

"Maybe so. What can you offer about Ted Esau?"

"Not much. Ted and I were good friends, I miss him a lot. It was just a normal thing he did with moving his boat. Everybody agreed it was what they would have done, too. I think he just slipped, hit his head, and fell in the water. Ted was a horrible swimmer. It was a terrible accident, at least that's what I thought it was. Now with Carolyn Waters' death and all these questions you're asking, seems there might be some other explanation. Peter Marrow has already been by, telling me I should be concerned. He's been drinking and he's afraid of his own shadow right now. All this baloney that he's spreading around about dead people from the lighthouse coming back for revenge is insane. Revenge for what? I think he's lost his marbles, which surprises me, because he's not that type of guy. For some reason, this Carolyn Waters thing has really put him over the edge. What do you think, Brad?"

"I don't know what to think, but you're right about one thing: this all seems out of character for Peter Marrow. He was never much of drinker and now he can't drink enough. Puzzling. One last question; anybody in your crew left handed?"

"What" a squinting puzzling look on Dave's face. He thought a bit; "nah, but Bernie Caswell the light house keeper was. Know that for sure. It was always funny the way he signed paperwork that Peter gave him. Why do you ask."

"Just asking. Okay, Dave, if you think of anything else, let me know. Take care."

Brad headed back to his Chevy pickup. Bernie Caswell left handed, a big man too, but he drowned sixteen years ago. Brad would not go down that road. Settling into the front seat, he lit up one of his Parodis. He'd been starting to smoke a lot more of them the last couple of weeks. That would need to slow down.

"Hey, Brad." Dave Brooks had followed Brad back to his truck. Turning his gaze to the ground and then quickly back to Brad's now questioning expression, he began to put the words together and then stopped.

"What's on your mind, Dave?" Brad said, knowing that he needed and wanted a little nudge.

"Do you think I'm next?"

"Nah, I wouldn't worry about that, but don't go fishing in the next hurricane." Dave chuckled.

"You've been listening to Peter Marrow and the rest of the wannabe detectives way too much. Peter's drinking is warping his sense of reality and the rest of it is all just a lot of baseless speculation."

"Maybe so," he said sullenly, not entirely convinced.

"Relax, Dave. Anything else before I go?"

The other man's face suddenly lit up as he remembered. "Oh yeah, I just remembered! Peter and the lighthouse keeper had a pretty good argument near the end of the project. They were inside the house and the rest of us were at the trucks, putting all the tools away. It was the end of the day."

Brad's attention was captured, if only mildly. "What were they arguing about?"

"Don't know really, we couldn't hear that much," said Dave. "Didn't last very long, but it was pretty heated. Tom Tuttle asked him what all the fuss was about. Peter said Bernie was mad that we were taking too long to finish the project. He didn't want to talk about it anymore. The thing was, we were right on schedule. Didn't make much sense to me."

"Did they have any more arguments after that?"

"Nah, nothing was ever said after that. Now that I think about it, though, they *were* a little cool to each other after that."

"Interesting!" Brad said, and then with a dusting of irony, he added, "Can I go now or do you have anything else you want to share with me?"

Dave shrugged his shoulders and held his arms and hands out to the sides. "Only trying to help, Brad."

"I know you are, Dave. Thanks for that help. Take care." Brad pulled away, hoping he had comforted Dave, but knowing that

Dave had every reason to be concerned. Only a few short weeks ago an unpredictable event had suddenly begun to make very bizarre outcomes eerily predictable.

Chapter 6

C arolyn Waters' funeral service was held at the Union Church on Pier Road. The whole island was unified in their sadness. Reverend Bob Lite from the west side presided over the proceedings and gave a very moving eulogy. There were a lot of tears. Others who wanted to speak to Carolyn's legacy were invited to share their reflections with the overflowing congregation. There were many who did exactly that. She had touched a lot of people's lives.

Carolyn was buried next to her beloved Freddie at the small island cemetery on Golding Road. Her casket was lowered into the open ground and numerous people slowly filed by and paid their last respects. Some dropped flowers, others dropped trinkets or seashells onto her casket.

Brad was there with Milly; Morris and Mary, too, were among the mourners. Chief Anthony also made the trip to the island to express his condolences to Carolyn's close circle of friends, and to meet with the Wheeler brothers prior to the funeral service. They would need to see who attended the service, and the attendees' actions observed. They would spread themselves out and take it all in. Chief Anthony had called the night before and reinforced the obvious: this was a homicide investigation and they needed to start treating it like one. He would be there taking his own mental notes, but he would also be there to give Brad the right advice on how to go about it.

"This is your flock, Brad," he had said. "You know just about everyone there and they all know you. They were all shocked by what happened and they're all gonna want to help you in any way they can. Probably end up getting in your way. But we really need to pay attention to the people who attend the service today. You should focus on only that. Maybe you can get your brother Morris to make notes on those who don't attend. I'll be there to offer my insights at the end of the day."

Brad, Morris, and Chief Anthony did not join the ranks of mourners as they filed past the open grave. They stood off to the side at their separate stations. Everything seemed normal for the type of setting. People were saying goodbye to a special friend. Buck Taylor and George Caswell were near the end of the line of mourners. They stopped at the edge of the grave and looked down at the casket. They stood there for a while and said nothing. Finally, Buck leaned over, whispered something in George's ear, and patted him on the back. George smiled, softly nodded and returned the pat. They moved on and soon were far removed from the gathering.

Morris was quickly next to his brother's side. Leaning in, he whispered in disbelief. "Did you just see that?"

"Oh, I saw that all right, but I'm not sure if anyone else saw it."

He was wrong. Peter Marrow was upon the two of them immediately after the service. Most of the mourners had gone on their way. Brad and Morris had sent their wives home and Chief Anthony stood with them, reviewing their observations.

"Brad, what the hell are you going to do about those two fuckin' nutjobs? You saw them there yukking it up next to Carolyn Waters' grave." Peter was drunk, quite drunk. His eyes were bloodshot and he slurred his words.

"What should I do, Peter? I told you to take it easy on the booze. Apparently, you didn't take the advice."

"Arrest the fuckers, charge them with murder!"

50

"Based on what? Peter, you need to go home and sleep this one off."

"Sleep! I can't sleep. I'm never gonna sleep again as long as you're walking around with your thumb up your ass."

Chief Anthony had heard enough. "Listen here, Mr. Peter, or whatever your name is. Brad has been pretty patient with you here. But I'm done with you. One more asinine remark from you and I'll slap some cuffs on you so fast your head will spin. Take Brad's advice; go home, and don't you dare get in a car and drive there."

Peter puffed up in indignation. "How am I supposed to get home, big shot?"

"I don't care if you roll home or stumble with every step you take. Just don't drive in the condition you're in. I'm just dying to throw your sorry ass in jail."

Peter's wife Lillian suddenly appeared from where the cars were parked. "I'll take care of him. He's been drinking so much lately. He's convinced himself that he's next. My Peter is a shell of what he used to be. Brad, can you stop by sometime so just you and I can talk?"

"Sure Lily, I'll stop by in a couple of days"

Peter suddenly became a beaten man. Lily led Peter back to their car. They got in and drove off.

"What the hell was that all about?" Chief Anthony asked.

"It's something that's surfaced in the last couple of weeks. Peter is convinced that the lighthouse family that perished in the '38 hurricane is out for revenge. In his mind, it's why everyone who worked with him on that project is slowly being bumped off. He's convinced he's the next target."

"Any truth to that, Brad? I know it's not ghosts from sixteen years ago, but are these people all connected to Peter's work crew from back then?"

"Yeah, Bill, they are. And as crazy as it might sound, it's the only thing that makes any sense right now. I just don't have anything that leads anywhere."

Morris finally decided to enter the conversation. Brad had smelled the whiskey on his breath from the very moment he arrived at the funeral. It was an all-too-familiar odor. He was hoping that Chief Anthony hadn't smelled it, too. "Don't tell me you believe in that hogwash. Ghost and spirits from the past bullshit. You gotta be kidding me."

"Of course I don't, Morris. Maybe there's something else just below the surface. I mean, why is Peter Marrow so convinced that these are all revenge drownings? Revenge for what? He seems to have one big guilty conscience. I think something happened sixteen years ago that no one knows about except Peter. But Peter's wrong; someone else knows what happened sixteen years ago and they are just loving what this is all doing to us, and him."

"All right, Brad! Now you're thinking like a top-notch detective," said Chief Anthony jokingly, but with encouragement.

"I was about ready to share this with you, but there just isn't enough to sink my teeth into. It's all speculation at this point. Any half-competent D.A. would throw me out of his office."

"Maybe so, but stay with your gut on this one. I think you might be onto something. I would keep that Buck Taylor and Crazy what's-his-name in your crosshairs. Wish I could send you somebody to help, but I'm still short on manpower. Hang in there."

Brad and Morris dropped Chief Anthony at the ferry, and thanked him for his advice and support. There were just a few minutes before the boat left. They continued their drive to the farm and discussed the little lovefest that Buck and Crazy George had shared at Carolyn's graveside.

"It was just plain weird," said Morris, shaking his head in disbelief.

"I know," said Brad, "just real out of place. I don't think too many people picked up on it. The fact that they were near the last to file past her grave had a lot to do with that."

"Fuckers had it planned that way, and it sure put a hair across Peter's ass."

Morris was driving and had taken the westerly route, past the salt marshes at Nag Creek with its resident white egrets and nesting osprey, along Bay Avenue skirting the old stone pavilion and pier, remnants of a time when New York steamers bound for Providence would tie off and offer their passengers the decadence of bath houses and casinos. They drove past the tiny one-room schoolhouse where Priscilla Marshall prepared daily lessons for her two second-, one fifth-, and one ninth-graders. Brad asked him to drop him off at his house instead of going all the way up to the farm.

"Get me a list of the people who did not attend the funeral. You remember you were supposed to have a handle on that. I didn't see you taking any notes."

"Yeah, yeah."

"And another thing: if you're going to be working with me, lay off the booze. I could smell it all over you and I know Chief Anthony could, too," Brad said, his frustration about to boil over. "He didn't say anything this time, but next time he will. I'm not going to have you compromise my relationship with him."

"Oh, fuck that. He didn't smell anything."

With biting sarcasm, Brad replied, "Noticed you didn't deny you were drinking. This is it, Moe, no more booze when you're working with me on this case. You got that? Christ, you're all over the place with your driving right now and you don't even know it. Makes me nervous as hell just riding with you."

"Let it go, Brad. This is where you get out. I'll have the list for you tomorrow. Bye." He hit the gas pedal and sped off, his tires throwing stones. Brad wondered if any of it had sunk in. He would need his older brother's help.

* * *

Buck would have to be careful from now on. It was out there. They had forced the fools to connect the dots and now the cretins were scrambling. It would be fun to watch. But now they would have to back off a bit, lie low for a while. Brad Wheeler was already snooping around and asking questions. He was no dummy. Buck knew not to sell him short. But now they would be looking at events that happened four and eight years ago, events that were labeled mysterious, and as much as people might suspect foul play, they could never, never prove a thing. Buck and his partner had made sure of that and once more they would just sit back and watch all the drama. Good luck trying to solve the murders.

Buck also knew that Brad's brother Morris would be a problem for as long as Brad could tolerate his participation in the investigation. Moe was always sticking his nose where it didn't belong, fancied himself a first-class detective after he discovered that Deno Sullivan was the one who broke into Chalmer's store one night to steal cigarettes and money from the register. Brad and Milly had gone to her grandmother's funeral in New Hampshire and Morris was the only semblance of authority on the island. But everybody knew that Deno left his pocket knife on the counter next to the cash register when he jimmied it open. The knife had his initials on the handle. 'Lightning' wasn't Deno's middle name.

Morris loved his whiskey jug, more than Buck ever did, and yet they all thought Buck was the one with the drinking problem, although he never saw his drinking as a problem. Too much hard liquor at night might leave you a little queasy the next morning, but that was only a temporary problem. By the time evening rolled around you were already looking forward to its biting taste and soothing effect.

* * *

It was Moe Wheeler himself who had introduced Buck to the sweet taste of Kentucky bourbon. Brad and Morris had hired the young lad to help around the farm for a few hours every Saturday. Riding his bike to the Wheeler farm, Buck would arrive at 8:00 a.m. At twelve years old, Buck was responsible for cleaning the animal stalls and chicken coop. Fresh hay for bedding was needed, and the weekly reward of grain pellets was placed in their feed troughs. Big Ben's stall was at the top of Buck's list. He began every Saturday cleaning the huge Persian draft horse's stall, and would end the day feeding and brushing the big gelding down. Big Ben knew the routine, and he followed Buck around the barn with his eyes as Buck completed his tasks, sometimes announcing his impatience by throaty grumbles and scuffing his front hoofs on his paddock door. Only when Buck approached Ben with a curry comb and a bag of oats did he stop his protests. The big gray equine was Morris's pride and joy. Morris and Mary never had any children, and so Big Ben became the only pleasant diversion Morris had. On Sundays he would ride his mighty steed around his now unproductive fields with his flask tucked into his canvas saddlebag. He was lord of the manor.

Buck was there one Saturday morning brushing down Big Ben in his stall. Often, he used one of the rugged chairs that were in the barn office to stand on. It was the only way he could reach the top of Big Ben's massive head. As he approached the office, he could hear soft grunts and subtle moaning. He quietly peeked in the partially-open door. Morris was standing there with his pants down around his knees. Kneeling in front of him was Buck's neighbor Angela Wilcox. She was several years older than Buck, not very pretty, but she had the biggest breasts he'd ever seen. She was always catching him staring. She never said anything, but always gave him dirty looks. Buck knew she worked at the farm helping Morris's wife Mary with jobs around the house. *Don't think Mary had this on her of list of things to do*, he thought.

His neighbor's shirt was unbuttoned and peeled back and her bra was pulled up. Her head was going back and forth on Morris's johnson, her huge breasts gently swaying with the motion. Morris's massive hands gently guided her head back and forth. The whole scene captivated Buck; he was galvanized where he stood. Morris began to roll his head back, his face flushed with ecstasy. Then he saw Buck standing at the partially-open door. His eyes widened and he waved him away with an angry finger. Buck quickly retreated to Big Ben's stall and resumed his brushing without the chair. In a few minutes, Angela scampered by. She gave him a quick glance, said 'hi!' and was out the door. It was obvious she had not seen her little friend standing there. Morris then called him from the office.

"Buck, come on down here. I got something I want to share with you."

Buck became nervous and he slowly walked to the office.

"Come on in, Buck, that ain't no big deal what you saw. That kind of stuff happens all the time with men and women. I suppose you just ain't never seen it before. There comes the day in every girl's life when she realizes her pussy ain't just used for pissin' through. You gotta pecker, too, what the hell you think it's there for? Here, have a drink of this fine Kentucky mash."

Morris had a couple of old coffee mugs on the desk and he poured a good portion from his ceramic jug into each.

"Here now, just pull on this real slow. It's got a kick but you'll like it."

Buck took a mouthful and swallowed slowly. It burned a little, and he briefly thought about spitting it out, but then it was down, and then there was the kick that Morris had predicted. The next feeling he had was just heavenly. An unexpected warmth steadily spread across his body and with it a relaxing, numbing feeling — hands that were always clenching now hung loose, shoulders that bore a burden too heavy for such a young boy were suddenly upright and square. The knot in his chest, one that he never knew he had, quickly evaporated. He was at peace, floating on a cloud. Buck instantly understood all the years of physical and emotional pain his mother had subjected him to had exacted a fearful cost. He took another drink from his mug and then another.

"Easy, Buck, easy! Damn if you ain't a drinker! You can finish what's in that cup, but that's all for now. You keep what you saw with me and young Angela a secret and you can have a pull on this jug every Saturday. Is that a deal?"

Buck could hardly wait until the following Saturday and every Saturday after that. The provocative scene he had witnessed with his neighbor had captivated him and instinctively he knew Morris wanted his twisted tryst to remain a guarded secret. The newfound, calming warmth that Morris's bourbon provided had become a powerful bribe.

"It's a deal, sure is," Buck replied, and he knew a deal with the devil had just been made.

George's Hurricane

* * *

After leaving Brad, Morris and Chief Anthony at the cemetery, Peter and Lilian drove the short distance to their home in silence. Peter rested his lifeless face against the side window with half-closed eyes. Lillian, glaring straight ahead, kept her two hands together and tight at the top of the steering wheel. She desperately wanted to scream at her husband. His new, odd, and embarrassing behavior frustrated and angered her. She would save her wrath until they were home and in their living room; in the meantime, she tightened her grip and envisioned her hands around the throat of her very intoxicated husband.

Lillian helped Peter out of their car and into the house. Peter Marrow fell into his recliner, hoping it might provide protection from Lillian's angry words. Her body language and icy stares promised fire and brimstone. Perhaps his throne might provide some sanctuary. It did not. With an angry countenance and an accusing finger, Lillian began her verbal assault.

"You nearly got yourself arrested, you goddamn fool! What the hell is going on? Talk to me. You've become someone I don't even know. Don't you dare push me away!"

"It's all gotten to be too much," Peter said, his words slurred with booze and exhaustion. He hadn't slept in nearly two days. Sleep only brought the bizarre nightmares. "Can you please get me some coffee? I need to think this all through. I'm not sure if even I can make sense of this." His voice was sad and pleading.

Lillian stood silent, focused on her mission of confrontation. Then her anger slowly melted away and she turned toward the kitchen, dropped her shoulders in defeat, and headed for the pantry coffeepot.

Peter would never have an issue with making sense of the last few days. In times like these, most people would ask, How did this happen? Where did it all go wrong? But Peter knew exactly how it had all turned so ugly because he was the one who had put the whole thing in motion. It was all his fault and sadly knew that he could never tell his wife what he had done.

Peter Marrow sat there wallowing in paranoia and self-pity, he desperately wished his father could be there just once more to offer the sound advice that had always been there at the center of his growth as young man. But his father was dead, taken from him by the influenza in 1920. He missed him terribly.

Peter Marrow grew up on York Avenue in Pawtucket, Rhode Island with three older sisters. Peter was the baby of the family. His father was a general contractor, and insisted that Peter learn the skills of the trade. He began to bring the boy along on many of his summer jobs when Peter was only twelve. Peter didn't really mind. There were times when he wished he could horse around with his friends, and his father often let him have a day off during the week, usually after some strong coaxing from his mother. But there were times Peter declined the day off. He enjoyed the work and the time with his father. His father had a strong and nurturing presence in his life. He was a compassionate and understanding man with the biggest hands he had ever seen.

His dad was always there with life lessons. Peter vividly remembered how his father taught him to deal with the school bully. Peter was in eighth grade at Goff Junior High and he was being persecuted almost daily by David Zaluski, the school screw-up. Zaluski was always doing something to reinforce his loser position, too.

He had somehow chosen Peter to torment on an almost daily basis. He would sneak up behind Peter in the corridors and knock the books out of his hands. Zaluski's loser friends thought it was hilarious. Lunch time was especially torturous. Zaluski always took Peter's lunch box and shared its contents with his pack of morons. Then he'd toss the remains at Peter's feet with his predictable parting shot: "Hey, Marrow, see you toooo *marrow*!" The goon pack all laughed. It had become more than Peter could bear. He approached his father with his dilemma.

It had been an especially tough week at school and Zaluski was incessant with his persecution. One late Friday afternoon found

Peter's father in his work shed. A small fire in the old pot-bellied stove took the chill off the frigid January day. His father looked up from his workbench when his son hesitated before venturing in. His khaki work jacket was unzipped and a knitted woolen hat was pushed back on his scalp. Large, hard-worked hands returned a hefty wood plane to its proper location and his dad waved Peter into the room.

"Come on in, son, close that door quick. It's just starting to get warm in here," he said. "What's on your mind? And I can tell there's something."

Despondent, Peter settled onto a nearby stool and it all immediately spilled over. Recanting the harassment and bullying he had been subjected to these last six months, he struggled to hide his tears.

When he finished his embarrassing narrative he waited, uncertain of his father's response. Peter's father closed the distance between them in two large, determined steps. With a reassuring pat on the shoulders and an upward nudge of his son's chin, his father offered his insight.

"I've never met this punk nor have I ever heard you mention his name before, son. But I'll bet I can describe this loser pretty accurately. Let me see. First of all, he's probably a little on the short side. He's not the best-looking guy, I mean, he's not real popular with the girls. Probably got a skin condition, maybe a lot of acne, and this is probably his second go-round with the eighth grade after a couple of years in the seventh grade."

Peter was stunned with his Dad's clairvoyance. "How did you know all that?"

He told his son that bullies all have the same shameful qualities about them. They probably don't have the most secure environment at home and they're just overwhelmed by all their insecurities, physical and emotional. "You're everything he's not: tall, smart, and popular. It's just too much for his limited brain power."

Peter's father pulled over another work stool covered with various tones of wood stain and sat next to his son. He met his son's eyes and offered consolation, understanding, and warmth.

"The best way to deal with this loser David Zaluski is to confront him head-on. Don't wait for your books to take a tumble, or even for lunchtime. Just quietly walk up to him, almost like you don't see him, and then punch him in the nose as fast and as hard as you can. A good smack will make his nose bleed pretty easy. You want to embarrass him, and you want him to remember it. Then look him directly in the eyes and scream, 'Stay the fuck away from me!' It's okay to use those kinds of words, there are times when you have no choice. Your stomach will be doing flip-flops on you and you'll be a nervous wreck right up to that moment. But it will be over just like that, only a few seconds. He's a coward, all bullies are. Zaluski the loser will never bother you again."

The next day in school, Peter waited for David Zaluski outside his homeroom. He had hardly slept the night before and was a nervous wreck, just as his father had predicted. He hadn't even gone to his own homeroom; no doubt his own teacher had marked him absent, but he didn't care, he just wanted the whole thing over with. The first period bell rang and kids filed out of their rooms, heading for their first class. Peter saw Zaluski and Zaluski saw him.

"Hey look, everybody, it's toooo....*marrow* already," he said with his customary sneer.

Peter's right hand flew through the air and landed forcefully on the bridge of Zaluski's nose. Peter was amazed by how accurate his punch was; he felt the crack of cartilage under his fist. Zaluski was knocked to the floor and was quickly clutching a nose crimson with his own free-flowing blood.

Peter squatted over him and grabbed him by his hair.

"Leave me the fuck alone!" he shouted, and then tossed Zaluski's head back, straightened himself, and headed for his next class. He was quickly grabbed by a nearby teacher and marched down to the principal's office. After a long discussion with the principal and a follow-up meeting with his parents, the principal decided that no discipline was in order. The principal had been down that route with David Zaluski many times before.

Peter's father said he had done the right thing and his father was right: the bully Zaluski never bothered him again.

George's Hurricane

Peter left school when he turned sixteen. He remembered the night he told his parents of his decision. The Thursday night entree of kielbasa, baked potatoes and coleslaw had vanished from their dinner plates and they sipped on their hot tea. Peter wanted to work full time with his father. His mother expected him to finish school and told him he might regret his decision someday. His father, unsure if his son had chosen the right path was hesitant, but also knew he could make good use his son's participation. His work calendar was full and Peter was dependable and a quick study. But he did not want to be selfish with his son's future. The three sat and discussed the merits of Peter's decision. Peter was unyielding about what he wanted to do with his life.

* * *

"I want to learn as much as I can about carpentry, but I also want to be a complete contractor someday. I need to understand the electrical, the mechanical, and the plumbing parts of the job. I want to be more than just a carpenter and I want to start the process now. Waiting to finish high school won't do me any good."

His father was impressed with his son's insight and drive. His mother, however, had reservations. She pushed her dinner plate away and folded her arms on the kitchen table. Sage-like, familiar brown eyes that had raised four children and had witnessed a lifetime of lessons now focused on Peter. Understanding his mother was of few words, he knew she would be brief but on point.

"You should finish high school. I won't shy away from that opinion. But I know you are a lot like me, we all know that. It takes an act of God to change my mind about anything. So, I won't try to change the path you want to travel. Just think it through. Life comes at you quickly and it is not very forgiving."

Fetching her plate and tableware, she righted herself and headed to the kitchen sink, stopping only to kiss her youngest child on the crown of his thick brown hair. "You'll do just fine," she said lovingly.

Now Peter looked at his trembling wife and saw the panic in her eyes, he profoundly missed both his parents, perhaps they could have helped him through these dark days that lie ahead.

Chapter 7

Realizing several days later that he never had the follow-up conversation with Buck, Brad was mad with himself. He'd lost the initiative, and would have to start the process over again. He had every intention of going to see Buck the following morning at Joe Bearse's place, but there had been an abrupt change of plans. Chief Anthony had called the night before; he was sending over one of his officers to review the crime scene and was also sending someone from the Rhode Island State Police for fingerprints.

Meeting the two officers at the ferry, Brad drove them up to the Waters place and left them there to do their due diligence. The Portsmouth police officer, John Ferreira, was the one who'd had the emergency appendectomy right before the last storm; he was just starting to regain his strength and he'd come to the island to take more pictures and to go over the crime scene with a more focused intent. Brad doubted he would find anything; it had already been examined twice, but he had been overruled by Chief Anthony. The Rhode Island state trooper was a sergeant and all business. He impressively filled out his gray uniform with red banded epaulettes and his red striped jodhpurs. His brown campaign hat was squared up and was never in danger of being dislodged from his head. Brad was dressed in his green dickey pants and shirt and bore no visual indication that he was involved with law enforcement. He knew it probably drove Rhode Island's finest crazy — such lack of respect for the uniform and profession should not be condoned. When Brad asked the trooper how long his task would take and when he might see a final report, the sergeant replied,

"You'll have it as soon as it's ready. Can't tell you any more than that."

* * *

Late morning and Brad drove up to George Caswell's shack on Pennsylvania Road in the middle of the island. He knocked on the shabby front door, then rapped several more times, each with more conviction. Finally, George answered the door, still fuzzy from an interrupted late-morning slumber. He rubbed the sleep from his eyes.

"Oh, hi Brad, how you doing?" he said, his voice muffled.

George was thirty-four years old. He looked forty-four. He stood behind the half-open door in his plain brown chamois shirt and bib overalls. Most of his hair had disappeared, a victim of genetics and time. Only long thin strands remained, slicked straight back. A patchy, stubbly beard with flecks of gray here and there connected leathery ears to a squared, dimpled chin. Shaving was something George did not enjoy and there just wasn't that much to shave. It was how George typically looked.

George stood five-foot-nine, with a thin, reedy frame. Food was sometimes in short supply and Brad knew George depended a lot on the charity of the island folks. Not long after his little house was erected, someone built a small bench right at the beginning of the road to George's shack. No one but George lived on Pennsylvania Road, and people started leaving food on the bench after he had taken up residency there. Lots of tinned Spam and corned beef, canned vegetables, and once in a while a leftover casserole, some beef stew, or a lasagna. George always washed the container and returned it to the bench for its owner to retrieve. After all the years, it had become a way of life for everyone involved.

"Hey, George, I was hoping I might find Buck here. Wanted to ask him a few questions, but maybe you can help me. Do you mind, George?" Brad asked.

"Kinda early, ain't it?"

Brad looked at his wristwatch. "It's nine-forty-five, George, not that early."

"Guess not. I was up late last night, talking."

"Talking to who, George?"

"Well, my family of course." He opened the door, let Brad in, and pointed to the walls at the back of the room, behind the wood stove.

Brad was frozen in his steps, his mouth hanging open. The two corner walls were covered with pictures of all sizes and shapes. Some pictures were framed, most were not, and they were all attached to the wall by galvanized roofing nails. There wasn't a square inch of free space on either wall. Many of the pictures had begun to curl up at the bottom.

"What's the matter, Brad, ain't you ever seen family pictures before?"

Taking small steps into the room, Brad was stunned by all the images before him: there were hundreds of pictures of the Caswell family in various stages of their lives. There were pictures of George's parents when they were married, at family get-togethers, pictures of George and his siblings when they were just infants, images at birthdays, on Thanksgiving and Christmas. Pictures of their move into the lighthouse. And there were five large individual pictures of his father and mother, brother, sister and him, standing alone in front of the lighthouse.

"My oh my, George, where did you get all these pictures? Did these survive the storm?"

"Hell no, Brad. People just started leaving pictures on the bench. Guess they thought I would want them — and I do. Then I started hearing from relatives, most of them I knew, but there were some from kin I didn't even know I had, and they all were sending me pictures of a little while ago or of long before. The *Providence Journal*, the ones that did the story on our family right before we moved into the lighthouse, sent a few pictures, plus those five big ones on the back wall there," and he pointed like he was giving directions.

That's when Brad saw the splintered glass and fractured frame surrounding the picture of George's mother. It had been put back together with scotch tape and glue.

"What happened to your Mom's picture? It seems like a nice picture, too bad."

"Oh her, that don't matter, I still got good memories of her from before."

"Before what, George?"

"Just before."

"Well anyways, I want to ask you about a few things that happened right before you and your family moved into the lighthouse. Hope that's okay."

"It's okay, Brad, they're all here with me now anyways. We won't mind."

Brad thought the comment bizarre and once again stared at the pictures on the wall — they all seemed to be staring at him. Made him feel a little creepy. He turned his attention to George.

"Listen, George, you've obviously heard about what happened to Carolyn Waters." Brad told him about all the speculation and how they were starting to rethink some of the events surrounding Ted Esau and Tom Tuttle's deaths. Brad also shared with him the conversation he'd had with Dave Brooks about the heated argument he and the other members of the crew overheard between Peter Marrow and George's father.

"Do you remember that argument, or did your father ever mention it?"

"No, don't remember anything about that. What did Dave Brooks have to say?"

"He just remembers an angry confrontation between your father and Peter. He was too far away to hear much of anything.

Claims Peter told him your father was complaining about being behind schedule."

"My father never said a word about Peter being behind schedule. I think Dave is making that whole story up. It's best to let the dead rest in peace."

"Why would he make up that story?"

"Don't know. Suppose you should ask Dave that."

"Maybe I'll do that. Well, thanks for now, George. If you think of anything, let me know."

"Can't say I will, but maybe *they* will." He turned and nodded to all the pictures on the walls.

Once again Brad turned and witnessed the bizarre scene before him; he decided he would keep his puzzling thoughts to himself. He said goodbye to George with a nod of his head and walked backed to his truck. George stood on the front porch near the door and started to wave goodbye as Brad drove off and then suddenly stopped, turning his head as if someone from within had called his name. He slowly returned his arm to his side and stood there rigid, like an admonished teenager. Brad had always thought it was a little cruel that most of the island called him Crazy George, but this visit had only reinforced why he may have earned the moniker.

Brad drove down the hill on Pier Road. At the bottom, he took a right on Narragansett and headed home. There were no street signs on the island, didn't really need them. Most people knew the important roads: Narragansett, Broadway, Bay, Daniel, and Pier. The rest of the time you simply navigated by who lived where: there were the Voses, Fairweathers, and Williamses on the west side; the Moshers, Garrisons, and Lincolns in Bristol Colony; Sand Point had the Caymans, the Chases, and the Holmans; Homestead connected with the Bains, Starkes, Rices, and Beechums; and so forth throughout the island. There were a lot more people than that, especially in the summer, when there were almost a thousand people enjoying their dog days without competing for spots on crowded beaches, or fishing and clamming in secret family locations passed down for generations. Everybody knew each other, and sometimes seeing too much of one's neighbors could escalate into a cold shoulder for the rest of the summer, but there never appeared to be any lasting bitterness — people were on the island to relax and briefly escape the pressures of their lives.

This was why it was so hard for Brad to comprehend the death of Carolyn Waters. There had never been a murder on Prudence before, and it would probably be a very long time before there would be another — certainly not in Brad's lifetime.

There had been the casualties of conflict in the Revolutionary War, when British troops had stormed ashore and burned farms and outbuildings suspected of being ammunition storages for the Continental Army. There was a brief skirmish, and several colonists had been killed. But that was almost two hundred years ago, and now one of sweetest women on the island had been brutally murdered and possibly two other men had suffered the same fate. It just didn't make any sense.

Brad needed to get home to Milly. She had been his sounding board from the day they were married.

* * *

It was an early Saturday evening when Brad finally asked Milly to be his wife. He remembered it like it was yesterday.

He first noticed Millie at the Swansea Harvest Festival where she was singing with a local a cappella group. Long red hair and a voice of gifted talents separated her from her vocal companions. She was a peacock among the crows, and Brad was smitten. Fate intervened for a young lad too timid to approach the young lady who had stolen his heart. Several weeks later, he was signing up for guitar instruction and was astonished to find his queen behind the counter of her father's music store. Milly handled minor cash sales, scheduled lessons, and collected fees before classes. Brad soon found reasons to be there before his lessons every Saturday morning, and was just as inclined to hang around after his instruction. They were soon dating and found every opportunity to spend time with each other. Two years later, he surprised Milly one early evening when she was closing and

68

locking up her father's emporium. He had been anxious all day and was near panic with the words nearly bursting from his lips. He hoped twilight on a perfect summer's day, a simple silver band, and a question from the heart would seal the deal.

Brad had always known marriage would be a welcomed event in his life. Knowing who and when would be the only obstacle. Mildred Truant would be his who and April 29, 1925 became the when. He knew he would love this beautiful woman with the strawberry-blonde hair for the rest of his life and she would love him.

* * *

Twenty years later, they still lived in their cozy little cottage. The plan was to add on to their diminutive bungalow as their family grew, but the household numbers never expanded.

Having a family, a big family, was something that both Brad and Milly had wanted. Milly had been raised an only child and Brad had only his brother Morris; both felt a lack of family interaction and closeness; they felt cheated. Immediately after their marriage, they tried to have children, but month after month Milly's cycle always arrived on the expected day.

"My God, why do I have to be so predictable?" she would complain to her husband. "You could set your watch by me."

It frustrated and saddened her. Every month there was the anticipation and every month there was the disappointment. Four years of mounting anguish had become a dark cloud over their happy little life.

Chapter 8

Tropical storm warnings were again issued just three weeks later. It was the second hurricane in succession to approach the coast of southeastern New England, certainly a foul weather phenomenon, but weather officials were confident it wouldn't be worth the paper.

As far as Brad and the folks of Prudence were concerned, it might as well have been the storm of the century. It was as if a very selective and deadly plague was about to descend on the island. People immediately began to speculate who was next, who had drawn the black spot; someone was about to be drowned and found washed up on a deserted beach and no one tortured themselves more than Peter Marrow.

This following hurricane was too immediate and too emotionally challenging for Peter. As a community, they had just buried Carolyn Waters, and Peter struggled with her loss and the sadness it brought. Peter had moved ahead only marginally, the healing process barely begun. His drinking had slowed down but he was still a very restless man. Sleep was now an elusive component in his life. Peter sought to bring routine back into his life.

Carolyn Waters' older brother Arthur came to the island and contracted Peter to make repairs to the cottage. It needed a new roof and the south side needed new cedar shingles. Arthur had no real connection to the island, but since he was the sole beneficiary of her will, it was his intent to sell all her assets and property. He only needed to wait for his sister's will to clear probate.

Peter's wife hoped that getting back into a routine, and the passage of time, might help her psychologically fragile husband. But another threatening hurricane, quickly about to descend upon them, and the potential for another death, possibly his own, had diminished all those hopes. Peter had only recently replaced the damaged door at Carolyn's home when weather bureaus began tracking the tropical storm. It pushed Peter closer to a breakdown and there was nothing Lillian could do. Something dark had taken possession of her husband's soul, an invisible entity created by the fears, insecurities, and suspicions that now inhabited the spirit of her once strong and fearless mate. Sleeping at night became difficult for her; no position seemed comfortable and Lillian started each day tired and despondent. Her eyes were bloodshot, and the flesh of her face hung pale and slack. Culinary treats lost their appeal and her cherished tulips and daffodils did not seem as bright.

* * *

Steering clear of Peter Marrow became an annoying burden for Brad; sometimes the island was just too damn small. Besides, it's tough trying to avoid someone when they're purposely looking for you. And, inviting as it might sound, hiding from Peter was not an option.

Brad tried to vary his daily trips to the post office to avoid all the island's wannabe detectives, especially Peter Marrow. He never went at ferry time, and sometimes Milly or his brother Morris picked up the mail for him. But today he had a package from the state that required his signature.

Brad got to the post office just before closing time. He hoped that Peter would be at home with his wife, cleaning up after a day of work and getting ready to sit down to dinner. They always took their evening meals early; Peter and Lillian were early risers and were usually in bed by 8:30 or 9:00.

As Brad feared, Peter was waiting for him in the parking lot, pacing around his black Chevy pickup. There was a hint of fall in the air, with a cool, dry, gentle breeze out of the northwest. Goldenrod was in bloom all around the edges of the dirt and gravel parking lot. Brad reluctantly accepted the day's destiny and slowly steered his pickup next to Peter's. He looked like a beaten man. There was no energy in his gait and, although he was there to talk with Brad, he seemed oblivious to Brad's arrival into the parking lot. Aimless in his wandering, he seemed startled when he stumbled into Brad.

His hair was a mess and he hadn't shaved in several days. Clothes that were soiled and tattered gave Peter the image of a hobo and not the man that Brad had long respected. Peter's eyes were bloodshot and he reeked of alcohol. He had been crying a lot. He appeared like a man who was about to attend his own funeral. Empathy and sadness was all Brad could feel for him.

This shattered man was no one Brad recognized. Peter was once a focused and ambitious man. He had built a successful contracting business and had hired many of the young men on the island and taught them the skills of the trade. Several had gone on to start their own businesses and some had actually gone on to compete against Peter. Brad thought it rather ironic. Peter wasn't a big man but he had always been deceptively strong. He had won the arm wrestling contest at the Christmas Fair at the Union Church five years in a row. Now he stood in front of Brad and seemed small, fragile, and vulnerable.

Peter took a tentative step back as if bouncing off an unseen wall. Brad could see Peter struggling with his recognition, thought and speech.

Finally, he blurted out, "I swear to God, Brad, I'm gonna fuckin' kill them. Or maybe just one of them."

"Kill who, Peter? You need to calm down. What the hell have you been doing to yourself? I almost don't recognize you."

Slowly raising his head as if it was the last thing he wanted to do, he stared at Brad through inflamed eyes. "You know who the fuck I am," he said with quiet rage. "And I'm gonna kill fuckin' Crazy George and that fuckin' loser friend of his, Buck Taylor. They think they got something on me? They ain't got shit."

"What are you talking about? Got what on you? You can't keep drinking like this, Peter, it's gonna kill you. Looks like you're already halfway there."

"Those fuckers, you know they're behind all of this. They think something happened a long time ago, but nothing happened."

"Peter, what do they think happened a long time ago? You're all over the place." Brad was once again trying to converse with a drunk. Slobbering drunks were from another planet, where common sense and comprehension were the rarest of natural minerals.

"Nothing happened! Nothing, nothing, NOTHING!" Peter shouted.

"Sounds like something did happen, Peter. Do you want to talk about it?"

Brad, from the corner of his eye saw Peter's wife Lillian quietly pull into the lot in her 1940 Dodge. When she parked the car and got out, it was obvious she'd been crying, too.

"Oh Brad, thanks so much. It never gets any better, it only gets worse. I am so afraid how this might end."

"Hi, Lil. Come on, Peter, let's get you into your wife's car, she can get you home." Brad could see that Peter was about to protest, but even in his inebriated state he thought better of it and allowed himself to be led into the front passenger seat. He hung his head and stared at his dirty hands with half-closed eyes.

Brad walked Lillian around the back of the Dodge and stopped her halfway.

"Say, listen, Lil. Peter was just now talking about something that happened a long time ago, although he also claims whatever it was, it never happened. Not sure I made sense of the whole thing. You know anything about that?"

73

"The only thing I can tell you is that Buck Taylor came to see Peter right after Carolyn Waters died. They had a conversation out by Peter's pickup and it just escalated from there. They had some words, and Peter seemed a little animated, but it didn't appear to be anything at first. But Peter's mood did change soon after that, his anger was always close to the surface and he appeared distant and kind of sad. Every time I ask him about it he just gets angry. Says his conversation with Buck was just about some advice on a job he was about to do. I avoid it now. But with this second hurricane on the way he's just beside himself. He's convinced that he will be the next one to die. And to tell you the truth, I'm concerned, too. Our house is like an armed fortress. Peter has got his shotguns and rifles all loaded and at the ready. He double-bolts the doors at night and he blocks all the windows with two-by-fours."

"I never knew about this. Wonder why Peter never mentioned it?" Brad asked, perplexed by this new information. "God knows he's been in my face enough. Get him home and see if you can get him to bed. The second storm is due to hit tomorrow evening. It's not supposed to be much of anything. Last I heard, it had been downgraded to a tropical depression, but I'll make a point to stop by several times. Try not to get too worked up. I know it's really easy for me to say that, but we'll figure this thing out and no one else will get hurt."

"I hope you're right, Brad," she said dejectedly and gently squeezed Brad's left hand. She started her old Dodge and slowly drove away from the parking lot and north up Narragansett Avenue.

What a lonely, sad, and mystifying car ride that must be, Brad thought to himself.

Chapter 9

Brad had just learned that Buck dragged up something from the past and threw it back in Peter Marrow's face. Peter denied everything but fooled no one with his over-aggressive defense. Whatever it was, it had a very emotional connection to Peter and had convinced him that he would be the next casualty of the storm that was due tomorrow evening. Suddenly it all seemed like a Hollywood movie: three mysterious deaths, a dark secret, a family's destiny taken in an apocalyptic storm. And now a whole community frozen in fear. *Revenge of the Lighthouse Family* or *Hurricane Terror*. But this was real, and as much as he tried to dismiss all the half-baked (as well as practical) theories, privately he accepted there would be another twisted murder tomorrow night and he knew there was nothing he could do to stop it.

* * *

Buck drove his tired Hudson up to George's house as soon as he heard people talking at Chalmer's Store at Homestead about the second unexpected hurricane that was to be so quickly upon them. Folks milled about in front of the counter as they always did when an island issue was worthy of debate. Whoever worked behind the counter would hold court. Today it was Meredith Souza, Bill Chalmer's young cousin. She filled in whenever Mary Wheeler had the day off. A collective consensus had been reached: another hurricane meant another dead body, somewhere along the Prudence Island shoreline.

Don't see how it could be any other way," Meredith stated, as if being informed of the verdict by the jury before her.

Buck knew there would be the typical gathering at the shack on Pennsylvania Avenue. This time a little hasty and urgent in its agenda. The sudden development of a second hurricane had caught them off guard.

The national weather bureau tried to be as accurate as possible with their forecasts and assessments of impending storms, but their warnings often left folks with little time to prepare for nature's angriest moment. George was insistent that each and every member of the rat pack suffer the same fate as his family did. They should be made to feel the same terror and helplessness that his own kin must have experienced that day in September of 1938. They must feel the rage of the storm as it approached, fear its deadly potential as its winds become deafening and the seas violent, then be tossed into the middle of the tempest like a June bug cast into an early summer campfire, the remaining seconds of their lifes marked by absolute terror.

Knocking on the front door and not waiting for a reply, Buck strode in with purpose and found George sitting in his chair facing his pictures. George was in that other dimension, lost in communication with his family, and once more Buck saw and heard nothing. George turned to look at Buck and then quickly swiveled back to face his family on the wall as if he had suddenly heard his name called. Apparently, the family dialogue was not complete.

He seemed to be listening more closely, and when Buck asked, "Are they talking to you now?" George brought his index finger to his lips. Buck knew the routine; he had witnessed the family discussions before. He needed to be quiet and not hinder the dialogue that took place between George and his family. There was always an eerie silence in the beginning when George abruptly turned and regarded his family collage. First he would face his father's portrait and listened intently, often seeming to be entranced. Then he would turn and face his sister's likeness or his brother's, never moving his body, only turning his head, but always gaving his full intention. Buck never heard a sound, but the hair on the back of his neck tingled and the room turned cool, even before George heard his family's first words. Oh, they were in the shack, he never doubted that for a moment. George said most of the conversations were between him and his father, but Buck only heard George's side of the dialogue. Waiting for George to return to the moment was the only option he had.

A begrudging reply — "If that's what you really want" — and a quick nod of George's head told Buck that his friend was back in the present. He told George his concern about the impending storm.

"This is going to have to be a quick one, we don't have much time to figure out our plan of action. Sometimes I wonder how we pull these things off, but we always do. We usually have a few years in between, it gives things a chance to settle down, that way no one can make the connection with what happened to your family. How do you want to go about this?"

"We're not going to do anything with this storm. We'll just bide our time. There will be other hurricanes," George announced with disappointment in his voice.

Buck was astounded. "Not do anything? Wasn't this always your plan? We were going to make them pay for what they did! We'd wait for a hurricane and then, one by one, we'd have our revenge. These were your hurricanes, 'George's hurricanes,' you called them. Said your father gave them that name."

* * *

Buck remembered the night George revealed his family's plan for retribution. Over a year had gone by since the terrible hurricane had taken George's family from him. He had settled into his little hovel. One early winter evening, George and Buck were sitting close to the wood stove, dressed in their wool pants and long johns. George calmly laid out the intricate plan and Buck felt the plan was pure brilliance. Those fools on Peter Marrow's crew would meet their maker one death at a time, one hurricane at a time. Let the fools live in fear, year after year, and then, when nature's seasonal calamity approached, watch them squirm in their own terror. Witness their anxiety turn them into frightened, pathetic prisoners of their own homes. The plan might take twenty years or more to execute, but that was the beauty of it. It would exact a slow and painful recompense from its victims, who would know all the time their own terrifying death was a certainty, only the next hurricane away. It was a strategy for final justice for his family, and Buck understood George's reason and his need to bring about closure for the crime committed against his family.

"How did you come up with such a fuckin' great plan? Man, this thing is fuckin' brilliant. Can you imagine what those fuckers will be like every hurricane season? The fools will come undone. Count me in, I want to be part of the plan in any way I can."

"It was me and my father's idea," George had said with a small smile, "although it took a while to develop, and he wanted to be sure the punishment was equal to the crime. My father was already incensed at how easy our house crumbled in that storm and when I told him what you saw with my mother and Marrow it just put him over the edge, me too. My father knew we would have to have our revenge. He insisted that Peter Marrow should witness the deaths of each member of his crew, all the time knowing he would be the last to die and when that time came, he would welcome it. It's good that you want to help. My father is very pleased with that. These fools have been unfairly cruel to you, too. We will all have our retribution and be entertained at the same time."

Now George knew he had to convince Buck that the impending storm was not worthy of their plan. Blinking his cold grey eyes a few times, he slowly returned his gaze to Buck. He shook his head as if trying to refocus on the moment.

"The coming storm will not be fearsome enough for these fools. They must experience the same terror we did in the apocalypse of '38. Don't tell me you have already forgotten the horror of that day. We both thought it was the Judgment Day finally cast upon us."

"Oh, I ain't forgot the evil of that day. Ain't never going to forget, either. I'm the one that saved you from drowning that day with the rest of your family.

* * *

The Caswells had been living in the lighthouse for almost two years and Buck and George had become the best of friends. Buck remembered the day of tragedy as if it were yesterday. Attempts to date George's sister LouAnn hadn't gotten very far — she was still dating the loser Jeff Baxter — but she had become more accepting of Buck's presence in their home. He and George were always hanging out together and she now seemed to be reluctantly friendly to him. That was enough for Buck; maybe someday she'd wake up and realize what an airhead her boyfriend was, and then Buck would be there to show her the man he really was.

Buck and George had gotten jobs at the north end, digging holes for the footings and piers that Zebadiah Holcomb needed done for the new garage and workshop he was building. They also had to hand mix and pour several yards of concrete for those same piers; old Zeb Holcomb had an ancient hand-turn concrete mixer. Blending the sand and cement would be hard work.

They had finished the exhausting pickaxe and shoveling work the day before and were committed to completing the concrete work in one day. One single continuous pour pretty much guaranteed a good strong footing and pier — Buck knew it was the only way to do it. But it meant they would have to hump all day to stay ahead of it, lifting the hundred-pound bags of cement into the mixer followed by shovelfuls of the right sand and gravel mixture, and then the arm- and back-breaking hand-turn of the mixer as buckets of water were added to complete the recipe. When the right consistency was reached, they would tilt the mixer to pour the concrete into a wheelbarrow and move it to the next pier, funneling it in. Then the whole process was repeated, again and again, all day long.

There had been some talk about a hurricane in the area, but the weather bureau had downplayed their forecast, calling for gale force wind and rain. That type of prediction didn't get island people too concerned, least of all Buck. They decided to start their job early; it seemed like a normal day in late September with a clear sunrise, but there was an odd orange glow to the south and a feel of tropical air to it. They always put up a canvas tarp supported by four big posts to shelter them from potential rain or the draining, still powerful, late summer sunshine.

George and Buck began their mixing and pouring ritual and paid little attention to the changing weather. They had anticipated it and again they were sheltered under their big canvas tarp. They made steady progress, but then the wind had suddenly increased to a lethal level and blinding rain had descended upon them by late morning. They were working in a small grove of sturdy sassafras trees, protected from the strong winds, and had no view of the bay. The driving rains finally forced them to remove their heads from the sand, so to speak. Mixing and pouring concrete was no longer possible. They walked out from the shelter of the trees to see the tempest they were in. Enormous gusts of winds almost pushed them to the ground, and one look at the bay told them that they were in serious trouble.

"Holy shit, what the hell has happened?" Buck hollered against the wind. "This ain't no little squall. We need to get back home!"

Young George needed no encouragement to sense the seriousness of the moment. He knew he must return to his family as quickly as possible; they would need his help and would certainly be worried about him. It appeared they were in the midst of an event that could be catastrophic, and it was every man for himself.

He remembered his uncle telling him a story of his time in the Navy during the Great War, when his ship was torpedoed by a German U-boat. There was chaos all over the ship, and many of his shipmates were already dead or severely wounded. There were fires everywhere and it would only be minutes before the ammunition room would blow. The order to abandon ship had been quickly directed and men were leaping into the sea. He had stopped to help a terribly burned shipmate when Chief Ponterelli forcefully grabbed him by the back of his blue fatigues and pulled him to his feet.

"You can't do anything for him, it's every man for himself right now. You can be a good guy later on, but first save yourself. We'll need that compassion later when we're still bobbing in the ocean, days from now. Go!"

He ran to railing and threw himself into the inferno that was floating below. He was only in the water moments when there was a sudden explosion as the gunpowder room finally blew and a three-hundred-twenty-foot destroyer escort was split in half and was quickly sinking at the bow and stern. He never saw Chief Ponterelli again, but understood that he had saved his life and taught him a tragic lesson. He was one of the few sailors who had entered the water unscathed and was able to care for the many that were not so fortunate. They were lucky they were only in their life rafts about eighteen hours before they were rescued, but George's uncle had been instrumental in keeping several men alive. His chief would have been proud.

George and Buck left their tools and cement bags where they lay and jumped into Buck's maroon and brown Hudson. Now completely layered in thick mud, with potholes and ruts filled with rainwater, the winding side road ahead of them, would be difficult to traverse. Buck needed to keep his car moving quickly — any loss of momentum would guarantee becoming mired in deep sludge. The Hudson jumped up and down with every hole it encountered and weaved wildly back and forth across the width of the road. Buck's arms flailed wildly as he fought to control his car. George, riding shotgun, shouted his encouragement.

They finally reached the main drag, which was just a hard-packed gravel road. The rain had been more severe than they realized and the main road wasn't in any better condition. The firm-packed aggregate was a loose, waterlogged clod. There were no deep holes, but traction would still be an issue. Buck kept the old Hudson's gas pedal to the floor, and he fished tailed madly onto the main road, desperate to maintain his forward progress.

"Nag Creek is gonna be a mess!" shouted Buck, trying to see through his rain-soaked windshield. The Hudson's wipers pumped madly against the flood.

"I know!" said George. "Just keep going! I gotta get home, my family needs me."

Nag Creek was a low point where Prudence was almost divided in two. On a full moon tide, Bay Road was just a few feet above the high-water mark. Both Buck and George knew this and anticipated something a lot worse. There was a slow-sweeping turndown into that low spot and Buck had the old Hudson struggling for every foot of progress. They made the turn and what they saw ahead was frightening. At least one hundred feet of the road was gone, disappeared into a churning sea.

"We gotta stop!" screamed Buck.

"No, we don't," challenged George. "We gotta ride this bucket of rust as far as it will take us. I'll make sure you get another car. Please just go Buck, please!"

"Damn if this ain't turned into one crazy day. Oh, I'll drive this old gal as far as she'll take us. Roll down the windows and get ready to swim!" And once again, he slammed the gas pedal to the floor.

The car lurched forward and gained some downward momentum as it turned lower into the waiting waters. Their vehicle plunged in and pushed a sudden wave in front of itself — salt water shot up through rusted floor boards and soaked the two men. Dashboard, ceiling, and seats were immediately soaked. Intense winds and driving rain tore through the open windows, but the car kept going, the road still there just a couple of feet below. The Hudson coughed and sputtered but still crawled along.

"Baby Doll must have swallowed some salt water." It was what Buck called his tired old Hudson. They crawled along through the encroaching water. Seawater found its way through the door seams as well. Buck's feet, working the gas and the brake pedals, were completely submerged. George had changed positions and squatted in the passenger's seat.

"I think Baby Doll is going to make it!" Buck crowed. "The water don't seem to be getting any deeper. As long as it don't get in the carburetor and things don't start shorting out, we'll make it." George didn't say a thing — he was intently focused on the road ahead.

They finally emerged from the rapidly-formed river and stopped briefly to open the doors to release all the seawater. Empty whiskey and beer bottles streamed out of the car from their hiding places and fell onto the open road. Both passengers said nothing. Buck took his seat again and tried revving the car to clear it out. He was convinced that Baby Doll, his six-cylinder conveyance, was only firing on three or four of the cylinders. Putting the Hudson in first gear, he slowly released the clutch, and the car lurched forward as it bucked back and forth. The car jumped forward a few feet and then coughed, sputtered, and backfired several times. It was slow, desperate progress.

They were several hundred feet from where they left the water. The wind and rain lashed at them and rocked their car. George looked back to where they had emerged from the water and suddenly there was another powerful surge of water. It quickly swelled from only inches to an engulfing wall of water, like a Hollywood movie monster. It moved silently but powerfully forward, swallowing everything in its path. There was no wave, no terrifying, unchained element of nature, only a rapidly, inexorably rising tide, quiet but savage and deadly. The surge swiftly moved along, pushing saplings, decayed tree stumps, and dead wood ahead of it. Vines of wild grape, bull brier, and bittersweet churned and tumbled along like thousands of stringy tentacles, attaching to anything in a death grip. Buck and George knew their car was about to be consumed by the surge.

"Buck, get us out of here, we need higher ground!" George screamed.

Buck once again engaged the clutch, and Baby Doll sputtered and lurched forward, only to sputter again. They were on a slow, inclining hill — safety was only a hundred and fifty feet away.

"Buck, get us going!" George screamed again. And then Baby Doll cleared herself of the choking salt water in her lungs and roared to life. Her rear tires spun in the muddy road and then caught solid ground as they raced away as fast as they could. A soothing, grateful smile spread across Buck's grim visage. He stared straight ahead with his face and head covered in rain and salt spray. His white-knuckle grip on the steering wheel said everything about their attempt to outrun the demon that was chasing them.

The wall of water was almost up to them, the rear tires churning in the brackish slime. Buck power-shifted into second gear, and then the wall faded into the background. They were gaining higher ground, and finally the surge peaked and the riot of debris settled into the surrounding ground like grazing sheep on a hillside. There was no time to reflect on their escape; George pushed Buck to make it to his lighthouse home and family as quickly as they could. He sensed their state was perilous.

They drove on, swerving and fishtailing as they went, down Aldrich Hill, going off the road at the bottom turn, heading north. Buck strong-armed his Hudson back on the road and they approached the crest of Sand Point Hill. The sight below numbed them both. Through the driving rain and salty spray they could see the lighthouse was gone and tragically George's family gone with it, too.

"Holy fuck," Buck said, his voice shaky. "I'm so sorry, George."

George stared at the scene below them in disbelief. His mouth hung open and his eyes welled up. Where the lighthouse once stood there was only turbulent sea water. Wave after wave pounded on what remained of the foundation. He did not want to think about what could have happened to his family.

"Buck, bring me down there."

"What are you going to do? There ain't nothing there."

"Just get me down there!" George screamed. But when Buck hesitated, he spat out, "Fuck it, I'll walk."

George reached for the door handle.

Buck stretched across and grabbed his arm.

"Okay, okay, George, I'll get you down there." Buck nudged Baby Doll down the hill.

They were at the bottom in moments. Buck parked the car about a hundred feet from the newly-created shoreline. The storm had claimed many feet of a once beautiful beachfront. Sand Point dock, there just a few hours ago, was now a crumpled wreck, crossbeams and planking stuck out at bizarre angles or were simply gone. Once tall pilings were bent almost parallel with the bay water. Wave after wave pounded mercilessly on what remained.

The two friends sat in silence and once again stared in shock at the scene before them. Their car rocked back and forth in the lethal winds. The windshield wipers fought a lost engagement against the drenching rain and spray; it was difficult to see clear images of the destruction before them, but it was enough to understand the devastation was complete.

Then George was suddenly out the door and running toward what was left of his home.

"I have to save them!" he shouted back to Buck. The wind knocked him down and he scrambled to his feet. He ran a short distance and was knocked down again.

"There ain't nobody there," Buck whispered. He watched the scene in front of him in complete, horrific disbelief. His best friend ran against winds and rain that bashed him to the ground with every step forward, running toward an angry surf, running toward certain death.

He had to stop him. Buck jumped from his car and he, too, was immediately pushed to the ground.

He barreled along the ground like a child rolling down a hill. Walking in the dangerous winds would be fruitless. He scrambled along on his hands and feet.

Buck stole a look at George and could see his friend was at the water's edge, positioned on his knees with arms held high, as if pleading with his god for deliverance. Huge rollers crashed all along the beach and surged around him, trying to drag him into the tempest. George disappeared in the undertow and then reemerged from the water, still beseeching his lord for relief from all the anguish.

Buck was almost to his friend's side when the breaker that promised George his redemption reached out like a giant evil hand and dragged him out into the sea. Buck knew his friend needed his help. He did not hesitate. He threw himself into the thrashing surf and was soon next to his buddy.

"Buck, I've done it now, killed myself and killed you!" George shouted.

The ocean madness that surrounded them guaranteed they would be drowned or separated in mere seconds. Buck spied a large plank floating nearby — it must have torn free from the adjacent dock, and he gripped the timber, pulling it into them. George threw his arms around it and they held on for their lives. The peninsula that was once home to the lighthouse was just a short distance away. Buck prayed that the wind and tide would push them onto that stretch of land. The elements were in their favor and they were soon being buffeted against an angry shoreline, pushed ashore at intervals by huge swells, only to be sucked back out again by the powerful undertow. They were helpless to change their deadly predicament and knew their own horrific demise would at any moment be upon them. Another roller grabbed them and tossed them against the shoreline. Buck drove the end of the plank into the sea floor, trying to secure a grip. The board slid along the bottom and then caught something and held just long enough for the two friends to break free of the forceful return current. They crawled ashore and crept to their car. They were battered, cut, and bruised — but they were alive.

Buck started Baby Doll and they slowly drove to Buck's little shack at the top of Pier Road. Forceful wind and rain buffeted the car along the way. Nearing his sanctuary, he deliberately turned his car off the road and onto his now swampy lawn. The tires dug deep ruts across his lawn as he drove his car right up against the front porch. Buck turned the car off and it coughed and shuddered to a stop. They sat in silence, Buck searching for the right words and George not capable of any. Finally, Buck reached across and rested his hand on his friend's shoulder.

"We should go inside, George." He could not remember a sadder day.

George only nodded. They staggered from the car, onto the front porch and through the front door, the wind nearly tearing it from its hinges. They threw themselves onto the two army cots that Buck always had set up. They sat there exhausted, battered, and hungry. His spirit now fractured and void, George stared vacantly out Buck's front window. Tears began to flow and he wrapped his arms around his upper torso and slowly rocked himself back and forth on his cot.

Knowing that time would be the only thing to heal his terrible hurt, Buck could say and do little at the moment. He wondered if the healing would ever begin.

"I'm so sorry, George," he finally offered, finding in his friend a pain similar to the one that had tormented him years ago after his mother's desertion and his father's unexpected death.

George did not answer but only sat there numb, wrapped in his own arms, private tears consoling him. Buck watched his compatriot struggle for hours with a world that had suddenly collapsed around him. Finally, no longer able to keep his fatigue at bay, Buck lay down on his cot and fell asleep. His last vision was of George rocking back and forth, soaked in rain and seawater, physically and emotionally drained from a hellish day that no one could ever have imagined.

* * *

Several days later Brad was contacted by the Rhode Island State Police. There was more disturbing news: state authorities had recovered two bodies on a shoreline south of the Terrace section of Riverside. They had recovered hundreds of bodies scattered all about Narragansett Bay and Rhode Island Sound. They were having difficulty identifying bodies, but felt the remains of an adult male and adolescent boy might be part of the missing family from the Prudence Island lighthouse. They would need George Caswell to assist in that grim task.

Brad Wheeler drove directly to Buck's to share the disturbing news that authorities believed they had recovered the bodies of

George's father and younger brother, many miles up the bay on the East Providence shoreline. They were partially decomposed from their time in the water, and the state medical examiner hoped that George could identify the bodies. The thought of looking at his family members in such a state unnerved George and he wished he did not have that responsibility, but he knew he owed that accountability to his family. Allowing his family to be buried in an unmarked grave in a common burial ground was something he would not permit. Their spirits should not be left to wander aimlessly in the afterlife. They needed to be brought back home, although George was not sure if Prudence Island had become their home. They had only lived there for a short while. He wanted Buck to go with him, but Buck said he'd get the "willies" if forced to do that. "No sir, not me," he had said sheepishly. "It just ain't in me, George."

So Brad, George, and a state police sergeant accompanied a naval petty officer who piloted a launch up the bay to Providence the next morning with a grim task at hand.

* * *

George was led down a flight of stairs into a cool room in the basement of the Goodwin Elementary School in East Providence. Just outside the room they had set up a temporary office with an old wooden card table and filing cabinets. An extension cord was run out to a tarnished brass floor lamp that illuminated a stack of folders on the table. A short thin man in a white tee-shirt with a grey stubbly beard greeted them. He could have been the janitor pulled out of retirement for the forbidding task of babysitting the deceased until they were identified and processed. The state police sergeant explained why they were there.

The attendant stood and lit a cigarette. "This helps a little. It's starting to get a bit uncomfortable in there, if you know what I mean." He led them into a large open room.

Numerous bodies lay on sturdy wooden tables, all covered in dingy bed sheets. Other bodies lay on the concrete floor near a door at the back of the room. Tags inscribed with names were attached to their feet. Several pedestal fans hummed in unison, trying to circulate the pungent, stagnant air that now filled the room. The attendant walked briskly to two tables near the entrance.

"I believe these are the remains of your loved ones," he said in a practiced and mechanical voice as he pulled the sheets back.

George walked over to the bodies with conflicting and wandering emotions; he was unsure if he would cry, laugh, or tremble with fear. Brad and the police sergeant remained a few steps away, allowing him the privacy required for such trying moments. His father and brother's upper torso were a lifeless green-grey pigment and their arms lay limp at their sides. They were without any clothing. Their faces, carved with deep wrinkles, seemed to have aged ten years. Numerous abrasions covered their heads, shoulders, and chests. George did not want to think about what they must have been subjected to. Eyelids that seemed to have gently closed only moments before and lips that offered soft, peaceful smiles pleaded with George not to believe his senses — they were still alive.

"Are these your loved ones?" came the rehearsed voice of the retired janitor as he blew cigarette smoke into the air.

"Yes, they are," George said. Then his father slowly turned his head and spoke in a soft whisper. "This is all Peter Marrow's doing, and we will make him pay dearly for it." He then winked his right eye and softly returned his head to its lifeless position. George was suddenly alive on the inside. His heart erupted in panic and his eyes bulged. The hair on the back of his neck stood rigid and goose bumps traveled along his arms. His sadness was quickly gone, replaced with a bizarre mixture of fear, anxiety, and hope.

"And how do you wish to honor their remains?" offered the mechanical voice.

No one said a thing. They all were waiting for George's response, but George was numb, his speech frozen. He would not bury the living.

"Mr. Caswell, what do want to do with the bodies of your family members?" asked the attendant. his voice a bit more demanding this time.

Again, George said nothing, but Brad stepped over to George, grabbed his arm and pulled him to the side, away from the others.

"You got to decide what you're going to do with your dad and brother's bodies."

George turned to Brad, his eyes wide with disbelief, his words quiet but filled with conviction. "They ain't dead. I ain't gonna bury my family if they're still alive. I don't know what to tell you."

Brad couldn't believe what he had just heard, but the look on George's face confirmed his disturbing condition. He turned to the attendant. "Why don't we get back to you in a bit?"

"Okay, but please make a decision by tomorrow," said the attendant. "After that, the state will have to make that pronouncement for you, I'm sorry."

"We'll have a decision by the end of the day," Brad said and with a gentle hand on his back, he steered George out of the room.

In the end, after a lengthy, frustrating discussion with George, and only after convincing him that if he didn't do something the board of health would and since his father was a veteran, he was entitled to all those attached benefits, it was decided to have the bodies moved and buried in Groton, Connecticut. There was a graveside service and a select few from the island were there. Peter Marrow and his crew were in attendance, their wives and girlfriends standing with them. Not one of them shed a tear. Oh, they were respectful and stoic in their presence. Heads were bowed and hats removed when they were required. Prayers were mumbled and empty handshakes were offered at the conclusion, but George knew they had come together for themselves and not for him.

George stood alone above the open graves of his father and brother. On an overcast day, the air heavy with humidity, George for the first time began his dialogue with his father and family.

That day had forever altered his view of the world; he was no longer grounded.

Brad made the mistake of sharing the disturbing conversation with his brother about George at the temporary morgue. Morris agreed the brief discussion was bizarre.

"This whole thing has put him over the edge," Morris had said. "Guess he's just gone crazy now." He inevitably shared the episode and his observation with the rest of the island. People now pitied him, and kept their distance. Isolating him, thinking he would want his space, his time to mourn, George would have preferred a tender word or a caring touch, but no one saw that need. Or maybe they did and just didn't care. He was crazy now.

* * *

In the spring following the Hurricane of '38, several of Peter Marrow's crew got together and started building a hovel for the now desolate and only remaining member of the Caswell family. Other islanders helped on weekends and donated whatever materials they could spare for George's new home. They hadn't started calling him Crazy George yet. That distinguishing title would evolve over time. The state of Rhode Island, as part of their disaster relief plan, provided windows, roofing supplies, and siding, although it was a mishmash of materials. Not one of the five windows was a match. The roofing asphalt was of two different colors and manufacturers. There was a bedroom and a main room which included a kitchen with a white cast-iron sink and hand pump, a potbelly stove for cooking, and a sitting area with a Vermont Castings coal and wood stove. The stove barely provided enough heat in the biting days of January and February. Sometimes during those brutally cold months, George slept in the small loft he had built above it. It was supposed to be a storage area, but often it was the only place that could provide the warmth he needed on those bitter nights.

George and Buck hand-dug the well themselves. It was the dead of summer and it had been a dry one. They had to go down about thirty-five feet before they got a decent amount of seepage. Actually, Buck did most of the digging once they got beyond fifteen feet. Confined in a small space, the light diminishing with every foot they dug, George's nerves had begun to fray.

"I'll take it from here, George, being down there don't bother me at all. You just keep the buckets moving." Buck was a wiry young man and deceivingly strong. Hard work became his only saving grace, and when forced into it, he never demonstrated any lack of commitment.

"I'm gonna have a good pull on the bottle every now and then, but I know that don't bother you too much. Wish more people could be like you, George."

When the bungalow was finished, it was just a few steps up from a hunting shack.

But George loved his little shack; he could hide up there and no one ever bothered him. Buck Taylor visited a lot, but that was okay; he liked Buck and so did his family. George and Buck talked to his family a lot in his shack. They did a lot of planning there — years of planning, with more to come.

Chapter 10

Winds did blow at gale force for most of the night, and there were some heavy downpours with intermittent thunder and lightning, but it was, for the most part, a non-event. Peter Marrow sat at his kitchen table with his bottle of Four Roses, his shotgun at his side, waiting for his rendezvous with the angel of death. His wife sat on the family couch in the living room frozen with fear. Unable to see her husband — he had demanded all the lights be turned off — she heard the clink of his whiskey glass every time he took a sip and returned it to the oaken, drop-leaf kitchen table. Every so often she heard the soft gurgling of his bottle as he refilled his glass. They were only a few steps from each other, but tonight they were worlds apart. Her Peter had opened a door and entered a separate world, a dark world. She wanted so much to save him from himself, but the booze had locked that door behind him and he had no idea that he was a man standing in quicksand. No one could help him now and she wondered if he even wanted to be saved.

She pleaded with him to stop the destructive binge he was on.

"Peter, this can't go on. How will tonight be different than the next night, and the one after that? Are we going to live in fear like this the rest of our lives? I can't do this. I will leave you," she said, her voice wavering. Trembling hands gently massaged her agitated and sour stomach.

It was as if he stood behind a huge glass wall: Lillian could see him and his pain, she could hear his desperate conversation and his empty sighs, but the invisible barrier stopped her from touching and comforting him.

There was no sound from the kitchen, only the clink of his glass.

They sat there in their dark, self-imposed prison, with the hours measured only by the chimes of the family grandfather clock in the living room. The winds began to die down and the rain had briefly stopped. Peter had finally fallen asleep at the kitchen table. Lillian listened to his snoring and tortured sleep. She softly rose from the couch and like a blind woman, slowly made her way to where Peter sat and carefully took the shotgun away from her wheezing husband.

Retracing her steps to the couch, she gingerly sat on the sofa and placed the rifle next to her. Its dull grey gun metal glinted morosely in the low light of the living room. Securing the gun from her fragile, paranoid husband allowed Lillian to bring her tortured anxiety down just a bit. It allowed her to reflect.

She remembered the night she met Peter Jerome Marrow. Bobby's Rollaway on Daggett Avenue in Pawtucket, Rhode Island, was the place to be on a Saturday afternoon or evening. Lillian Camire and her friends from the York Avenue and Dailey Street neighborhood decided to gather their numbers and try to break out from the winter doldrums they seemed to be mired in. It was near the end of February — school vacation week — and they had just begun to dig out from back-to-back snowstorms. The street and sidewalks were barely passable. Lillian, Helen Schofield, Muriel Keating, Bill Stewart, and Tinker Millson bundled up in their woolen coats, scarves, hats, and mittens, their roller-skates slung over their shoulders, and set off for an evening of fun at the popular indoor roller-skating rink. Dusk had come about an hour before, and there were remnants of a lonely winter sunset way off in the southwestern horizon. Streetlights were on and the stars shone brightly in the cold, clear sky. Their boots made a crunching noise on the soft, dry snow, and their voices echoed off the icicle-trimmed, double- and triple-decker tenement houses in the neighborhood.

A lone figure soon joined them on the opposite side of the street. It was Peter Marrow. His mother had convinced him that a night at the roller-skating rink would be good for him. He was supposed to meet up with a couple of his buddies. The previous week, he'd had an altercation at school with Zaluski the school bully, and Peter was still trying to put the unsettling encounter behind him. He had made himself the center of attention at school and it was a role he was not comfortable with. Faculty members and classmates were re-evaluating his character. It had been a sudden and violent attack, even if it was on a person of questionable moral fiber. There were many who were not aware of the events that had led up to the confrontation in the hallway, all they knew was that Zaluski was walking the corridors with a bandaged nose and bloodshot raccoon eyes. Peter was worried that he had reversed the roles, that he was now perceived as the aggressor — and who might be his next victim? His father told him he was reading too much into it, that he should just give it a couple of weeks and his friends and kids he didn't really know would be reaching out to him with support.

Helen Schofield was the first to recognize Peter and she whispered to her group, "Hey, is that Peter Marrow? Isn't he the one who punched out that jerk Zaluski?"

"Yeah, that's him," said Bill Stewart. "I saw the whole thing. Don't know what brought it on but he nailed Zaluski real good."

"People said it was a sucker punch, kind of a dirty trick if you ask me. He's a little creepy."

"Muriel, you really don't know much about the guy. I heard that Zaluski had been bullying him for some time and Peter finally had enough," Lillian said in quick defense.

"Yeah, Lillian, but a sucker punch?"

"I don't care. Zaluski is a jerk, always has been. Besides, I think Peter's cute and I'm going to say hi to him right now." And then she was crossing the street before her friends could say another word. Something about Peter drew her in.

"Hi, Peter, looks like you're heading to Bobby's. So are we."
She pointed to her friends on the other side of the street.

"Hi ah, Lillian, right?" She was a year behind him in school.
"Aren't you in my U.S. History class?"

"Yes, I am, didn't think you would remember me. I'm only a
sophomore."

"Oh, I remember you. My friends talked me into going to
Bobby's tonight. I have a good dose of cabin fever right about now."

"I know what you mean. After all this snow, I've been
bouncing off the walls, too."

They walked together to the roller rink and spent the rest of
the evening together. Lillian couldn't believe how easily the
conversation flowed. They were never far from each other's side the
whole night, often holding hands to secure the closeness they both
wanted. Sore from hysterically laughing at the silliest things and
bruised from all the tumbles they took, the pair leisurely made their
way home, this time without their chaperoning friends. Peter walked
Lillian to her door, said goodnight, and softly stole the kiss that
Lillian had been hoping for all night. There is no felony with a gift.
Her insides tingled and her cheeks and neck flushed. Lillian knew she
had met her soul mate.

It all seemed like a lifetime ago and a world away.

* * *

The long, terrifying night had caught up with her. Sleep
slowly secured its grip on her. Soon Lillian would be its captive —
but would she be rewarded with a much needed, peaceful, deep
slumber, or would it be more disturbing nightmares, she and Peter
pursued by some hideous creature trying to kill them both, or Peter's
body once again washed ashore on some unknown beach, naked,
scraped, bloodied and battered, almost unrecognizable?

In her dreams, he would always rise from the beach and
follow her everywhere, stumbling with nearly every step he took, but
never falling. People would stop her and ask why he followed her

around so much. "Doesn't he know he's dead?" they would say. And always she would reply, "I think he likes being dead. It's what he's always wanted." Lillian thought it a bizarre thing to say, but those in her dreams seemed very comfortable with her answers and often replied, "Oh, that's true, he always wanted to be dead, he seems a lot happier now."

Tonight, they were sitting on a park bench on another beautiful deserted beach. It was not a beach she recognized from Prudence. The winds were out of the south and were balmy; there wasn't a cloud in the sky, and the water was the most pristine blue she could ever remember seeing. Lillian could smell smoke, and then Carolyn Waters was standing there, her hair still dirty, wild and tangled with seaweed, her lower jaw quivered, revealing jagged teeth crawling with sea worms and infant rock crabs. They were alive with their normal shoreline colors and contrasted starkly with her lifeless alabaster pigment. Above that tortured mouth, bulging eyes peered out from behind a milky film, and her lips and complexion were also without color. She could have been a porcelain statue.

Carolyn still wore the dress that she drowned in but it was in shreds, and barely covered her; her breasts hung freely and her large buttocks were bare and covered with scrapes, bruises, and seaweed. She cared little about her nakedness — she stood shaking an angry, accusing index finger at Lillian.

"Your Peter doesn't smoke, why do you let him smoke now?" she snarled. "It's a dirty habit, especially those horrible cigar things." Tom Tuttle and Ted Esau suddenly joined the group and they were in the same state of disarray, their clothes torn, almost naked, with the same chalky color — animated, ghostly white, ceramic statues, all of them.

Peter just stood there, almost lifeless, his hands to his side, no cigarette or cigar in his grip. He offered no explanation.

They all poked Lillian and demanded she do something about Peter's new unhealthy habit. She wanted them to leave her alone and she told them she would talk to Peter the first chance she got.

"You know he never smoked before! Never in his life!" she said, trying to deflect the verbal attack by these unholy beings.

Then Carolyn Waters was in her face again, screaming, "No, you need to tell him now!" She had the smell of a marshy low tide and her breath was even more stagnant.

Lillian Marrow was quickly awake and she could smell smoke. It smelled like wood, but not like wood burning in the fireplace, and it had a strange aroma mixed in with it, like rubber or plastic. Then she saw the smallest flicker of a flame near the electrical panel in the kitchen on the north wall. She grabbed the shotgun and rushed to her husband's side, knocking over an end table next to Peter's big leather recliner in her haste. It sent his books, radio, coffee cup, and reading glasses crashing to the floor and it sent her stumbling into her husband.

Peter was instantly awake from a deep drunken stupor. He tried to stand but only fell into the kitchen table and then onto the floor, his arms and legs flailing wildly. The demon that had tortured him in his dreams for the last several weeks was right in front of him and he would have his revenge. He grabbed and punched at anything he could; his hands quickly closed around his wife's neck. They rolled back and forth on the kitchen linoleum and Lillian screamed Peter's name over and over. The whiskey bottle had shattered when it hit the floor. Her dress soaked up the spilled bourbon and Lillian felt the shards of glass cut her skin as Peter struggled against her. The right side of her face and forehead were cut and she felt the blood as it ran down. Her hair and the neckline of her dress became soaked.

About to pass out and unable to call out his name, she desperately reached out to Peter's head with her fingers and dug her nails into both sides of his face. Pulling with what little strength she had left, Lillian felt her husband's skin tear, felt the warm blood flowing between her fingers. It was enough. The sudden, intense pain brought Peter to his senses and he screamed in agony. He released the death grip on his wife's throat as he knelt over her. He immediately realized what he had almost done and was stunned. Then Lillian saw the silhouette of a man on the other side of the slider to the back porch. The figure pounded on the glass door. Then it stopped and turned back into the gloom.

"Oh my God, Peter, there he is!" she screamed.

Peter was now a man in control of all his actions. He grabbed the shotgun from the floor and had it at his hip in an instant. He shouted, "Hell will have you!" and fired both barrels at the fleeing shadow. The rear slider exploded and they heard the scream and saw the body collapse to the deck floor.

* * *

Brad had decided he should keep an eye on the Marrow place during the storm. Everyone was certain that something would happen and so was Brad. He worked it out with his brother: Morris would handle the eight p.m. to one a.m. shift. Brad knew his brother would have his jug with him and would be lucky if he lasted even that long. He arrived just after midnight — no sense in tempting the gods — and his brother reeked of Jim Beam but said nothing had happened. In fact, the lights never came on when it got dark. They were still off.

"Wondered if they were even home, but I saw them come out around nine to pick up a rocking chair that got blown off the rear porch. Didn't look like Peter was up to the task, though; he was stumbling around. Lillian did most of the work. Never turned a light on the whole time, but I could see them."

"Okay, Moe, thanks. I'll take it from here. You can head on home. Be careful, the roads are a little washed out."

"It ain't the roads that you're worried about. You're wondering how many pulls I took from my jug. Just start being honest about it."

"You smell of booze. When you start to be honest about it, I will."

Morris didn't say a word, he just started his pickup and drove off.

* * *

Brad sat listening to the portable radio he had brought with him. WPRO out of Providence was on all night and they were giving updates on the progress of the storm. In the early hours, the winds started to back off ever so slightly and the weather apprises confirmed that the worst was over. Familiar songs were soon being played and Brad found himself humming along to his radio station. Milly had filled a couple of thermoses with strong-brewed coffee and Brad was not holding back on how much he drank. He felt as if he was hovering about two inches above the front seat of his truck. The caffeine had taken possession of his body and his senses were on fire, his thoughts racing.

At around three in the morning he thought he glimpsed a small flicker of a flame near the outside kitchen wall. A rain-streaked windshield made it difficult to be sure.

He had just gotten out of the truck to take a closer look when he saw and heard the flash of a shotgun. The porch glass slider shattered and the silhouette of a man was knocked to the porch floor.

Through the steady rain and wind, Brad raced to Peter's rear deck. He had his .38 removed from its holster and held his big Coleman flashlight in his left hand. Brad felt sure he was about to fire his service revolver in the line of duty for the first time in his career. He crossed the swampy, rain-sodden back yard and was standing on the deck in mere seconds. Searching the back porch with the broad beam of his lamp, he illuminated two people standing over a writhing man lying face down on the rain-drenched deck. It was like a scene from a Hollywood horror movie: Lillian's face had deep cuts and was streaked scarlet with her own blood, as was her silver hair. Her dress was torn and was also heavily stained the same crimson color. Peter's wild, terror-stricken face had deep vertical scratches that ran from just below both eyes all the way down to the collar of his work shirt. He appeared as a man possessed, almost rabid. Brad thought briefly that shooting this man might be the humane thing to do.

Peter was standing there with Lillian at his side holding on to left arm. When the beam of the flashlight focused on him, he instinctively raised his shotgun and pulled the trigger.

Two loud clicks, brief snapping sounds of metal on metal contact, instantly stopped Brad's world from turning, but nothing happened, no explosion or flash of light.

The hand that had quickly reached out and stopped Brad's life from turning on the Victrola suddenly released its momentary grip. He was alive and all his senses surged in their efforts to process the scene before him. He had been given a second chance.

With his eyes bulging and red, with raw scratches slashed down his face like war paint, Peter quickly searched his pants pockets for more shells.

"Easy, easy Peter! It's me, Brad. Put the gun down!" he yelled and brought his .38 level with Peter's midsection.

"Oh, thank God, it's you, Brad!" Lillian said, and tore the shotgun away from her now numb husband. "All of a sudden he was standing on our porch," and she pointed at the man lying at their feet. "He frightened us so much."

Brad shined his flashlight on the man and saw that most of the shotgun blast had hit him in the lower back. His rain jacket, shirt, and upper jeans were torn away; raw patches of flesh were exposed and blood seemed to be everywhere. The man was in intense pain and was trying to drag himself along the deck with just his arms, every pull bringing forth a deep agonizing scream. It appeared his legs were lifeless and would not participate in any escape effort. There was a trail of blood that led just a few feet back to where he had first fallen. Desperate to escape, the stranger continued his frantic crawl but was making little progress.

Brad stepped in front of the helpless intruder and challenged him. "You're hurt pretty bad, pal. You need to stay where you are."

But the wounded man seemed oblivious to it all. He scratched and crawled his way along the deck, consumed in his pain and his instinct to survive.

Brad reached down and grabbed the man's left ankle as he tried to pull himself along the floor. The trespasser screamed in agony and went limp. Brad focused his flashlight on the now unconscious man's face.

Brad was numb with what his flashlight revealed. "My God, is that who I think it is?" he wondered aloud, his voice shaky, and he reached down and rolled the wounded man over.

Lillian was horrified. "Oh my God, it's Dave Brooks! We just killed our neighbor! What have we done?"

Instinctively dropping to his knees, Brad put his right hand at Dave's neck and felt for a pulse. "He's still alive, his pulse is still fairly strong even with all the blood he's lost. We need to get him inside."

Peter and Lillian stood frozen in the tragedy of the moment. They would be of no use. Brad grabbed Dave by the shoulders and dragged him over the remnants of the porch slider and onto the living room floor. He flicked the switch on the near wall and the area was instantly flooded with light.

For just the briefest moment, Brad looked back at Peter and Lillian as they stood outside, oblivious to the wind and rain. The floodlights illuminated a disturbing image. Framed by a shattered glass door, bruised, cut and saturated in their own blood, they no longer seemed of this world. Peter and Lillian had abruptly taken up residence in a world where empathy and understanding no longer existed. Sadly, it was a world they had created themselves and it would have a lasting effect for the rest of their lives.

* * *

Dave Brooks knew his neighbors were nervous wrecks with the approaching storm, not because of its potential wrath — it was not much of weather event — but because every living soul on Prudence was expecting Peter or himself to be visited upon by the unforgiving spirits of lighthouse keeper and his family.

Dave had seen Peter's drinking escalate, and the strain on his marriage was clearly visible. Dave knew he was on that list of potential victims, but had stayed above the hysteria. There was no family from the grave exacting its revenge, no fiend or collection of demons marching to the orders of some dark figure. Dave had no room in his logic for such madness — fantasies and myths were for children and easily-manipulated minds. But he was not imprudent enough to deny that something evil was occurring on the island. The deadly events over the years were perpetrated by real living people. If he had to guess — hell, it wasn't even a guess, he *knew it was* Crazy George — and maybe George had enlisted the help of his dim-witted friend, Buck Taylor. He could not understand why they had not been arrested; apparently Portsmouth's finest had not put together a strong enough case.

Sitting in his living room with his .306 Marlin by his side, Dave stayed wide awake that night. His wife and two daughters had long since gone to bed. This was his vigil and his alone. Through the winds, rain, and intermittent lightning he waited; he knew the buffoons would come and he would be ready to put an end to it all.

He saw the small fire, just a flicker at first, right where the electrical panel was fixed to the side of the house. He knew his neighbor's home pretty thoroughly, had actually helped Peter install the panel. He watched the flicker grow into a small flame, but there was no sign of any activity, no lights coming on or a searching beam from a flashlight. Dave knew he had to move quickly. The rain was steady and the winds were strong, but the fire would feed on the dry interior structure. He grabbed his rain slicker and was quickly out the door. He ran to the rear deck with its big glass sliders near the electrical panel and peered through the doors with his hands to either side of his face.

There was a flash of lightning and the sight inside was horrific: Peter was kneeling over his wife with his buttocks on her hips and he seemed to have her in a death grip. Lillian was struggling against his stranglehold, her hands pulling at his face. There seemed to be blood everywhere. He pounded on the door — there was no reaction from Peter — and he turned to search for something to break the glass door. If he did not do something quickly, he feared Lillian would be killed. He saw a newly-fallen limb, a recent victim of the storm, and he turned to retrieve it. There was a blast and then he was face down on the deck, his lower back on fire with pain. He screamed with the agony and tried to stand, but his legs were no longer part of his body. A flashlight illuminated his head, something pulled at his leg and then a comforting blackness swiftly took all the pain and memory away.

Because of a simple act of caring and kindness, Dave Brooks' life had become a vacant existence, rendered that way in mere seconds. He had seen the small fire in the electrical panel at Peter and Lillian's home and had acted like anyone would have. That was the irony of it all: he had seen his neighbors in trouble and with little forethought had rushed to their aid. Now he was a cripple, chained to a wheelchair and a bedpan for the rest of his life.

* * *

The phone rang at his office up at the farm and Brad knew it was Chief Anthony from Portsmouth. They had been having too many conversations the past few weeks. Brad felt inept with the ways things were unfolding. Chief Anthony had never said anything critical or even implied that Brad was doing anything wrong. He knew that the state police sergeant had made note of Brad's absence of uniform and lack of respect for their profession — in fact, the trooper had noted it in his report. Chief Anthony cared little about a perceived dress code that had nothing to do with the very reason the state police were there; besides, he knew Brad's multi-role responsibilities and lack of support from his own office had handcuffed him. Brad was a good, smart man and was doing the best he could.

"Hey Brad, I just heard from the hospital, and it sounds like we got Dave Brooks there in time. He's in rough shape, but the doc says he'll make it. The bad news is, he will probably be paralyzed from the waist down."

"Oh, that is a shame, his wife will be traumatized. Their lives will be changed forever." Brad could only imagine the huge shifts that were dramatically put upon the Brooks family. Their world would be turned upside down. "I guess I'm not surprised. I saw the damage to his back from the shotgun."

"Yeah, doc says the X-rays show a real mess in his lower back. He'll never walk again. I understand there was a fire in the electrical panel that started the whole thing. Don't see that too often."

"Yeah, and it spread to the wood around it, but it never really got going once it breached the outside wall. Too much rain and wind, but it was enough for Dave Brooks to notice. He came running, only intent on helping. My God, what did he run into?"

"It's a real shame. Listen, Brad, we are going to have to arrest Peter Marrow for attempted murder. I hope it doesn't get ugly for you, but I don't have any leeway with this. Dave Brooks and his wife have pressed charges and the D.A. is going hard on it, too. I'll send a man over first thing tomorrow morning to help with that. I know it's been a crazy situation over there, with everybody looking over their shoulders, but Marrow's heavy drinking pushed him over the line. It always does, I've seen it a hundred times. He's lucky he didn't kill his neighbor, he could be looking at 30 years of hard time, maybe more."

Brad said goodbye and listened to the empty room. The following day would be difficult; Peter Marrow had invited tragedy into his life and tragedy never declines an invitation. Brad, with his Portsmouth counterpart, would pay a disturbing early morning visit. Peter would be up, breakfast would be finished and Lillian would be at her sink cleaning the remnants of eggs over easy and home fries. He would apologize for what he was about to do and the handcuffs he pulled from his waistline would be all the explanation required. Lillian would be devastated, he knew that. Brad wondered if they now sensed that life for them was about to change dramatically. Now burdened with a quickly approaching and unwanted task, he sighed deeply. "Sometimes I hate this job," he shared with his barren office.

Chapter 11

The state had prepared a solid case. Peter took the best deal his lawyer could negotiate. For his felony, Peter was sentenced to spend the next four years at the Adult Correctional Facility in Cranston, Rhode Island, a rather light sentence considering. Dave Brooks would spend the next four months at the Veteran's Hospital in Providence, and the rest of his life in a wheelchair.

Thankfully, Dave had enlisted in the Navy during World War II and his medical bills were not an issue, but he and his wife Darlene needed to move off the island. His days as a carpenter had been taken from him, and Darlene was their only source of income. They moved into a small four-room apartment off Hope Street in Bristol. Actually, it was once a large garage, but the woman who owned it had lost her husband in World War II and had it converted shortly after for the added income it provided. It did offer easy access for Darlene, Dave, and his wheelchair. Darlene began work on the second shift at the carpet mill on Thames Street.

George's Hurricane

* * *

Another family meeting, with the usual attendees: George, the Caswell family and Buck. Buck once again sensed his extended family's presence, only wishing he could hear or see them the way George could. But it was a good reason and a good spot to have a few beers. He could always sleep it off on the cot that George kept for him.

They had promised each other they would punish all the guilty participants and they knew it would be a slow, deliberate process, possibly consuming many years. They would have to be selective with the hurricanes they chose to punish the scumbags; they were prepared to be as patient as they had to be.

But now the idiots had actually participated in their own demise. How fortuitous! It was scripted beyond anything they could have imagined — how unbelievable was that? The fools had unknowingly aided the Caswell family in exacting the punishment on themselves for their despicable acts.

"This is better than we could ever have hoped for," Buck said. "Can you believe this, the fool Marrow actually shot his own neighbor. You gotta agree, George. These baboons are runnin' so scared, we got them trying to kill each other."

George faced the pictures and listened to his family. Once again, Buck was the outsider. He waited for George to share their conversation with him. George visually traversed the room, moving from picture to picture, much like the times before. This time, though, he shared his side of the conversation with Buck.

"He is a good friend, Dad, I know that." Still in his trance, George spoke to Buck in an almost mechanical monotone. "My father wants you to know how much he values all that you've done for us. It wasn't an easy thing to ask of you, but you have never backed away from anything we needed you to do. You need to know my whole family is indebted to you. They will always be watching over you." The large individual portraits of George's family swung slowly back

107

and forth on the wall where they hung together, their eyes suddenly focused on him, and there was an instant coolness to the room.

For the first time Buck was afraid. It was outside his comfort level, and he nervously stuttered his response. "T-tell your family, it, it was my pleasure."

George was quickly out of his trance. He sensed that his good friend Buck had reached a critical point.

"Don't get all nerved up, Buck, it's just my family. They like you a lot, even my sister LouAnn. They don't mean to scare you. Besides, my father says we're going to let things cool down a bit. He doesn't think there will be another hurricane for a long time. But those fools will always be on edge, just the way we want them, right, Buck?"

"Fuck yeah," said Buck.

Book II

Chapter 1

P eter Marrow completed his prison sentence and would return to the island. It had been four years of hell. At prison, he was weaned off alcohol and the withdrawal had been terrifying — hallucinations with cold sweats, uncontrollable shaking with painful retching and vomiting. It had lasted for days. There were times when his own death seemed a welcomed alternative.

Peter had been attacked and beaten twice, once for holding back on cigarettes he never had and another for just looking the wrong way at one of his fellow inmates. Staying alive became a daily struggle.

Lillian was always there for him. She visited with him whenever she could and brought baked goods and letters from friends and relatives and his monthly subscriptions to *Time* and *Popular Mechanics.*

Peter Marrow had paid his debt to society with his four years in the state penitentiary, but his obligation to Dave Brooks would never be paid in full. No subtraction from the principal and no interest would ever be credited to the tally sheet. Dave Brooks' new home in

Bristol was the first stop Peter and Lillian made when he was released from the state prison. Peter had insisted on it.

It was early afternoon and they had a couple of hours before the ferry for Prudence pulled away from the town pier. They knocked on the door of the converted garage, and they knocked again.

Lillian reinforced her criticism of the unannounced visit. "We should never have come here without letting Dave and Bethany know ahead of time." They turned to leave, but then the door slowly opened, almost without a sound.

"Hello, Mrs. Marrow," said a thin young girl, her long straight brown hair parted in the middle and hanging flatly and unwashed at the sides of her blemished face. It was Courtney, Dave and Bethany Brooks' youngest daughter. Courtney still remembered Lillian and Peter, though she had been just an adolescent girl when her father had been shot and the family moved away from the island in an unexpected and frantic upheaval. Lillian had been a sweet, nurturing woman in their lives, but she had abruptly taken up residence with the devil.

"Well hello, Courtney," Lillian said. "You've gotten so big, I almost did not recognize you."

"Yes, ma'am. If you want to see my father, he's in living room, sleeping in his chair. It's what he does most of the day," she offered matter-of-factly, like she was reading the recipe for Sloppy Joes. "It might smell a little bit, sometimes. Dad don't get to the bathroom as quick as he should." She would not look at Peter, then turned and led them to the back of the house. There was a mismatch of scratched and nicked furniture in every room and a patchwork of worn and dirty area rugs along the way. The room's air hung heavy with cigarette smoke and ashtrays overflowed with the evidence of an addiction. Unwashed windows reinforced the presence of a stale, smoky, and unsanitary aroma. The house gave all the indication of a family barely getting by.

Dave was still asleep in his wheelchair, his chin resting on his chest. Patches of grey stubble had accumulated on his thin face and complemented the dark circles under his eyes. He wore a tattered white undershirt speckled with food stains and cigarette burns. He looked ghostly white and his breathing was slow and labored. Hands heavily stained with nicotine, hanging from almost lifeless arms, nearly touched the floor at either side of his wheelchair. His swollen belly was nestled between the thin sticks that were now his unresponsive legs.

Courtney went to her father and poked his left shoulder. "He wakes up pretty easy from his naps when it gets around lunch time," she said, still reading her recipe. "Dad, you got company."

Dave Brooks lethargically raised his head and wiped the little bit of drool from the edge of mouth. He focused on the people in front of him.

"Hi, Dave," Peter said. "It's me and Lillian."

"I know who you are, lost my legs, not my freakin' eyesight," he grumbled. "Heard you was getting out. I was hoping you wouldn't stop by, but I figured you'd show up. Hope it was pure hell for you in the big house."

Peter looked down at the floor, searching for his next words. He had no idea how the meeting with Dave would go. He now knew it was the wrong decision. "I just wanted to stop by and tell you how sorry I am. I know I can never give you back what I took you from that night. It haunts me every day."

"Well it oughta haunt you every fuckin' day. Look at me, Peter, I spend every waking moment in this two-wheeled torture chamber and I sleep a lot in this goddamn thing, too. I can't work, either. My wife and daughter work at that hellhole of a factory on Thames Street and when they're not working, they're taking care of me. Look at this place. It ain't exactly the Taj Mahal. I used to be a carpenter and a damn good one, too." As he spoke, the tears began to flow, silently, running down his tawny cheeks and mixing with his stubbly beard. "I can barely wipe my ass now. Just leave, Peter. It ain't doing me any good, having you in my house." He dropped his head lower and sobbed.

Heartbroken and with tears in his eyes, Peter turned to Lillian and saw that she, too, was crying. He searched for the right words to say, any words, but there was nothing there. Then Lillian nudged him toward his old friend. Peter walked to Dave and stood next to him while he cried. Dave had come to Peter's aid because he was a loyal friend and a good man. But Peter Marrow had turned his own world upside down with paranoia and his own self-destructive immersion into alcohol, and he had shot Dave in the back on his own porch, making him a cripple for the rest of his life.

Peter reached down and laid his hand on Dave Brooks' shoulder.

"Peter, just go. You came here to unload a lot of guilt," Dave said in disgust. "Hope it worked for you. But I don't want no part of trying to help you clear your conscience."

"Ah, Dave," Peter offered. "Let me help you..."

Never raising his head, Dave cut him off. "I don't want your pity. Just get the fuck out of my house. Leave, before it gets ugly. Lillian don't need to see that."

Peter tenderly lifted his hand from his old friend's shoulder, looked at his wife despairingly, and nodded his head several times in complete acceptance of the pain he had caused. He knew that it was time to leave. Lillian turned and followed her husband. They left Dave Brooks alone, sitting in his grey, dingy living room like they had just paid their last respects to a fallen comrade, certainly fallen on the inside. The sad couple slowly walked to their car, not saying a word, as if they were mourners at a mutual friend's funeral, not knowing each other and only now connected by grief.

In the car, Lillian turned to her husband. "Dave looks terrible, Peter," she said. "He looks like a man close to death."

"I know," was all Peter could say.

* * *

Now Peter was back on the island and slowly regaining his sanity and self-respect. People on the island rallied around him and soon he and his new crew were busy with building and remodeling projects. There was a lot of support and understanding after the shooting of Dave Brooks.

Peter had been a respectable man before that and the good deeds attached to his name had a lot to do with that. Before he came unraveled after the death of Carolyn Waters, he was always involved in community events, often organizing and directing the schoolhouse and the Firemen's Fair. Singing in the Union Church choir helped keep him grounded. He sang every Sunday morning and every Wednesday evening for chorale practice.

But then it all fell apart after the Waters body washed ashore in Bristol Colony with hands tied behind her back Someone was sending a very clear message that her death and the deaths of Ted Esau and Tom Tuttle were no freak mishaps, they were all connected and everyone understood how they were linked. Peter Marrow and his work crew were the targets of a twisted mind and Peter knew the vendetta would only be complete when they were all dead.

* * *

People were baffled as to why, and it was always a topic of conversation. Folks speculated that it was the lighthouse family venturing back from the dead to seek retribution — after all, they perished in a structure that was supposed to be indestructible. Mary Platt was the biggest contributor to that theory. She was always consulting with her good friend Madame Alice. Madame Alice was the island mystic. She and her husband ran the small inn at Sand Point. Her gifted insight had told her that there was a lot of anger from beyond being directed at Peter Marrow, but she wasn't sure it was all about the tragic and unforeseen destruction of the Caswell family home.

People tried to keep their conversation and speculation away from Peter and Lillian, but that sort of gossip always finds its way to its source and Peter slowly began to pick up the bottle again.

* * *

Lillian was panicked at the possibility of returning to the drunken dark days before the horrible shooting of their neighbor. She would not go through that again and she approached Peter with what she had heard. They were sitting at the kitchen table and had just finished their dinner. For the fourth night in a row, Peter had gone to the liquor cabinet for his glass of Jack Daniels. Lillian knew the routine: Peter took his whiskey into the living room, eased into his chair, and worked on crossword puzzles that he never finished; in fact, the puzzles never kept his attention the way they used to, and soon, he was staring out their bay window at the opposite shoreline. The lights across the bay seemed to mesmerize him, and he became lost in his own world. Conversation became a rationed quantity. There was no 'how was your day?' or 'what do think about that?' Talk had to have a purpose with a finite result. Lillian wondered if being in the military was like her home life. She was convinced that one night soon Peter would refill his glass a second time and it would only escalate, along with his anxiety.

Lillian grabbed Peter's free hand as he walked to the living room. She stopped him and looked up at him with tear-filled eyes and trembling lips.

"Peter, what is it that you're not telling me?" she said. "It's all over the island that something occurred in that lighthouse that has left a sorrowful scourge on the family that once lived there, and you know what it is."

Peter stood in disbelief. His Lillian had become one of the accusers. He took a white handkerchief from his back pocket and wiped his brow and face. Denial was his first thought and he searched for the words.

"I have no idea what those fools are talking about, and how my name became mixed up in this is another mystery. I don't know of anything that happened there; nothing that involves me, anyway."

"Four years ago you and Buck Taylor had that private conversation in our yard and ever since, you have been a changed man. Your vocal denial of anything and everything connected to the Caswell family bothers me and it bothered Brad Wheeler years ago. Peter, I love you and I've stood by you through all of this, but I can't go back to living like we did. I can't believe you want that, too. Talk to me, tell me what's going on."

Peter's voice boomed. It startled Lillian and she withdrew her hand from her husband's as if she had burned it on a hot skillet. "There is nothing to say, nothing happened there, don't ask me about it ever again!" He gulped down his glass of bourbon and returned to the cabinet for a refill.

Lillian turned away from her husband and purposely walked to the spare bedroom. They would no longer share the same bed. Sitting on the edge of her new bed, she wrapped her arms around herself and gently rocked back and forth. She was overcome with a deep sadness and felt desperately alone. After a long while, Lillian took her mother's old woolen quilt from the foot of the bed and wrapped herself in it, softly crying herself to sleep.

* * *

It was five years since the murder of Carolyn Waters and the shooting of Dave Brooks. Peter Marrow had paid his debt to society for his stupidity with four years at the Adult Correctional Institute and they were no closer to solving her murder or the deaths of Tom Tuttle or Ted Esau. Too much time had gone by and the state police report on Carolyn Waters shed no new evidence or insight into her demise. The fingerprint analysis revealed no relevant information, a big fat nothing. Brad and Chief Anthony had walked the crime scene several more times and tried to approach it from every possible angle, but there was nothing to sink their teeth into. Eventually, they allowed Carolyn Waters' brother to sell the house and property. Peter had fixed the cottage up prior to the shooting mishap and it was a pretty little seaside cottage when it was finally listed. It didn't take long to sell; a friend of Preston and Marylou Clarke's who lived in the little community of Prudence had always liked the cottage and the view it offered. A deposit and then a Purchase and Sales agreement was quickly expedited and in less than three months the new owners were moved in. That's how houses sold on Prudence: anyone living there

— or who had come to visit family and friends — knew how special the island and its people were. There was no sales pitch — homes sold themselves.

Portsmouth and Chief Anthony had lost focus; the island murders just weren't on their radar screen, and hadn't been for quite some time. The chief sent Officer Souza over to the island every now and then and he and Brad would again discuss the case and review the file. Portsmouth police brought in Buck Taylor and George Caswell for questioning, and interviewed them together and separately. They stuck to their original story: they knew nothing about the deaths of Ted, Tom, or Carolyn. Buck often stayed with George at his little shack during the hurricanes. It was in the middle of the island and slightly sheltered. Buck could do his drinking up there and stay out of trouble.

The investigation was going nowhere and Chief Anthony told Brad that he had given him as much manpower as he could.

"I know you've got your hands full over there with one confirmed murder and possibly two more, but it's coming up on five years and I just can't commit anyone to that investigation any longer, even part time. I can spare a man every now and then if the need arises and of course, I'm always just a phone call away. Seems like you have had your suspicions right from the get go, that Buck Taylor and George Caswell were mixed up in it. Too bad we never got anything on them, but stay with your gut. You're probably on to something."

Chapter 2

Morris decided to pay a visit to the two conspirators at George's shack. He shared some details of the case with his drinking buddy Fenway Connors and had asked him to tag along. Fenway was a part-time fisherman, handyman, and town worker. He had wandered his way onto Prudence from Fall River to escape the responsibility of his badgering wife and the hungry mouths of his four children. His wife, Viola, never seemed happy with the amount of money he brought home to support his family; too many times she had seen him squander most of his weekly revenue and their livelihood with long nights at Dawley's tavern. Her harassing was incessant.

Fenway rented an old work shed from Morris near the southernmost corner of his property, installed a rugged wood stove, and managed to survive the harsh winters, although he had to pump his own water from a nearby well and be satisfied with the awkwardness of a not-so-nearby outhouse. He was a simple-minded man made simpler by his drinking. Fenway made sure that he agreed with everything that Morris postulated on and supported all of his actions. Mary, Morris's wife, disliked Fenway and was disgusted that her husband allowed him to live in the dilapidated shack on their property. Fenway knew his position was precarious. He was a suck ass and Morris knew it, but Fenway was someone he could depend on to share his jug. For the most part, Morris did not like drinking alone — too many demons waited to torture him when he was by himself.

They sat in Moe's pick up next to Fenway's dilapidated shack "You know, Fen," Morris said as he passed the jug, "I think we need to pay a little visit to Crazy George and his loony friend Buck. I think they know more than they're saying about all these mysterious deaths that've happened around here. You can't say nothing about this to my brother."

"Sure nuff, Moe, won't say nothin.' I'll have your back tonight, you don't got to worry about that. Should I bring my 12-gauge?"

"Hell, no. I hope we won't need that." He took the jug from Fenway and stared at it for a while. "Maybe we should lay off this for a bit before we go up there tonight."

"You really think so?" Fenway offered, disappointment in his voice.

* * *

They bounced along the dusty roads in Moe's pick-up. It was Saturday evening and Morris knew Buck Taylor would be well into his weekend binge. Some things were just that predictable. Maybe the alcohol might loosen Buck's tongue. As planned, Fenway was with him, but Moe wanted the two of them relatively sober. A shack full of drunks was a recipe for disaster.

"I need you sober and in control tonight", he reiterated to Fenway. "I'm going to be busting some balls. George won't be bothered at all, but I can see Buck getting hot under the collar and I don't need two drunks on my hands."

He believed his brother Brad would be proud of how he was thinking it through, although a surprise visit with Fenway Connors might not have been his brother's strategy. Moe hoped it would go well.

He parked the truck on George's lawn and confidently walked up to the front door, then knocked several times. No one answered. They knew Buck and George were in there, the lights were on and Buck's old Ford pickup was parked close to the shack. They heard George talking in a low voice; he seemed to be having a conversation with someone, but they never heard Buck's voice. Morris leaned into Fenway and whispered, "Who the hell is he talking to?"

Fenway shrugged his shoulders.

His patience gone, Morris had enough with polite knocking. "Fuck this, I ain't standing out here all night," he muttered, and pounded on the door with the side of his fist. Both the door and the cabin's front wall shook with each smack of his giant hand. Instantly there was movement inside the shack; they could hear the mumbling of Buck's voice as he stumbled to the door.

"Sounds like we woke him up," Morris said.

Buck opened the door. He stood with sleepy, bloodshot eyes, his hair looking like a feather duster and his white tee-shirt stained with grease and spotted with holes.

"It's time to have another little chat, Buck."

"Chat about what, Morris?" Bucks slurred.

"Mind if we come in?" Fenway asked.

Buck tried to collect himself, his thoughts still fuzzy. "Suppose you should ask George that, he's talking with his family right now," he said, and turned to where George was sitting.

It was an eerie sight. George sat in an old high-back rocker, facing the family pictures that were on the back wall, as he always did. There was an overhead spotlight that illuminated the black and white pictures and cast the silhouette of George's upper torso along the floor and partially up the wall. Each picture cast its own tiny shadow on the photograph below it. Every set of eyes in those portraits seemed to follow the two as they entered the room. They appeared angry by the unannounced visit.

George rocked back and forth, hypnotized in his trance, oblivious to the visitors in the room, only staring at the family snapshots.

Morris finally broke the silence. "Hey George, we want to ask you and Buck a few questions, hope you don't mind."

George continued his slow rocking, giving no indication that he had heard Morris at all.

"Guess he don't want to talk to you;" said Buck, still feeling quite drunk.

"Oh, he'll talk to us," said Fenway, suddenly stepping in front of George, his frame casting an enormous shadow on the wall and blocking George's view of his prized pictures. Fenway's face and hair were flooded with piercing light, and his forehead and nose cast eerie shadows on his leathered face and grey, stubbly beard. Fenway reached out to stop the rocking motion of George's chair but George's arm flashed out and grabbed Fenway's hand in a powerful grip. George slowly turned to Morris, still holding Fenway's hand in a vice-like grasp.

"I do mind your visit. And your friend's bad manners," he said in a cold and deliberate speech. A beat passed, then another. He released Fenway's hand.

Fenway took a step back and massaged his hand.

"You got a powerful grip for a skinny guy," he said.

"Move away from the light. Your shadow is offensive to me and my family," George replied.

Morris stopped his friend with a raised right palm.

"Listen, George and Buck," he began, sweetly but with a hint of menace just under the surface. "We need to ask some questions, and the sooner that's done the sooner you can go back to talking to your family and Buck can go back to his drinking."

"So, get on with it. Buck can answer if he wants, that's up to him," George challenged.

Morris relayed how rumors had surfaced over the years about something happening in the lighthouse right before the deadly Hurricane of '38. Peter Marrow had so vocally denied it that it only supported the theory that something had actually occurred.

"Peter's own work crew confirmed that there was a heated argument between him and your father; they thought it might have been over money, but you say it wasn't. Grown men usually fight over two things, money and women. Was there something going on between your mother and Peter?"

"Hey, you ain't got no right saying things about George's mother!" Buck said, and he stumbled toward Morris. Fenway stepped in to block his path.

"He ain't saying anything, he's only asking;" Fenway said, putting his left hand against Buck's chest, his right hand closing into a ready fist.

Morris stepped in again and calmed things down.

"My mother would have nothing to do with a scumbag like Marrow and I am pissed you're implying that," George said.

Morris turned to Buck and asked him about his conversation with Peter right before the hurricane that killed Carolyn Waters.

"Seems you went to see Peter at his house right after the storm that killed Carolyn Waters. His wife said she saw you two having a little conversation, got a bit heated, and he hasn't been himself since then. What do you know about that chit-chat?"

Buck paced nervously around the shack. "Nothing was said, I don't think so anyway. That was a long time ago. Peter was always getting too close to Mrs. Caswell, if you ask me."

"Buck, you shouldn't give your opinions to Morris," said George. "He's not looking for that, he wants only facts. Ain't that right, Morris?" George shot Buck an angry, warning look.

"No, no, that's all right Buck, tell me more about Peter getting too close to Mrs. Caswell."

But Buck had seen the anger in George's eyes and he was done talking.

"I didn't see a thing," he replied. "Anybody seen my bottle?" He looked under towels and blankets lying on the floor and on the cot where he had been stretched out.

"Never said a thing about you seeing anything, Buck," Morris replied.

"Enough of this bullshit!" Fenway shouted, his patience long gone. "You two losers better start answering some questions."

Buck found his bottle under his cot and gulped at it like a man dying of thirst. He sputtered over his next words, spitting, the bourbon still wet on his lips as he spoke.

"I went to see Peter Marrow that day about getting more hours or maybe getting some back pay, something like that."

"That's all bullshit and you know it," shouted Fenway, his face turning red with anger.

George quickly turned and walked to the back door and took the shotgun from the rack just above it. He turned and faced his family pictures and instantly slipped into another trance. Morris and Fenway stood there frozen.

Morris wished he had let Fenway bring his own shotgun. He cursed himself.

Morris grabbed Fenway by his arm and nodded toward the front door. "I think it's time to leave."

But Fenway's anger had consumed him and he was beyond any rational reasoning. He knocked the bottle from Buck's mouth, sending whiskey all over the room. The glass flask smashed against the wood stove.

"Fuck this, you little shit," he spat and he grabbed Buck by his ratty tee-shirt. It tore easily in his grip. "Time to 'fess up, you know there was something going on between Peter and George's mother, just say it."

Buck was petrified and tried to wipe the whiskey from his face and neck. He tore himself free of Fenway's grip and turned to confront his attacker. A shotgun barrel forcefully poked Fenway in the ribs. He winced and immediately grabbed his side. George moved the barrel to the front of Fenway's chest and pushed him toward the door.

"Like the big man said, it's time to leave," he said.

Morris and Fenway backed their way out onto the porch. Fenway was still spoiling for a fight and he challenged George.

"You can't threaten a police officer with a shotgun, you'll pay a price for that!"

"I can threaten him all I want. Besides, he ain't no police officer. Ain't that right, Morris? Your brother's a cop, but you ain't. You go around telling everybody you are, but it ain't so, is it? You got no right to be up here startin' all this bullshit. Wait 'til I tell your brother about all this crap. He won't be happy. Now get the fuck off my property."

Morris took a step toward George but then checked himself. George was right, he had fucked up and Brad would be furious when he heard about it. He turned to leave the shack but Fenway wanted more. "Morris, you can't take this—"

But Morris checked him. "Get in the goddamn boat, we're leaving."

"Boat!" Fenway repeated bewildered. "What are you talking about?"

"I said truck," Morris said, his patience beginning to wane.

* * *

Morris drove Fenway back to the farm in silence. He knew there would be hell to pay once Brad caught wind of what he and Fenway had done. He had been too impulsive, as he had been all his life. His intentions had been good, but getting Fenway involved was the wrong thing to do, his hindsight silently scolded him. Fenway Connors and good intentions were elements that would never mix together. He dropped Fenway off at his dilapidated hovel.

"Hey Moe, back there you told me to get in the boat, you really did, but it don't matter much. Come inside and have some mash with me," he said.

Funny, his wife had been telling him lately that he was mixing up his words a lot. Morris saw it as just a coincidence. "No, can't do that right now. Want to get back to my house and think this through. My brother is going to be pissed at me."

"What's to think over? They're just a couple of losers. We should have gone after them. I don't think that shotgun was even loaded. We could have gotten them to talk."

"Ah, Fen, sometimes you just don't get it. Go drink your mash. It's late. I'm going to bed." Morris drove off before Fenway could say anything more.

* * *

Buck found another bottle of bourbon not long after Morris and Fenway left and he shuffled back and forth, drunkenly venting his wrath with false bravado. He would make Fenway pay for grabbing him like that, he had done nothing to bring that on, and Morris was also just a hot-headed bully and he wasn't afraid of any bully, never had been. He would square things away, but it would be on his terms, the time and place would be of his choosing. He wobbled around the shack cursing Fenway and Morris and threatening them with all sorts of sadistic torture and humiliation.

George knew Buck needed to vent. He sat in his rocker and witnessed the spectacle. Sometimes he agreed with Buck's assessment of what happened and he encouraged Buck's plans for retribution. Trying to persuade Buck otherwise would have been futile. Besides, he knew the angry tirade would run its course and Buck would soon be asking him to play his Billie Holiday record. It was the only record he owned. "Miss Holiday touches my soul," Buck said. It was always the same routine. Buck took to his bottle and attacked the night as an angry young man, only to mutate into a sad and lonely old one, listening to his diva sing the blues. He would cry himself to sleep on his cot in the early morning hours.

It was funny how liquor had such different effects on people. Buck drank too much, George knew that — everybody knew that — but Buck was never mean-spirited when he was drinking. Sure, he could be a little goofy and stumble over his words, and there were times when his sadness and loneliness consumed him, and he retreated into a world of isolation and despair. But Buck always rose the next morning, and the next and the next. It was his only goal. George never pitied him, nor passed judgement; an abusive mother and an ugly childhood had sealed his fate, and booze was the only salve that Buck could apply to his hurt. George understood. Buck was his good friend, and a very loyal one.

* * *

Morris Wheeler, however, was a mean drunk, simple as that. He'd been that way as long as George could remember. He yelled at his wife for the littlest things, and George had seen the bruises on her arms and shoulders and the welts on her face. The whole island talked about it. Mary, Morris's wife, worked part-time at Chalmer's Variety, and she could be found there at the counter, courageously enough, her bruises and scrapes visible to all. She chalked it up to a fall or mishap and laugh, but the laughter never reached her eyes. A palpable melancholy seemed to live behind them, almost a surrendering despair. And fear too. George knew all about fear.

* * *

Over the years, George and Buck heard stories about the Wheeler boys. They'd even been witnesses to some of Morris's foul moods. Some people said that their father had been a mean son-of-a-bitch. There had to be a reason for Morris's nasty behavior and his bouts with alcohol. People wanted to think it was genetic, but George and Buck had learned over time that other factors were in play.

Morris's mean streak and bullying tactics had once again been visited upon them. Their first experience with Moe's dark side had been traumatic and disturbingly enlightening.

Hired on over the years for various town jobs, Buck and George had gotten to know both of the Wheeler brothers fairly well. Town dock and road maintenance, plowing the roads in winter, all of it had allowed them the intimacy that only comes with working alongside someone for long periods of time.

Brad was fair and open in his approach to work: show up on time, put in an honest day's work, and leave on time. It wasn't complicated. Brad wasn't much of a conversationalist and didn't really have much in common with two boys twenty years younger. But he did keep his brother in line and that wasn't always easy with a man so angry with the world. And when he drank he got angrier. Morris was always criticizing or second-guessing whatever municipal project they were involved in. The equipment that they used was always some second-hand piece of shit, or they didn't provide enough material for the job, and of course the pay was pathetic. Morris's complaining was constant and tiring.

Brad often tried to keep him in check. "Don't know why you bother to get out of bed in the morning," he would say. "All you do is piss and moan all day long. I don't know how Mary can live with you."

"If anything I'm saying ain't the truth, then just let me know where I'm wrong," Morris replied. And keep my wife out of this. She don't complain, I think she knows better."

"It just gets real old real fast, that's all. Besides, George and Buck get tired of it, too. You're filling their heads with a lot of nonsense."

"Might as well fill their heads with something. They're pretty empty right now."

Morris would say stuff like that in front of them. It was just his mean streak, and he made no effort to temper it. It came to define who he was.

The best time to approach Morris was at the end of the workday, late afternoon. The lengthening shadows meant it wouldn't be long until he could get to his jug. Just thinking about that approaching reward seemed to lift his spirits.

On a late September day, they had finished a grading job on the west side and Brad had sent Morris home early with the grader. He had the boys remain to finish a small shovel and raking project in the same area. "Bring the town truck back to the barn when you're done," was how he left it, and he headed for home.

George and Buck had the project done in about an hour and headed for the barn. They pulled into the usual spot. Buck turned the key and they gathered their lunchboxes and sweatshirts. Suddenly a large man in a white hood was standing in front of them. He held a black Colt .45 in his right hand, shiny in the afternoon sun. He was pointing it right at them. His left hand was behind his back.

"You boys best come with me." The hooded man motioned to the back of the barn with a casual wave of his pistol.

George and Buck stood stock still, the suddenness and the sheer abnormality of the situation freezing them in place. "Now move!" the hooded man yelled, breaking the spell, and they hustled out of the truck. The boys walked to the back of the barn followed closely by their armed escort.

George and Buck were convinced they were being marched to their death. Later they conceded that they thought it might be Morris dressed in his KKK outfit, but that thought brought them little comfort.

"Now turn and face the barn wall." Neither boy moved. Crippled with fright, they looked at each other, unsure of what to do. Then the voice boomed, "Do it now or face the consequences," and they turned to face the weathered red barn wall like they were mired in quicksand. Suddenly there were two quick gun shots — *Boom! Boom!* — like thunderous explosions that echoed off the tall oaks, maples, and pines at the end of the open field behind the barn.

Buck and George felt no pain, only the terror-stricken pounding of their hearts. Expecting to see the other one dead, they slowly turned their heads and looked towards each other.

They were both alive.

Their executioner was laughing hysterically. "It's all right boys, come on, turn around. I was just having a little fun with you. Shot about ten feet above your heads! Take a look, you can see the holes."

Numb with relief, they turned around to see their tormentor removing his white hood. It was Morris, his face red and sweaty underneath the disguise on such a hot day.

"Don't know how my Southern brothers can wear these things, it's hotter than hell down there." He held the still-smoking weapon in his right hand, but it was lowered, no longer a threat. His left hand revealed his pale brown ceramic jug. He brought it to his sweaty lips and took a long drink.

"Aaaaahhhh! Now that was good! Bet at least one of you boys pissed your pants," and he laughed even louder again.

It was obvious Morris was drunk. Buck turned and searched the back wall for the holes the Colt had made. George decided to confront Morris.

"You got no cause for doing such a thing. That was just plain mean. But then again, you're always mean, ain't you, Morris?"

"Now don't you get mouthy with me, young crazy, I might get even sloppier with my aim," and he fired three more rounds into the barn wall — *boom boom boom!* — the same thunderous echo, this time closer. Chips of wood from the outbuilding wall flew into the air and floated to the ground. Buck was petrified. He dropped to the ground and curled up against the barn wall. Trying to shield himself from whatever came next, he wrapped his arms around his head and upper torso.

It had just the opposite effect on George. He hated being called crazy, hated it like poison; somehow he felt the word erased his past, his frightful experiences, the very fact that he once had a living, loving family.

George gave Morris the middle finger and took several challenging steps towards him. "Fuck you, Morris, you're dressed up in some hooded clown outfit, stumbling around with a jug of rotgut and firing shots into the side of your barn, trying to scare two kids that ain't done nothing to you. You're the one that's fuckin' nuts."

Morris was about to say something but then his wife Mary walked around the corner of the barn and confronted her husband. She wore a light green cotton housedress, and her brown and gray hair was pulled back with a black ribbon. Her cheerful smile collapsed into a look of horror as she took in the scene before her.

* * *

Mary Wheeler had heard her husband return with the grader earlier that afternoon. From her kitchen window, she watched him park it under the elm tree and head toward his office in the barn. She knew the daily routine, except that on Friday, he started on his bourbon earlier. It would probably get ugly, and Mary knew she would have to be careful of what she said and how she said it.

She looked out on the neglected and overgrown fields that once had flourished with corn, potatoes, and squash. They had worked the land hard when they first came to the island, but then the demons from the Great War found Private Morris Wheeler and enslaved him. Years ago, they were young and so in love. She never was one of those confused housewives who wondered where it had all gone bad. There was no mystery. The Great War and the trenches of western Europe had gobbled up the gentle, handsome young man she'd married.

They had met at church and were drawn to each other. He was the big, strong, good-looking boy that every girl at the parish wanted to be courted by. But Morris saw only Mary. Her long platinum-blonde hair and piercing blue eyes mesmerized him, but her quiet, shy, accepting demeanor seemed to draw him in. She loved him so much and she told him and everybody she knew. He was her big strong champion and she felt safe in his arms. But then the Great War interrupted their love affair and Morris felt strongly that he had to go. She hadn't protested; it seemed like the patriotic course to take. She told Morris she would wait for his return from what was supposed to be a short engagement. Everyone said that once the Americans arrived overseas, the war would be over quickly. But Morris wanted to get married before he left for Europe and a quick, small wedding was arranged. Mary wasn't quite eighteen and her new husband was just nineteen. They had their whole lives in front of them.

But Morris had returned from Europe with deep wounds, both physical and emotional. The love that had ensnared the two in its happy grasp seemed to disappear overnight and Morris cared little about any life that lay before them.

* * *

"What's going on, Morris? Are you boys all right?" she asked.

"W-we're okay, m-ma'am," Buck stuttered. "We just want to go h-home." Still gripped with fear, he rose from his spot on the ground, never taking his eyes off the gun in Morris's hand.

"You boys go on home," she said, then wheeled on her husband. "Morris, what the hell are you doing? And why are you dressed like that?"

Seeing a weapon that had such a horrific history in the hands of her husband deeply saddened her. Years ago she had hidden it from him, hoping the pain attached to the deadly instrument would be enough to keep Morris from ever looking for it again. Obviously, he still had a morbid connection to the gun, and it frightened her to imagine the depth and contours of that obsession.

And now he stood in a hideous outfit that Mary had hoped was no longer part of her husband's dark identity. It had been years since Morris had worn the evil swathe. She detested the disgusting ensemble, hated what it represented, and it saddened her that Morris still fostered a connection with such a despicable movement. The man she had married would never have aligned himself with such a bigoted organization.

But her Morris had returned from a barbaric struggle with a severe upper leg wound. The wound would eventually heal, but there would be a lasting impairment — their ability to have children had been forever taken from them. The emotional wounds that Morris suffered would never heal. The first six months after his return from the European campaign had been nerve-wracking. Cars that backfired or slamming doors had Morris cowering in the nearest corner or frozen where he stood, his eyes rapidly scanning the sky above. Tense arms crossed against his chest and his hands sought the safety and warmth of his underarms. Mary's soft words and tender caresses assured him that everything was okay. She could bring him back from the sadistic trenches of France and the Maginot line.

But the nights were the worst. Mary could not protect him then. There were desperate, lonely screams and cold sweats. Morris thrashed in his bed and called out the names of comrades, often begging a Sergeant Connelly not to leave him. Many nights he woke and Mary held her once-proud champion, and he sobbed and shook in her arms like a frightened little boy. It broke her heart. Once, she asked Morris about the names he called out in his nightmares. It was Sunday and a frigid day in February. The yard and surrounding fields were covered in a deep snow, its top layer sparkling in the late morning sun. The night before had been typical. Saturday allowed Morris too much time for drinking, and that always translated into restless nights with the ghosts of long ago invading his dreams.

He became angry and defensive and told her to never ask anything about his time overseas. Mary had begged him not to hold it inside, and said that talking about the horrible events might help. If it was too difficult talking to her, then maybe he should talk to a psychiatrist. The suggestion only incensed him more. *Leave me alone,* he demanded; he would deal with it on his own terms.

Then Mary asked about Sergeant Connelly, the man who always seemed to be at the center of his nightmares. She had inquired too deeply — he turned to her, his head aflame with rage and his eyes cold and lifeless. Gripping her powerfully by the shoulders, he shook her like a ragdoll, then quickly released her. She fell to the floor, her legs tingling and numb. Both her shoulders felt bruised, and the material of her cotton blouse hung down, revealing quickly reddening welts. They had added another gloomy dimension to their empty relationship: it was the first time Morris had assaulted her. Sadly, Mary knew there would be more.

"Don't ever talk about Sergeant Connelly again," he said, his even voice belying the rage that simmered just under the surface.

But something deep inside told Morris he owed his Mary an explanation; the hurt he had just caused demanded it. He decided to tell her, just this one time, about that terrible night.

Morris painfully returned to the trenches. He sat before the fireplace, oblivious to the crackling logs being consumed by dancing red and orange flames. He moved his rocker slowly back and forth as if in a trance, staring straight ahead, seeing nothing before him but visualizing everything in his tortured past.

* * *

"He held us together, made us feel safe when none of us really were, and then I held him in my arms for hours and listened to his screams. We all listened to them. Both of his legs were torn away by a mortar shell.

"I dragged him back to our bunker. We applied more tourniquets, filthy rags, to both of his legs. There was no medication or morphine to help with his pain. I sat in the filth of our bunker with his twisted torso in my arms for longer than I want to remember.

"There was the briefest moment when Sergeant Connelly's mind could see through the pain. His thoughts became lucid. He reached down to his holstered .45 with a hand that was missing two fingers. With his trembling, disfigured hand, he placed the barrel against his chest and offered me the handle.

"His body turned and twisted with tremendous pain, and with his head and face drenched in his own sweat and splattered blood, he looked me in the eyes and said only one word: 'Please.'

"I looked around at the other men in the bunker who had witnessed the same horror and they all nodded their heads as if conceding the obvious, granting their approval and offering a blessing.

"One by one my comrades extinguished the lights or blew out the candles. There was total darkness, broken only by the flash of enemy artillery. It had begun to rain, and I could hear it, pelting the canvas drop cloth that hung near the entrance.

"In the darkness of our tortured shelter, Connelly squeezed my hand, pleading with me to end his agony. Somehow, I pulled the trigger. There was a blast and a quick flash of light, enough to see all those around me, their heads bent, looking at the ground at their feet.

"Never ask me ever again, never ask me to relive that pain," and he dropped his head to his chest and began to cry.

Mary scrambled to her feet and went to comfort him, but he stood and told her to stay away. "I need a drink," he said through tears and left the room.

George's Hurricane

The transformation that had begun that day in a deplorable bunker was complete. Mary's champion was gone, replaced by a bitter, lonely man, whose only friend was the nearest bottle of Kentucky sour mash.

* * *

"Hey now," Morris said to his wife. "Those boys don't got to leave now," and he grabbed Buck's arm as the boy tried to make his escape.

"Let the boy go, Moe," came another voice. It was Morris's younger brother Brad.

Morris let go of Buck's arm and the two boys scrambled back to their car. They were soon traveling back to their homes with a bizarre and frightening tale to share with their friends, never knowing how potentially dangerous a situation they had just escaped.

Brad had heard the boom of the big Colt. The loud report had echoed all around the open field behind the barn before engulfing his own home. It had been some time since the .45 had reaffirmed its presence. Brad also knew the weapon's tragic history. He wondered why his brother held on to it. There was so much pain attached. He remembered when his brother returned from the war, a frightened, timid shell of the young man he had been. He had aged ten years in about fourteen months, and his dark-circled eyes reflected all the horror and pain he had seen. Morris approached every day with a sour and cynical outlook and reinforced it with an unhealthy love affair with alcohol.

Over the past four years, Brad had watched his brother become an angry man trapped in a past that he relived every night and drank every day to forget. He had tried to talk to Morris about what had happened in France, but his brother made it clear that he would not share his experiences. Brad finally sought out a friend who had served with Morris overseas. Frank Carbone lived in Walpole, Massachusetts and had been by Morris's side through much of the action. Frank was also in the bunker during the last horrific hours of Sergeant Connelly's life.

* * *

They sat in a little coffee shop in the town square. Brad had traveled north along the bumpy roads of Route 1 to get there. They sipped their coffee and Frank recounted the horrors of what took place in those trenches. Frank told him it wasn't easy to talk about it all, but it was how he dealt with the shock and the pain. It was better than taking to the bottle. Time, and talking to his wife about those awful days, had allowed him to confront his demons and move forward. He would never be whole again, but he had a wife and a beautiful little daughter, and they had become his new happiness and redemption.

Frank told him how Morris and Mike, Sergeant Connelly's first name, had become good friends. They were both big powerful men. The sarge took an immediate liking to Morris and wanted to keep a close eye on him. Sarge was a true leader and tried to be there for all his men, but he seemed to take a special interest in Morris. The conditions in the trenches were horrible and the engagements were even more horrific. There were full frontal assaults across an open, barren land against an entrenched foe. Men were slaughtered by the hundreds and at night they heard the screams and moans of their dying comrades. Sergeant Connelly delegated himself and Morris to venture out in the early morning hours to retrieve what casualties they could, since, he reiterated once again, they were both sturdy, powerful men. Frank once witnessed Morris sprint the last few yards as he returned from a trip into no man's land — he had one soldier slung over his shoulder and he dragged another by his field pack. Morris and Sergeant Connely never shrank from that duty, although it was never an assigned responsibility. It was simply something they did, and they seemed to take strength from each other's moral actions.

On one of their rescue missions, Sergeant Connelly stepped on a mine or an unexploded mortar shell and his lower legs were torn free of his body. The men in the bunker all heard the explosion and then it was silent for several minutes. They waited anxiously. Then Morris was racing across the wasteland, naked from the waist down with Connelly in his arms. He had cut up his pants so that he could make tourniquets for the sergeant's butchered legs, which he secured as best he could to the ragged, bloody stumps. Then the lonely ordeal began for us as we witnessed the sergeant's slow, agonizing death. It was especially hard on Morris. I think you know how it ended. Several men requested the Silver Star for his actions that night, but he refused it. He did not want anything hanging from his chest to remind him of that terrible night.

"How is Morris doing?" asked Frank Carbone as his sad tale wound to a close. "The fact that we're here talking about him tells me he's not doing too well."

"No, no he's not. Every day is a struggle for him. He buries himself in his jug. He's abusive to his wife. The injury he received during that campaign prevented them from having children. In hindsight, I'm glad of that. He would have been an abusive father, too."

Carbone sighed heavily. "Seems this awful mixture of frayed nerves and alcohol are a deadly combination. So many men came back from the war like that. What a pity. I wrote Morris several times and never heard back from him. Obviously, he wants to be left alone."

* * *

"Hey Brad, now you spoiled our little party," Morris said, he speech slurred. He stumbled to his brother, waving the big Colt in the air.

"I don't think George and Buck thought they were at a party," Brad said flatly. "Why don't you let Mary get you a cup of coffee? Come on, let's go back to the house, I'll have one with you."

Morris stood pondering the question, his feet busy trying to keep him upright, his eyes half-closed and bloodshot and his breath reeking of booze. He waved the .45 back and forth, almost taunting, in front of his brother's face.

"Okay," he finally said, and stumbled toward the house. Mary was by his side, guiding him. Morris abruptly stopped and turned to Brad. "Okay, but no fucking lectures," and he once again motioned the pistol under Brad's nose. Brad reached up and removed the gun from his brother's fluttering hand, amazed at how easily it slipped from his grasp. He had heard the story before about Sergeant Connelly. "Don't think the sarge would ever want his gun being used like this."

Morris looked directly at his younger brother with a challenging stare. His expression slowly softened, his clenched teeth turned into a frown and his eyes began to well up. "No, no, he would not," and he looked around his property as if seeing it for the first time. Mary was at his side, trying to steady him. He turned back to his brother with tears running down his sun-leathered cheeks and asked with a pleading voice, "What have I become?"

Brad put his arm across Morris's broad back and privately cursed those who orchestrated war. "You'll be fine, Moe. Let's go get a cup of coffee." And the three trudged back to the farmhouse as if in a funeral procession for someone who had died long ago.

Chapter 3

George was a lot like him, guess that's why he and Buck were such good friends. They had both been stripped of their families, maybe for very different reasons, but they were alone and only had each other. George had never met Buck's parents. He had heard the stories about his mother, how she had abused her two children, especially Buck, and how she finally vanished with some young sailor from the island naval station. She had been a heavy drinker most of her life and supposedly continued her binging all through her pregnancy, right up to the time she delivered Buck in the back of Drew Dixon's Buick. Everyone thought it was why Buck drank so much and had other issues. People said he didn't stand a chance. Buck's father had been a good man and had tried to heal the deep wounds his wife had caused, but a fatal heart attack took him from Buck's life just a few years later. Buck was only fifteen. Aunt Dot, from his father's side, offered to take in his younger sister. There had been a lot of discussion about what to do with Buck. He insisted that he would not go to live with his aunt, and if they forced the issue he would simply run away and be on next ferry back to the island. They finally acquiesced and allowed Buck to continue to live in his father's cottage. His father had left a small savings account that would take care of property taxes and upkeep for a few years and by then Buck would be old enough to take care of those financial obligations himself.

They had done the same thing for George, but had been more caring and giving. They had built him his little shack up in the middle of the island. His parents had a small nest egg put aside and once it cleared probate, George had access to it.

* * *

After a while, Buck stopped his wandering about the shack and stared out the kitchen window; he saw nothing and felt numb. "Hey, George," he said in a sad and surrendering voice, "can you play Miss Holiday's blues for me?"

"Sure, Buck," George replied, and shuffled over to the old Victrola. It sat on an old upright lobster pot in the back corner to the right of the wood stove. The album was always there waiting for its cue. It was the only one they owned. George walked to the record player, turned it on and gently placed the needle on the spinning disc. Crackles and scratches introduced Billie again to her number one fan. George lit a small candle by Buck's cot and tip toed to the switch for the spotlight. He turned to his family, said goodnight, and flipped the light off. Buck was again lulled into a melancholy trance. He stood by the kitchen window and held onto the sink with both hands, rocking slowly back and forth. Soon the tears began, and he pushed his feet along the floor over to his cot and lay down. The crying continued, interrupted only by soft moans and sighs. Sometimes George heard Buck's lonely, sad pleading to a mother that had long ago left his life: "Why couldn't you love me, I was a good little boy."

George understood the emotional pain that Buck was feeling, the pain only a mother can cause. His own mother had caused his whole family a lot of anguish with her acts of infidelity. She had hurt George very deeply.

All those years thinking they were a close, happy family, never doubting that they weren't the most blessed family in the world.

Then Buck had told him the sad tale of what he had witnessed. It was a conversation that he would never forget.

* * *

Near the completion of their lighthouse project Buck had begun acting strangely, unengaged in conversation, even at night when they drove over to the stone pier on the west side to take in the sunset, he limited his chatter and focused more on his whiskey. George had had enough.

"Buck, I'm gonna ask you one more time, what the hell is going on with you? You're as tight-lipped as a corpse. You got nothing to say about anything and usually I can't shut you up, especially when you got your bottle with you. You ain't the Buck I know, and it seems to have happened overnight. One day you're okay and the next you're this weirdo. I've asked you a hundred times what's wrong and you say everything's okay, but it ain't and you know it. Something's gotta give or I don't know how we can stay friends."

"You ain't gonna like what I got to say," Buck replied. He took a slow sip of his whiskey, swallowed hard, and released a deep sigh. Staring straight ahead, he felt his heart sink along with the hazy sunset. Thin, wispy clouds stretched across the skyline to the west. There would be rain by the morning, Buck thought to himself.

"Something bad happened, George," Buck said, his eyes never looking at his friend.

"What?" George knew he would not like what he was about to hear.

"More like I saw something bad, George."

"This is freaking torture, Buck," and George grabbed him by the front of his work shirt and forced him to turn and face him.

"I can't look at you," Buck said, and he turned back to the comforting colors of the twilight. "Your mom and Peter Marrow were going at it, George, they were jumping each other's bones. Now it's out there."

The two friends sat in silence. Soft winds whispered the dark secret and the sea gulls screeched and echoed the terrible news.

Finally, George broke his silence with red, tearing eyes. He wanted to know every detail about his mother's infidelity.

"Ah! George, you don't want to hear that. What good will it do?" But George was relentless in his probing.

Buck told him of leaving work at the lighthouse. It had been an easy day and Peter let his crew go an hour early. Buck was going to enjoy the rest of a fine summer day and headed to Chalmer's store. There was sure to be a gathering of his friends there. They would be jumping off the dock at Homestead into the refreshing bay water. Buck parked his Hudson in the wide, dirt parking lot, grabbed his musty beach towel, slammed his driver's door closed, and sprinted down the wharf, finally yelling a conquering boast before leaping into the bay. It felt so good. He climbed the wooden ladder secured to the south side of the dock and stood among his friends. He toweled down and shook his long, dark hair free of the clinging saltwater.

"Hey, Buck, you playing hooky from work?" asked his friend Al Buckley, slapping Buck's briny back at the same time.

"Hey, Al. Not me, Marrow let us go a little early today and that water looked mighty good on the drive home, just couldn't pass it up. A little sip of whiskey would make it complete. I'm gonna grab my flask, you want a pull?"

"Too early for me, Buck, but you go ahead."

The warm summer sun felt good, and Buck strode back to his car. He always kept his bottle under his front seat. But there was no flask there, nor was it under the passenger's side. He checked the back seat, nothing there. The glove compartment, under the front seat again and the back again, nothing. Maybe the trunk, in his box of rags and quart containers of Harris motor oil — but still nothing. Buck panicked; it was a fresh quart of Imperial whiskey and he hadn't even cracked the seal yet. Standing next to his old Hudson, he scratched his head and wondered if someone had stolen his bottle. He paced along the side of his car (it was how Buck did his best thinking) and then he remembered he had brought it to work that morning. He had wrapped it up in his sweatshirt and stuffed it behind some plastering lattice just inside the back door.

Shouting to his friends that he'd be right back, he hopped in his car and headed for the job site at Sand Point. He was surprised to see Peter's truck still there as he turned down Landing Lane and into the parking area next to the lighthouse. The job was nearing completion, but there was still a lot of lumber and shingles stacked at various spots; half-used-up electrical spools were still stacked near the back door. He'd have to be careful how he retrieved his bottle, he didn't want Peter knowing about that. He hoped Peter was on the second floor, busy with job planning. Through the open second floor windows he could hear the radio that Peter always kept on. WSAR out of Fall River was treating their listeners to the crooning of Frank Sinatra.

As Buck tiptoed up the back stairs and quietly opened the back door, the sounds of heated passion suddenly engulfed him. Whoever the amorous couple was, they were making no attempt to be discrete. Buck stole into the back room and retrieved his sweatshirt and bottle. He was about to close the door behind him when his curiosity got the better of him. He guessed it had to be Peter, but who was his partner in their boisterous love dance? He crept back into the house and passed the back room. The noise was coming from the kitchen. He peeked around the corner and his heart sank; there on the floor were Peter and Connie Caswell, George's mother. Peter had put a heavy canvas drop cloth on the floor and the heated couple were writhing on it. They were completely oblivious to the world around them. Peter was naked from the waist down and Mrs. Caswell had her dress hiked well above her waist, her underwear off to the side. Peter had his arms locked behind her knees, and her legs were pulled back and spread wide. Peter thrust hard and deep and Mrs. Caswell had her arms wrapped around his broad back, lost in her desire.

Buck pulled his head back and stared out the window that faced south toward Sand Point dock and further down the bay. Children played along a shoreline speckled with sandpipers, and a soft, gentle breeze made the bay sparkle with a million diamond crystals. A glorious New England summer day cast its spell on a grateful gathering, but Buck stood frozen, numb with anxiety. In turmoil, he turned away from the blissful scene in front of him. Knowing he had to leave before he was discovered, he sneaked back to his car like a combatant behind enemy lines and drove off toward home. How could he ever talk to George again with that image of his mother burned into his memory? With his knees bracing the steering wheel and his hands shaking, he broke the seal and twisted off the cap of his whiskey bottle. He took several deep swallows and a familiar comforting feeling, like a soft warm blanket on a frigid night, slowly engulfed him. Bourbon made him numb and when he was numb he didn't feel pain. Buck learned that a long time ago.

The sun had long ago finished its day and only a faint glow outlined the distant shoreline. Buck finished his sad tale and the two friends could barely look at each other. "I'm sorry, George, I just didn't know how to handle it. I ain't really good with complicated things like that."

"It's alright, Buck, I knew something was up, it just ain't what I expected to hear. It hurts a lot, a lot; can't imagine what my mother could see in such a jerk as Marrow."

"Are we gonna be okay?" Buck begged him. "I don't want to lose you as a friend."

"We'll be okay, but I can tell you, Peter Marrow will pay for what he has done. My father will see to that.

"You ain't gonna tell him, are you?" said Buck, stunned with George's intent to share the news with his father. "That's only gonna make things worse. Your family is gonna hate me."

"This news as awful as it is, belongs to my family, it's out of your hands now, and not to worry Buck, my family could never hate you. Let's go home, I need some time by myself."

Chapter 4

Bernie Caswell demanded a family discussion.

The darkness spread throughout the tiny shack as the sun sank down below the horizon. Soon a single candle on a table next to George's small sleeping palette would be the only light available. George sat in the old recliner with the family pictorial towering above him. In the flickering candlelight, their eyes took on an animated quality and seemed to dart about suspiciously, longingly, as if taking worth of this world they no longer were a part of.

Most of the time it was George and his father reviewing what actions would be taken and when and how they would be carried out. George knew the whole family was involved, but his father always remained the spokesperson. This time was different: everyone was offended by Morris's and especially Fenway's actions. Their sanctuary had been invaded, Morris and Fenway had been rude, and Fenway had been physically abusive to their good friend. It demanded recompense. Everyone insisted that Buck be in attendance.

* * *

George had seen Buck early the next morning and had asked him to stop by that evening.

When Buck arrived at the shack, the sun had long set and the moon had begun its rise in the east. He swung open the rickety door without knocking, as was his custom. "Hey, George, hope I ain't too late," he said as he entered with a clamor. "Had a few drinks and got to reading some of my magazines." Buck was apologetic and a little nervous. "The time just flew by."

"No problem, Buck. You sit there, have another drink. I got something I want to share with you; matter of fact, my whole family wants to share it with you. Heck, I even got some Seagram's that I been saving for special occasions." He hustled over to kitchen and reached into the cabinet under the sink and retrieved a new bottle of Seagram's Seven. "Let's pour us a glass of this."

"Your whole family? Is that okay? Don't know what I'm supposed to do. I don't know if I'm ready for this." Buck nervously stumbled over his concerns.

"It's okay Buck, don't be nervous. Have a seat. Here, have some of this." George handed Buck a full glass of whiskey. "My family is just real pissed off at the way those boys behaved, especially that pig Fenway. You don't have to say anything; I'll do all the talking."

Sitting under the blank consternation of George's framed family, Buck became more and more restless. He gulped down the whiskey that George handed him. He pushed his glass toward George for a refill.

"Hey, George, how come I can never hear your family?"

George refilled Buck's glass and handed it back to him, then paused for a bit. "Don't know," he said.

George turned off the light above the dark gray slate sink in the kitchen and the floor light near his caned rocking chair. The whole room was instantly pitch black, but Buck could hear George as he moved across the cottage floor, heard the click of an electrical switch and the overhead light illuminated all of his family pictures on the back walls. Their eyes became energized, and Buck felt as if he were suddenly standing in a very crowded room. He could feel people

146

pressing in on him from all sides and yet he saw and heard no one. It unnerved him, and he sensed it would be a night of strange conversations and bizarre events.

His legs trembled with fear of the unknown and pushed him toward the only rocking chair in the room. He sat down, steadied his hand, and threw back his glass of Seagram's. His reliable, longtime friend within the bottle once again warmed and relaxed him.

George paced back and forth in front of the wall-mounted family pictorial. The four big portraits of his father, George Sr., Constance his mother, his sister LouAnn, and Trevor his brother hung in the center of the collage at about eye level with George. He pressed in on his father's portrait and stared directly into his eyes. He seemed to listen intently, nodding his head as if both comprehending and agreeing with his father's thought process.

"Yes, Dad, Wheeler is a scumbag."

Then George turned to his sister's likeness. "No, you are right LouAnn, they are not boys, just grown men acting like adolescent teens." George turned to Buck. "My sister says hello."

"Your sister is talking to me?" Buck asked. The images on the wall seemed to move in and out on him, their eyes piercing. "She's in the room with us?"

"In a way, Buck. She's just very bothered by the way you were roughed up by Fenway."

"Oh, fuck him, LouAnn," Buck replied. "He ain't nothing. I ain't oughta be cussing in front of you, although I ain't really sure where you are. George says you're here somewhere." He took another drink.

Things were getting blurry for Buck; the pictures on the wall began to sway back and forth as they continued to press in on him. Some of the faces smiled at him, some of them moved their lips as if speaking to him. The room seemed to spin very slowly. Buck wondered if he had drunk too much liquor. He held his hands in front of his face, and counted the fingers. Ten and all visible, although if he did move his hands too quickly he could see the trails they left in the air. He had seen those hallucinations before. Yeah, I'm getting a little drunk, he thought to himself.

"But I've been drunker than this before, a lot drunker," he said out loud, almost proud of himself.

"Why do you drink so much, Buck?" said a whispering, soft, sultry voice.

Buck slowly turned his head toward the hypnotizing voice. LouAnn was there, a floating, ghostly image. She was dressed in pastel green shorts and a white short-sleeved blouse that accented her girlish figure. It was her outfit of choice that summer before the hurricane. Buck was so jealous of Jeff Baxter, her island boyfriend. He thought about LouAnn incessantly that summer, always envisioning her in a passionate, naked lovemaking rendezvous with Jeff, always wishing it was his own hands caressing her firm breasts, his lips exploring her secret areas.

"Those kinds of thoughts will serve no purpose any longer. Besides, you are making them into much more than they ever were," LouAnn added.

Buck, like a child caught with his hand in the cookie jar, answered, his speech slurred and unsteady. "I don't know what you're talking about. I ain't thinking about nothing."

"Oh, Buck, I know exactly what you're thinking," she said. "Look at me now! I think it would be difficult to have those thoughts of me again."

She floated before Buck, her long blonde hair a snarly mess filled with seaweed and seagrass, her face cut and scraped. Several teeth from the most beautiful smile Buck had ever seen were gone, and only jagged stumps remained. Her nose was displaced and contorted. Deep lacerations, scratches, and dried blood covered both her hands — she held them out to Buck like an offering.

"Do I seem so appealing to you now?" she asked in a sad, empty voice.

Buck reacted instinctively. "Oh LouAnn, what happened," and he took another long drink from his bottle.

"I drowned, and all of this is evidence of my struggle to avoid that horrible fate." She turned her head side to side and once again held out her arms for Buck to see.

As much as he tried, Buck could not focus on LouAnn's ghostly presence; her image became more indistinct as she floated in front of him. His mind began to swirl. Was he dreaming? Or was heavy drinking warping his vision, his very mind? Trying to make sense of it all, he closed his eyes and pressed his sweaty palms and trembling fingers to either side of his head. Terror had now taken possession of his body and it began to spasm. Buck no longer wanted to be in the bizarre world that George found so comforting.

"Ah, George," Buck slurred. "I can't do this n'more. I think I should leave."

"You can't leave now," George said.

"Yes, you should stay," Louann pleaded. "You must hear our plans for Morris Wheeler."

"Plans! What freakin' plans?!" Buck demanded. The room and all the ghostly images were swirling around him.

"Our family has been insulted, and you were horribly mistreated," said George, his ghostly kin pressing in on him. "Morris must pay a heavy price for his rudeness, and only his death will suffice. You will help us collect our retribution."

"Whoa!! I don't want no part of that. I gotta get out of here." And Buck stood, but his balance and coordination had long ago deserted him. He fell instantly to the hard wood floor and struggled to find his vision in a tilting room. Images of George's father, his wife and children floated around him, their hair and clothes all tattered and torn. Eelgrass and small seashells clung to their locks and clothing. Their skin was a lifeless pale blue color, wrinkled, like dried moldy plums.

"No, I can't be part of that! Killing Morris Wheeler was never part of the freakin' plan. No! No!" Buck shook his head vigorously.

LouAnn's ethereal spirit was again before him. "Yes, you can do this, Buck. But it will be at a time and a place of our choosing."

The whole Caswell family surrounded him again, telling him he should do it. It would be all right, they said, they would all be there to help.

Buck rolled on the floor in terror. He shouted in a stuttering voice that he wanted nothing to do with whatever they were plotting.

149

K.W. Garlick

He pleaded with them to leave him out of their plans, then he felt a wet warmth bloom at his crotch and spread down his legs.

"Oh my shit, I've pissed my pants."

Buck struggled to stop the room from spinning. The images before him were overpowering. He felt light-headed. The warm puddle under him had grown. There was a small flash of light and the Caswell family faded from his vision, turning slowly from grey to a complete and empty black.

Chapter 5

Peter cursed the day he strayed off the path, cursed the deceptive act that immediately compromised his marriage to a special woman, one certainly not deserving of his infidelity. He should have been a stronger person. He believed he had greater moral fiber than that. Disrespecting his loyal wife that day with a sinful act had led him down a path that spiraled out of control. He felt helpless.

Peter had been spending a lot of time with Bernie Caswell, the lighthouse keeper. The federal government contract mandated that Bernie be on the job site each day to monitor the project, and he took the ferry daily to the island except for bi-weekly meetings at the federal building in Providence, where he was to provide updated reports on the quality and progress of the construction. Mrs. Caswell — Constance — often accompanied her husband to the island. She wanted to get to know the island folks a little bit at a time, rather than abruptly immersing herself in the close-knit community.

Connie Caswell sometimes sat in on the weekly lighthouse project meetings, especially near the end, when a woman's perspective seemed appropriate. Peter often found her agreeing with many of his views on aesthetic issues, much to the obvious dismay of her husband. She was a smart woman and quite pleasing to the eye. A mutual attraction took root.

Peter was potentially damaging his own marriage. He and Connie had kept their affair a secret, although he was unsure just how much Constance wanted to keep it a surreptitious relationship. She was very unhappy in her marriage.

Their affair began at choir practice of all places. Peter was a respectable tenor, and he and Matt Sears were the only men who could provide a balanced sound to the Union Church choir. He was surprised and pleased to see that Connie, with Mary Wheeler's assistance, had become a member of the choir.

Connie had gotten to know Mary Wheeler, Morris's wife, at Chalmer's store at Homestead. Connie often stopped by to pick up drinks for the lunches she had with her husband. She had also begun to stock up on staples they would need in their new lighthouse home

"Say, aren't you the new lighthouse keeper's wife?" Mary finally said after a few visits. "Bernie Caswell, I think they said that was his name. Very nice to meet you." She extended her hand. Mary would turn 35 that July, a short woman with some added pounds well distributed over her diminutive frame. She had a loud, gravelly voice, but it was always welcoming.

"Yes, my name is Connie, and it's nice to meet you, too," she said, and they shook hands. Something told Connie that Mary was a good person, and they quickly became friends. Mary began to include Connie in some of the activities at the Union Church and often invited her for morning coffee at her home on days that Connie came to the island. Involved in town work or with some farm-related project, Mary's husband Morris was rarely there. The intimate settings allowed Mary and Connie to quickly become good friends. They soon found out that they had one sad element in common: neither had the most loving relationship with their husband.

Connie Caswell, with Mary Wheeler's invitation, began to stay overnight on the island. Wednesday night was choir practice and Connie wanted to lend her voice to the small gathering. She had always been involved with the choir at her previous church. Her voice was strong and clear and it always lifted her spirits. She and her family would soon be year-round residents of the island and she would welcome the gratifying distraction. Connie told her husband of her intention to stay overnight at Mary's, and he saw no issue with her becoming involved with the church and island community ahead of schedule. Bernie and the kids would be fine with brief excursions to the island. The fact was, the couple had been slowly drifting apart over the years. George had been a great father but had shunned his duties as a husband, always had, and their marriage had begun to suffer with the loss of intimacy.

To help simplify Connie's participation, Peter had innocently offered her a ride back to Mary's after choir practice. It was as practical as that. Peter was building their home and was good friends with her husband; no one gave it an extra thought. But Peter had been smitten months before and had tried to suppress his charged feelings. Connie Caswell was an attractive woman and had unknowingly cast her spell over him. Her movements enticed him and thoughts of her began to creep into his day. Peter sensed that it had blossomed beyond his single-sided fantasy. Often, he caught her looking at him, and a brief smile would confirm her guilt. When she toured the work site with her husband, she took Peter's extended hand to navigate a tight passage and was slow to release her grip. Her touch electrified him. She continually found reasons to be around Peter and concocted ways to touch him.

Her husband appeared to be oblivious. He was no longer the sort of man who paid attention to those types of actions. He had long ago emotionally disconnected from Connie — any possible intimacy had vanished from their life.

Connie Caswell remembered the day her husband announced that they would be sharing separate beds. His statement was not shocking, and, oddly enough, she welcomed it. The physical side of their marriage had never been what she had envisioned, although she had no real reference to gauge it by. Bernard had been the only man in her life.

* * *

K.W. Garlick

Connie and Bernie met at Fitch High school in New London, Connecticut. They actually met in homeroom where they had been assigned seats next to each other. Since their teacher organized the seating alphabetically, Constance Coleman and Bernard Caswell had been destined to meet. They were from the same neighborhood, but their paths had never crossed. They did discover soon after that as a boy, Bernie had delivered the newspaper to her parents' home. Connie and Bernie talked freely in class and began walking home together after school. Asking Connie to the junior prom seemed like the most natural thing to do. In his senior year, Bernie made the varsity basketball team and Connie went to the games with her girlfriends. Sometimes Bernie was lucky enough to get the family car and they drove over to Lover's Lane on Groton Long Point.

Their interludes never progressed to the point that Connie hoped they would. She never protested or hindered any of his physical advances — in fact, she tried her best to encourage any sexual curiosity her boyfriend might have. He didn't seem to have any. He always insisted that preserving the innocence of his male sexuality was something he took very seriously, as should she of her own virginity. It would make their first night together all the more special. It was a warning sign she should have picked up on, but she convinced herself that Bernie's noble principles were to be admired and respected. It did, however, leave her frustrated and confused on many nights.

Bernie and Connie were married eight months after they graduated from high school. It had become a simple progression; most high school romances are just that. Junior prom, senior reception, marriage, and then enlistment. Bernard joined the Coast Guard six months after their marriage. After boot camp, Bernie was fortunate to be assigned to the Coast Guard station in Bristol, Rhode Island. Connie was seven months pregnant when they moved into their second-floor apartment on Wood Street in Bristol.

She was aglow with her pregnancy but puzzled with its conception.

Their honeymoon night was shallow, with little intimacy. Leaving in the morning for three days in New York City, Connie lay in their large nuptial bed at the Biltmore Hotel in Providence, Rhode Island. Her skin tingled and her face and bosom flushed with anticipation; every fiber of her womanhood was alive with pleasure. Bernie was in the bathroom. She was naked under the satin sheets. Her loins quivered and she could barely control herself. He finally emerged from the bathroom in only his boxers. He pulled the sheets back and briefly took in her nakedness. Connie met his eyes with all the warmth and longing she felt any woman could ever offer. He was quickly under the sheets and reached over and turned off the light on the nightstand. The room was dark and she felt his hand reach between her legs. A soft primal moan of longing whispered from her throat. She heard and felt him fumbling with his shorts and then he was on top of her. She opened her legs, wanting him to take her, and then she could feel him, he seemed large, she thought, but she had no reference. He slowly entered her. Connie was alive with a sexual energy she had only imagined. He moved again inside her and then his body stiffened, spasmed and shuddered. Bernard was quickly off her, rolling to his side with his back to her. He turned his head slightly back. "New York should be fun! See you in the morning, sweetheart."

Connie felt empty. Lying in the dark, she stared at the ceiling wondering if it had really happened. Their tryst had lasted but a few seconds and then the warm semen that slowly ebbed from between her legs cruelly validated the disappointing experience. She turned toward her husband. Perhaps his lack of intimacy had not been lost on him. Maybe he could offer an explanation; certainly he could not be satisfied with their meager closeness. But he was already asleep, and soft throaty grumblings affirmed a deep slumber.

Soft, silent tears dripped from the corners of her eyes. Connie sensed that this was the best their lovemaking was ever going to be, and she knew her acceptance of the brief, empty, and mechanical interludes would determine if their marriage would survive.

The next morning, they had room service deliver a delicious brunch. The late morning sun flooded their room and they sipped coffee. They soon would board a train to New York City for their honeymoon. Connie thought the moment was right; she gently probed about the previous night's intimacy.

"I hope I was everything you expected last night, my love," she offered. "I was so nervous with anticipation. I sensed your uneasiness, too."

"No, everything was fine last night," he countered, like a man unsure of his words and actions. "You're making too much of it. You were just wonderful. I'm sure we will have many children."

There would be other nights just as fleetingly repetitive as the night they consummated their marriage. All disappointing and all leaving her so void of the sexual and emotional nurturing she desperately sought.

Soon, Connie was pregnant and Bernie was all aglow when she shared the good news.

"This is really good news," he told his wife. "We have started our family. It will be a boy, I am sure of it. I can't wait to tell our parents." It seemed Bernie drew more pleasure from the results of their lovemaking than the actual act itself. It was simply a means to an end — children — and Bernie wanted children.

The physical side of their marriage was predictable and unfulfilling: brief, empty early-evening interludes were orchestrated until Connie became pregnant, then there was complete abstinence on Bernard's part until his wife delivered the newest member of their family. Bernie would then play the part of the proud father and the grateful family man. After their third child was born, all their intimacy disappeared completely. Connie had slowly been uncovered of any loving feeling she had for her husband — like a lonely pine tree on an exposed precipice, cold raw winds had stripped its limbs bare, leaving little evidence of life on its exterior and complementing little vitality on the inside. There were no loving gestures, no holding hands, no soft caresses in the night, not even an endearing, tender word for her during their brief sexual moments.

Bernie was a good father, always supportive of his children, and he provided guidance when he deemed it necessary or when called upon to do so. The man was just incapable of intimacy, but what tore at Connie and eventually destroyed her love for Bernie was his lack of caring, his complete disregard for how that absence of intimacy affected her. She had married a very selfish and cold man.

* * *

In the later years of their marriage, Connie talked to her mother about her husband's lack of intimacy. She was surprised at how open her mother was; for so long Connie had stayed away from the subject, always afraid her mother would not be receptive to such an intimate and private part of her daughter's marriage.

"You know, your father and I had a very good physical relationship. Bet you didn't know that, or even want to know it, but we did," her mother said. "But I had a good friend who told me how disappointing her lovemaking was with her husband. The sex lasted mere seconds and then it was over. She had been married briefly before and her first husband was killed in a horrible work accident, so she knew it wasn't normal. She approached her husband several times about his problem, but it always caused embarrassment and made him shut down. They finally saw a doctor about his issue — some doctor up in Boston — and he told them it was a real thing, and not as rare as you might think. A thing called 'premature' something. Nothing he could do about it — the doctor suggested they should experiment in their lovemaking. Entertain different approaches to their sex. I don't think it worked, because she left her husband about a year later. Just up and disappeared. They didn't have any children so it wasn't complicated."

"That sounds exactly like what's going on with Bernie," Connie told her mother.

"Do you think you could get him to talk to a doctor?" her mother asked.

"No," she said, then paused for a moment. "That would never happen. I have tried to talk to him about it, but he won't hear it! The conversation is over quicker than our lovemaking." She laughed bitterly and without mirth. "I don't know why I call it lovemaking, there's no love involved at all."

"I am so sorry, some people don't place much importance on that kind of stuff. But you are my daughter and the apple did not fall far from the tree. You need that intimacy, and sooner or later you will look for it. It's only natural. But be careful. You have children now."

"I don't know about that," Connie said. But she was lying to her mother and to herself. She was already looking for it, and in all her fantasies there were numerous imaginary lovers.

But now there was a man, a very real man who made her skin tingle, and he was standing right in front of her.

* * *

Peter and Connie sensed that they were trains on the same track, heading madly towards each other and impatiently wishing for the collision.

Their first choir practice was instantly sexually charged and it only escalated from there. Dark blue eyes locked in on Peter every time he looked up from his sheet music, and they seemed to reach into him and ignite a flame that was his raw, instinctual sensual appetite. His virility was as energized as it had ever been. Then the purest ruby-red lips softened into a delicate and enticing smile. She coyishly lowered her blue eyes to feign interest in her sheet music, only to quickly return to search the room for the man who made her body quiver with carnal energy and anticipation.

Connie intermittently flipped her long auburn hair back with delicate alabaster hands with nails highlighted the same fervent red color as her lipstick. They were the hands of a sensuous angel. Her every gesture intrigued him, and he lingered on each feature of her face and form. Her physical presence had captured him and her pheromones had rendered him helpless.

Connie felt his eyes slowly undressing her and she tingled with excitement. She wished him to see all of her and to take whatever he wanted from her. Her breasts ached and tingled and she secretively moved herself against the back of the choir pew in front of her. She was alive as never before. Peter was the hunter, she the hunted, but there would be no hunt.

Choir practice seemed to last forever: the hands on the clock in the vestry appeared frozen, and only the separated soon-to-be lovers were aware of its every teasing tick.

And then mercifully rehearsal was over. Music needed to be put away and folding chairs returned to the storage closet. Light switches clicked off and polite goodnights and goodbyes finally signaled the end of the torture that none were aware of but Peter Marrow and Constance Caswell. They slowly walked back to their car, shallowly discussing the beautiful summer evening they had been blessed with, knowing that a storm of their own making was about to consume them both.

Getting into Peter's car, they knew they were alone in the small church parking lot. The sound of Connie's soft cotton skirt as it moved across the front seat was all he heard before she reached down and stopped him from starting his car. Her hand was alive with heat and erotic energy. Blood rushed to his loins. Peter instantly embraced her and their mouths found each other in the darkness. His hands sought and quickly found her breasts, and she helped him undo her blouse and fed them to his hungry mouth and lips, her nipples erect and hard, easy for his nipping teeth to find and tease. No man had ever touched her like that, and she only wanted more. She had become the woman that she always knew she was, alive and reckless in her desire.

Peter, too, was alive. His hands moved all over her body and he could not stop them. Her breath was hot and heavy and her lips mated with his. He kissed her breasts and teased her nipples with his tongue. They were alive and yearning for his touch. His hands reached under her skirt and pulled at her underwear. She hoisted her skirt with frantic hands, raising her hips and arching her back so that he might easily remove the last obstacle to her femininity. His hand was soon between her legs and his fingers were inside her, moving easily in and out with her dampness. A deep primal moan escaped her lips.

"Let's go to the lighthouse, we're too old for this backseat," Peter said, struggling against his own words.

"I want you now," Connie said, her breath labored and her face flushed and sweaty. "But I can tolerate a short drive."

Peter started the car and they drove quickly towards the lighthouse. They made no effort to straighten their clothes or put them back on. They drove with the windows down and in the moonlight that flashed from between the passing trees, Peter could see her form. Her beautiful breasts gently swayed and moved with the contour of the road and Connie sat with her legs slightly parted, letting the summer breeze stimulate her. Peter thought the scene erotic and almost magical.

"My god, you are beautiful," he said, and groaned.

Then she was upon him, her face at his loins. She undid his pants and released his erect penis. It throbbed in her soft hands. She took him in her mouth. She had never tasted a man before and it was wonderful. It only hypnotized her more.

They pulled into the sand lot behind the lighthouse, away from prying eyes. They ran from the car, their clothes missing or re-arranged like teenagers on a Saturday night. They hurried to the living room and Peter threw a work tarp on the floor while Connie found a blanket that she often used when sitting on the beach. They shed the rest of their clothes in a rush and tumbled to the floor. Connie opened her legs wide and then he was inside her, thrusting hard. A muffled screamed escaped her lips, as every fiber of her body erupted in pleasure. Tears ran down the sides of her cheeks, but not from the frustration and disappointment she had experienced so many times for so many years. This time from release, relief and joy.

* * *

He had built a lighthouse and Constance Caswell, from another place, another world, had softly, seductively penetrated his own domain.

Peter Marrow remembered the day he had been contacted by the United States Coast Guard by formal document. He had to sign for it at the island post office. It was an FBP, a Federal Bid Proposal, to build an addition to an existing lighthouse. That lighthouse was on Prudence Island at Sandy Point. They wanted to construct a living area for the future lighthouse keeper and potential family members. Peter reviewed the documents over the next few days. There were drawings with various plan and elevation views. Engineering specifications that detailed materials to be used, and method of construction were also provided. Daily job site monitoring with weekly federal inspections were mandated.

Peter thought the whole thing was laughable. He knew that they had to go through the motions, but who the hell would bid against him? He was the only builder on the island, and any off-island contractor didn't stand a chance; most of the general contractors on the bid list would decline. The contract was his for the taking and he anticipated a healthy profit. Peter was feeling quite pleased with himself.

They began construction of the lighthouse addition in the spring of 1937. That was when Peter decided to hire Buck Taylor in order to meet the Coast Guard's aggressive scheduled completion date. Peter had expected it might be the break Buck needed. He hoped it would go well. It did not.

Buck was damaged goods before he even had a chance in life. His mother had seen to that. His hand had long ago been played out.

Not long into the building schedule, Buck reverted back to his wayward behavior. Two to three times a week he showed up late for work, and it was obvious he had been drinking the night before. Sometimes he returned from his lunch break with the smell of alcohol on his breath. Only weeks into the schedule and Peter was in a quandary. Could he overlook Buck's misguided actions? Buck was a hard worker when he was there and on time, but Buck had also quickly become good friends with the lighthouse keeper's oldest son. Federal Guidelines required that the soon-to-be lighthouse keeper, a man named Bernard Caswell, be on site to monitor the progress of the construction. Caswell took the ferry to the island daily and oversaw the build out. When summer arrived and school was out, he often brought his oldest son, George, with him. The two adolescents quickly struck up a friendship. Soon, George was passing tools or fetching needed material for Buck or other members of the crew. Buck and George's chatter was lively and constant.

Bernie Caswell enjoyed the new friendship his quiet, shy son had found with Buck. He made several comments to Peter, explaining how his son was always anxious to return to the island, especially when he allowed George to visit with Buck over the weekend. Peter could only imagine what Buck was exposing his new young friend to; surely alcohol would be in that mix of intriguing incentives behind George's weekend visits with Buck. Peter decided he would tolerate Buck's misbehavior; it hadn't become too disruptive, and his client seemed comforted with his son's new friendship. Keeping his customer happy was the more important issue here. The construction schedule was aggressive, and maintaining it with Buck involved would be challenging. But for the time, Peter kept Buck on the payroll.

The real dilemma with Buck was that he never saw himself as doing anything wrong. Sure, he drank a lot, especially for a young kid; he was often late for work or appointments, he acted goofy and said a lot of stupid stuff, and he always spent his last dollar on a bottle of booze. But he never borrowed money from anyone, he was always prepared to stay after work to make up for his lost time, and acting a little crazy and babbling on about ridiculous things wasn't a crime. He just couldn't understand why people had a problem with his drinking. Some people drink water when they're thirsty, Buck reasoned — he drank alcohol when he was thirsty and he was thirsty a lot. But most of all, Buck drank to stay alive.

Chapter 6

Dave Brooks was well aware of Hurricane Donna. It had been six years since the last hurricane and those same years in his wheelchair. He and Bethany had followed its progress up the east coast on their little black-and-white TV. Watching TV was all he did. Although he did have one minor indulgence: a neighbor sometimes brought him down to the town pier to do a little fishing. He had always enjoyed casting his jig before the incident at Peter and Lillian's. But now it was an involved a process, usually taking place on a Sunday afternoon. His neighbor would arrive and pack all of Dave's fishing gear in the back of his pickup, lift him from his wheelchair into the front seat, and then put the wheelchair in the bed with the rest of the gear. His neighbor's son was a quahogger and provided plenty of hard and soft-shell clams for bait. It was always degrading for Dave to be lifted in and out of the pickup like he was a sick, old dog. His neighbor would unpack Dave and his gear at the pier, make sure he had ample cigarettes, and would leave him there for a couple of hours, then return and repeat the process all over again. If Dave caught any fish, it complicated things. Sometimes he threw his catch back before his neighbor returned.

Bethany didn't like cleaning fish and it was difficult for Dave to reach the sink. Besides, hooking and reeling them in was enough for him.

Now Dave did not care to fish anymore, he didn't seem to have the energy for it. The last time his neighbor dropped him off, he hadn't actually fished, just chain-smoked his butts and took in the sights and sounds of the harbor. The last few months, he had started to feel a shortness of breath, and there were times when his heart raced for no apparent reason. Often there was a sense of pressure in his upper torso, as if someone was pushing a strong hand against his chest.

* * *

Dave heard the stories. Bethany had been caught up in all the drama of George's hurricanes. That's what the people on Prudence began to call the storms. She still kept in touch with her old island friends and was dialed in to the gossip line. Every hurricane since 1938 had taken a living soul from Prudence, and Bethany had heard all the whispers and rumors: namely, the deaths were all targeted victims of the vindictive spirit of Bernie Caswell, who returned from the grave with every hurricane that threatened the tranquility of Narragansett Bay.

Hogwash. Pure bullshit, Dave thought. He had felt that way from the day they had discovered Carolyn Waters' body. Oh, the people were definitely murdered, but they were not the target of some evil spirit bent on revenge. No, Crazy George Caswell and his mentally-deficient friend Buck Taylor were the twisted minds that orchestrated the meaningless murders.

* * *

Now, years later, Dave still stood by his theory, although he hadn't shared it with anyone and only casually mentioned it to his wife and daughters. Confined to a wheelchair and housebound, Dave didn't get out much, and didn't receive many visitors, especially with his sour and cynical outlook on life. Besides, people don't want to hear the truth. It's more intriguing to buy into the ghosts-and-goblins theory that was out there. The whole thing was ridiculous and made little sense, but it captured and captivated people. Hell, when the cops finally did apprehend and convict the nitwits George and Buck, there would always be those who still believed in the ghost-of-the-lighthouse-keeper-come-back-from-the-grave theory. It was far more compelling than the truth; fools, all of them.

But recently, Dave's thoughts were getting mixed up, and sometimes his memory played tricks on him. He wondered if there weren't some evil souls from another universe contributing to the bizarre act of revenge. Maybe there *was* something to the story of George's hurricanes. Often, he woke from deep slumbers to find George and Buck in his living room, pointing their fingers at him, telling him he was next. Dave yelled, challenging them to try and take their revenge. He was ready. Occasionally, Crazy George mutated into his father's form and rushed him, threatening him with death, then disappearing. Dave would continue his verbal assault on the intruders until Bethany ran into the room, trying to calm him down, telling him there was no one there. She'd bring him a small glass of ginger brandy and light a cigarette for him.

"There's no one in the room, Dave," she would tell him. "It's just a bad dream that you held onto a little bit too long."

He would shake his head and tell his wife, "No, no, no." Because Dave had seen them and knew their threats were real. It made his heart race again and the ever-present pressure in his chest radiated out to his arms. There was a dull ache in his groin and urinating had become difficult. Dave knew he was falling apart, but he had to settle the score with George and Buck, because they had invaded his home. For the past few days, Dave had begun to suspect that George and Buck had indeed retrieved Bernie Caswell from beyond and included his wrath in their twisted vendetta.

* * *

Dave Brooks was certain it would be his turn next. There could be no denying it, not when George and Buck were in his own living room confessing to their horrible deeds, almost proud about it, and declaring that he would be their next victim. Other than Peter, Dave was the only one who remained of the Marrow crew that had labored on the lighthouse project. People liked the theory that it was the Caswell family; they had been led to believe that the structure was indestructible, and they had felt safe inside its thick walls. But now all but George of the Caswell family were dead, and the family would make those who had built the faulty lighthouse pay for their ineptness and deceit. But the Sand Point lighthouse, from what he knew, had been built exactly to specifications. No shoddy workmanship, no inferior materials covertly substituted. Now there was the rumor that the lighthouse keeper had somehow discovered that Peter Marrow and his wife were having an affair. Dave wasn't so convinced of that, but he had witnessed a very heated argument between Peter and Bernie Caswell near the end of the project. Peter downplayed the incident, insisting that the disagreement was about project cost and schedule, which seemed odd, because they had all been told that things were on time and on budget. Kind of peculiar!

Dave would be ready for the fools when they came for him. He would turn the tables on them. No one really understood who the murderers were and what their twisted motive was, but he did.

A simple phone call would put things in play. Dave knew the Heckle and Jeckle team all too well; he had worked with Buck for many years and had visited with him at George's shack numerous times. Dave knew their routine. At boat time, they would all be down at Chalmer's, hanging around the store, sitting on the rails with their feet resting on the benches below. The ferry would arrive and everyone would see who was coming to the island and who was leaving. It stimulated rumors and conversation. Family and friends were there to help others with their packages or to see friends off. There was a flurry of activity as people said their hellos and goodbyes, and it was usually over in about twenty minutes. Then it would settle back to the dependable small crowd that hung around the store on a summer's day. There would be a little more activity with the approaching storm. And there would be all sorts of speculation.

The payphone rang, its loud, clanging noise startling everyone. Buck had been sitting on an old milk crate, whittling on a piece of weathered oak he had found on the beach, and he jumped when the phone rang, slightly nicking his left index finger.

"Damn," he said and shook his left hand in the wind. He stuck his finger in his mouth, trying to ease the discomfort.

Butch Cramer, in his Bazooka Joe hat, a jovial regular at Chalmer's, answered the phone. "Road kill cafe, you kill 'em, we grill 'em," he said with a grin. Then a blank expression spread across his face.

"Ah, ah sure," he said, mystified, and he held the phone out toward Buck. "Some guy wants to talk to you."

Butch, Chris Fernandez, Melanie Baxter, and others in the group stopped their chatter and locked their eyes on the scratched, shiny black phone being passed to Buck.

Buck took the phone with his right hand, still holding his cut left finger to his lips. "Hello, who is this?" he demanded.

"Buck, this is Dave Brooks. Just wanted to say a quick hello, now pass the phone to your moron friend George. I know he's there, so don't fuck with me. You two are always together, probably jerk each other off, too. Don't say anything, just pass him the phone. Enjoy what little time you have left."

Buck was numb. The brief, dark dialogue had instantly frightened him and taken his speech. He turned to George. "It's for you," he said, as if he had just received devastating news from his doctor, and handed the phone to George.

"What's wrong?" asked George as he took the phone "Who is it?"

Buck said nothing. He stepped down from the landing and walked numbly to his car. The onlookers, now even more captivated, focused intently on George and the call he was about to take.

"Hello, who is this?" George challenged the mystery man.

"I'll tell you who the fuck this is. It's me, Dave Brooks, and I'll tell you something else, you ain't fooled me one bit. I know it's been you and fucknuts that's been killing all these innocent folks and now you even got the balls to come to my home and tell me that I'm next. You and your twisted mind have concocted this murderous payback, which brings me to the reason for this call. Well, I guess if I'm next on your list, there's only Marrow left after me. Wish you'd go after his sorry ass first, but that ain't how your plan works, is it? Well anyway, I'll be waiting for you and fucknuts, and I'll be ready. You won't have to look for me, I'll make it easy for you. I'll be at my fishing spot on the town dock when the storm hits and I'll wait for as long as it takes. Enjoy what little time you have left." He hung up.

George slowly returned the phone to its cradle. He appeared to have received even more devastating news from the doctor that had spoken to Buck. His face was without expression and he stared straight ahead, never looking at anyone.

"Are you all right, George? You look like you just saw a ghost," Melanie Baxter said. "Who was that?"

George walked across the plank way, down the short run of stairs and out to Buck's car. Settling into the front seat, he softly closed the car door. He turned to Buck. "Just start the car and head to my place."

Buck started the car and leisurely pulled out of the parking lot, leaving those who remained standing with their mouths open, wondering what had just happened.

They drove in silence for a while. Finally, Buck inquired, "What did he say to you, George?"

"I think he's really lost it, he claims we both went to see him."

"I guess he has. What are you going to do?"

"I'm not really sure. Guess I'll talk to my father."

A stricken look crossed Buck's face, and he was suddenly as pale as a bed sheet. "I don't need to be there for that, do I?" Buck pleaded.

George only looked at him, saying nothing.

Chapter 7

Another hurricane and another storm, internal to Dave Brooks. His weathered spirit could tolerate no more. Weather forecasters said it might be a bad one, but they also felt it could turn out to the east. Folks on Prudence wondered how Bethany Brooks was getting on with the anticipation of an approaching hurricane, the fourth one since 1938, seeking a fourth victim. She would have her hands full with Dave's escalating dread. Bethany had done her shopping for the extra staples they might need. Coolers were packed with ice. Candles and flashlights were pulled out of crowded drawers.

Dave Brooks hoped he could find the moment when his wife and daughters might be distracted just long enough to orchestrate his escape, although escape wasn't quite the right word for it. It was more of a rendezvous with fate.

* * *

Howling winds and a horizontal rain pelted their south facing windows, and told Dave and Bethany that foul weather had finally arrived in their neighborhood. It was hard to listen to the radio or TV with all the threatening background noise. Dave suggested that the girls should attempt a little reading time in their bedroom.

"Probably should give it a try while we still have power," he encouraged. He needed to get to the town wharf. They would be waiting for him. The girls looked at each other, shrugged their shoulders, and trudged off to their room.

After a while, Dave suggested that Bethany should check their storage room in the small half cellar they had below the kitchen.

"You'll need to move things around if we start to get rainwater in there," he said.

Bethany thought the idea sound and made her way to the basement door in the kitchen. She grabbed a flashlight on the counter and headed down the stairs. There was a light switch in the room below.

Dave waited for Bethany to get to the bottom of the stairs and then closed the door behind her, locking it with its deadbolt. He quickly wheeled himself to the radio on the kitchen table, turned the volume up and scurried to the back door. He opened the back door and it nearly tore free of its hinges in the punishing winds. Grabbing either side of the doorway, he propelled himself out into the fury. He could hear his wife pounding on the basement door and yelling for their daughters. Obsessed with his mission of confronting his soon-to-be assailants, Dave was beyond rational thought. With wind tearing at his clothes and a driving rain stinging his face, he guided his wheelchair out of the driveway and down his street as fast as his grinding arms could propel him. His sudden freedom excited him and he pushed himself even harder. He was oblivious to the elements that nearly capsized his wheelchair, nor did he hear the screams of his wife and daughters as they chased him down the road. Dave was more alive than he had been in years. His heart pounded in his chest and the driving rain teased his fiery complexion. Then his oldest daughter grabbed his chair, slowing him down and changing his course. He felt like a cornered animal and he fought against her, screaming obscenities. Soon his wife and other daughter were there and then all the fight left him. He hung his head like a beaten man.

"What the hell are you doing, where are you going?" his wife screamed above the wind and rain. "Can you imagine what our neighbors are saying right now?"

Shaking his head in defeat, he whispered, "I don't care."

The neighbors were indeed witnesses to the spectacle. Many of them were at their windows watching a family as they battled the elements to bring their wheel chaired father back to the safety of their home.

* * *

Dave had only been delayed, not denied. His wife and daughters got him back home and had vocally scolded him. The absolute absurdity of it all had infuriated and embarrassed them in front of their neighbors.

"Where were you going, especially on a day like this?" his wife demanded as she helped him out of his rain-soaked clothing. "Why did you lock me in the basement?"

"I have my reasons," was all he would offer.

"You have your reasons," she repeated. "Have you gone mad? On a day like this, you have your reasons. Does that mean you will do this again? Do we need to lock you in your room?"

"I won't do it again, I promise." But he was lying.

"Your daughters are just as angry with you as I am," his wife continued. "You caused them so much embarrassment."

"Just leave me alone, please," he pleaded and hung his head in false shame. He was not humiliated at all. Maybe a little angry and disappointed that he had not completed his escape, it had been impulsive and poorly planned. Because he was driven by a vigilante justice to thwart thirty years of a twisted vendetta that had culminated in his own crippling injury, Dave Brooks was not thinking rationally. Now back in his dingy living room, he understood the foolery of his efforts. There would be another attempt, that same night, in the early hours, when his family was asleep. He would sneak away to confront the fools. They would be there waiting for him. He was sure of that.

Then suddenly the lights and radio were off. They had lost power and his wife left to find their candles.

Chapter 8

Buck stood frozen on George's front porch. He was stunned by what George had just told him.

"How the hell do you expect to do *that?*" Buck asked in utter amazement. "You want me to swim to Bristol with you, in the middle of a hurricane? I think this has gotten out of hand. You're not thinking straight, George." Buck began his nervous pacing — he would be looking for his bottle shortly.

"You know I can't back down from that kind of a challenge," George said to Buck as if it was an event that had been prophesied long ago and was finally upon them. They had been told of the coming apocalypse and knew they must confront it. It was a threat to their lineage, their integrity, and moral fiber.

"Aren't you making a little too much of a stupid freakin' phone call from a stupid, angry and bitter man?" Buck countered. "He's in a freakin' wheelchair and will be for the rest of his life. And I hear he's not doing too well, slowly losing his mind. What kind of a threat can he possibly be?"

"Buck, it is much more than an idle threat."

"Oh, come on, George," he said. "Dave Brooks calls you at the pay phone and all of a sudden your pride is all out of joint. The guy is a physical wreck. He sits in a wheelchair and chain smokes all day long. They say he has lung cancer and they think it has spread to his brain. He can't keep his thoughts straight. Why do you even care? It's time to let it go. Ain't there been enough death and sadness around here? That was all wrong what happened to Carolyn Waters. It's been a real steady, slow hurt on the inside for me."

George knew only that the task of revenge was not complete. It had consumed him and his family. He grew angry with Buck, certainly frustrated that Buck did not seem to understand — there was no other option for them.

"Time is making you forget what happened to my family, all of them. What about the pain I've been living with the last twenty-two years? They built me a rat shack. It's a wonder that I don't freeze to death in the wintertime. I imagine Brad Wheeler will find my frozen corpse there some day. And then these wonderful islanders call me Crazy George behind my back, although they ain't real careful about it. Sometimes it just slips out. It ain't even George anymore, it's become 'Crazy' or just 'Craze.'

"We can swim to Bristol. I know it seems like an insane thing to do, but I know we can do it. It has to be done this way. It was decreed by my father and you know it. I don't have a choice. This storm will soon be upon us and Dave Brooks knows he is now the critical character in a play that was scripted long ago. I know how we can do this, just hear me out."

George knew sooner or later they would have to go to Bristol and confront Dave Brooks, adding his name to the list of those who had paid for their sins. He had worked it out in his head a thousand times. They would use the inner tubes of the old tires from his pickup. They would lash them together and ride the waves, tide, and winds out of the south, right up the bay into Bristol Harbor. He told all of this to Buck. "You forget that we were both dragged into an angry ocean back in '38 and we lived to talk about it."

Buck was convinced that George had oversimplified things. It would be a ride through hell. The waves would be tremendous and the wind would be damaging.

"We're not the nineteen-year-old boys who survived a powerful storm more than twenty years ago, and you forget we were only in the water for a few short minutes." Back then, they had stumbled into the tempest, naïve and unprepared; this time they would think it through and be ready for the deadly elements. A lumber yard close to the town pier had on its property some abandoned storage sheds near the water's edge. Buck had spent many a night in those same shelters when he had been drinking too long at Crosby's Tavern and missed the last ferry to the island. They could hole up in there until the time was right to send Dave Brooks to join his other friends in hell and then return to their secret den, wait for the winds to switch to out of the north and once again ride those same gusts back to the island.

"Ah, George, you got to let go of this. I believed in it when we first started a long time ago," said Buck, his head shaking in disbelief at what he just heard. "But I'm not so sure I can be part of this evil plan much longer, especially this harebrained scheme. I know you really believe we can do this, but we can't. It's a suicide mission."

"No, it ain't," George said, and he angrily punched the dashboard of his pickup. "We can do it. Like I said, we can use the truck tubes, lash them together. They're big tires, even tie a fifty-pound weight to the tubes, that will keep us from being tossed around in the waves. I have life vests, swim fins and masks we can use. It's not supposed to be anywhere near the strength of that devil storm in '38."

"George, do you even hear what you're saying?" Buck asked him. "You sound like a mad man, it's a good thing I know you."

"I'm not a freakin' mad man," he said, his feelings hurt. "I don't like being called that and you know why. The winds and tides will be just like I said and you know it. How many times now have we seen what these storms do? And we've used all of that to help plot my family's revenge."

Buck still could not believe what he was hearing, and then he knew that George's father had placed his palmprint on the foolhardy adventure. George was convinced the trip through hell was viable by someone who resided in hell. It all made sense, certainly not their chances of success in the ridiculous journey, but in that instant Buck knew that George's father had schemed the lunatic trip.

"This insanity has all the markings of your father's heavy-handedness," Buck told him, relieved that he had finally solved a family conundrum. "This is your father's idea, isn't it, George? I wonder how receptive you were of its worthiness when you first heard it. Your reaction was probably the same as mine, how could it not have been? Your father has been after you day and night over this matter. I think he just finally wore you down, and now you mean to do the same thing to me."

"Okay, Buck, you got me," George said evenly, he too was relieved they had arrived at a point where there would be an honest dialogue. "Yeah, it's my father's idea, and he has been on me about it like a tick on a dog."

"So, you're willing to admit it's a harebrained scheme?" Buck challenged.

"I guess it might be," he said, his shoulders slumped and his posture weakened. "But I have to do this. I was hoping you would help me, you're a strong swimmer, stronger than me. I could do it with your help." George's eyes teared up. "I would probably think the idea insane if I were you, but I ain't you. My whole family was taken from me. I don't think you will ever understand how this drags at me, it has for over almost twenty-two years." George made no attempt to hold back the tears, twenty-two years of suffering, pain, and loneliness finally spilled over, and he sobbed, his body heaving with the emotional weight, interrupted only by deep breaths that sought to hold him from falling off the precipice. Finally, George collected himself, his eyes swollen and red from baring his soul. He turned to his friend. "You don't need to worry about this anymore. I will do it myself, guess I always knew that."

Buck stood and embraced his old friend, just like he did twenty-two years ago when George was a scared, naive eighteen-year-old kid, when family and home had been violently torn from his life. Buck had sensed the urgency to stand by his friend on that terrible day and now again he sensed that same resolve. They had been through so much together, they only had each other.

"No, George, you ain't gonna do this by yourself. I'll go with you, guess I always knew that."

* * *

Just south of Bristol Colony, George and Buck stood on a rocky shoreline on a small jetty away from the wind, two lonely gladiators about to forsake their lives against an evil wind created by Jupiter himself. Two large rubber tubes strapped together with rope and planking floated before them. Several large cinder blocks sat on the single two-by-twelve planking and were attached with rugged line in the hope that it would be the sea drag they would need to keep them upright. They were dressed in cutoffs and navy blue, heavy, cotton, long-sleeve jerseys. George, as promised, had located swim fins and masks. The diving masks would keep the sting of salt water from their eyes and help maintain clear vision, and the fins would allow their legs to be more responsive to the demanding task ahead of them.

They had waited for dusk to better hide their desperate launch. No one would see these two dark figures being tossed about in the stormy twilight. The wind and rain pushed at them, and large, fuming waves waited just beyond the breakwater.

"Here, Buck, put this little backpack on," George shouted into the wind. "I packed a few sandwiches and a little water. It ain't that heavy, it shouldn't be a problem, but just in case, you're the better swimmer."

"Sure, George, guess it would be a good idea to bring it," Buck yelled back, and he secured the small pack to his waist and shoulders.

Buck looked straight ahead into the darkening horizon in front of him. He tried not to think about the fury that awaited him. He reached into his back pocket and retrieved his half-pint, took one last drink of whiskey — like kamikaze pilots in the war of the Pacific, this was their fated mission. Angrily, he tossed the empty bottle into the boiling bay.

"George, I just can't think about this anymore," he said stoically. "Let's go if we're going," and he waded deeper into the water. George offered no response but was instantly by his side. They moved past the jetty and were engulfed in chaotic turmoil. Punishing winds, driving rain, and demon waves all fought for possession of their souls. They were helpless passengers on a Nantucket sleigh ride from hell.

Towering waves with huge white crowns pushed them along like dry brown leaves at the mercy of a harsh New England winter gale. They would be tossed around until they either crumbled or the wind finally exhausted itself. Roller after roller crashed over them, and they hung on dearly to their raft. The swim masks they wore allowed them to clearly see the insanity that was all around them. Perhaps such clarity was not what they needed now. Mountains and valleys, valleys and mountains were the only topography they had before them. They were continuously torn free from the safety of their raft and only the lifelines they had attached to themselves saved them from keeping company with Poseidon. They took turns searching the turbulent water and retrieving the other when one of them lost his grip on the raft. Their bodies bobbed up and down, sometimes disappearing completely in the violent aquatic juggernaut. They screamed each other's names in the dark and wildly flailed their arms, hoping to be the beacon that guided them back to their floating, fragile solace. Sometimes they pushed themselves up onto the raft, stood, and quickly searched the foaming chaos around them, only to be tossed violently back into the sea to continue their self-inflicted examination of their survival skills and their desire to live.

Their journey of destiny seemed endless: booming waves, separated by torrential rain driven by a livid and treacherous wind, were their only measure of distance and time. George wondered if this had been the fate his family had suffered so many years ago. Stars and a near-harvest moon obscured by towering, thick clouds were of little value. George and Buck sensed that they were moving northh and, hopefully, into Bristol Harbor. Their perilous condition allowed only brief moments of clarity to gauge where they were and what lay ahead. Instinct to survive does not permit time for reflection.

Suddenly they were smashed up against a dark metal wall. Was it a boat's hull? The wooden planking that held the inner tubes together shattered and the inner tubes were quickly free of each other. George and Buck had tied each tube to their belts, and they reined in their life rafts. Soon they heard the clanging of the bell that was secured to the top of the channel buoy they had just hit. The wind and rain had hidden its distinctive calling. They were quickly by the harbor marker, its coast guard number and barnacles fading into the night.

But the bay marker had brightened their mood; they both knew the buoy revealed the entrance into Bristol Harbor. The elements prevented them from sharing their elation, but it marked the beginning of the end of their journey. Waves shrank and lessened their impact — soon they would be pushed up against the very shoreline sheds that would be their hideaway. They had survived the voyage.

* * *

Staggering from a pounding surf, they sat shivering in the abandoned storage sheds while the storm ravaged outside. They lit a candle that Buck had left in the shed and it flickered bravely in the drafty shelter. Their shadows danced on the walls. Their ordeal in the bay had left them cold and exhausted, but the warm tropical air that is at the root of all hurricanes soon had them revived.

"What do we do now?" asked Buck, no longer shivering but shaking for a different reason. "I think I need a drink."

"We'll just sit tight for a while. I will know when the dirtbag Brooks makes his appearance. This is the shed that you sometimes stay in, why don't you look around, maybe you left a bottle here."

"Hey, that's a good idea," said Buck, energized, and he scavenged the hard-packed clay floor for his salvation. After several attempts of finding bottles and shaking them for their contents, he found a half-full bottle. "Now ain't this a sweet surprise," he exclaimed.

Buck took a long drink and it soothed his torment. "Hey George, how you gonna know when Dave Brooks shows up?"

"My father will let me know when the fool has presented himself," George replied.

"Is your father here?" Buck asked, and began to look around the room.

"Yes," George answered, as if it were obvious.

Once again Buck searched the room. Maybe George's father was hiding among their pirouetting shadows.

I-I don't see him, George," Buck stuttered

"You don't need to see him, Buck."

Chapter 9

ave, Bethany, and their two daughters sat, hidden in the dark living room with candles that cast their own little world of shadows. They listened to the storm with its howling winds and pelting rain. They watched as trees all along the street tried to stand their ground against the fury, their limbs flaying wildly, trying their best to deflect rather than confront in their desperate battle. Their neighbor's majestic sycamore lost its engagement, taking power and telephone lines with it. Random lightning made it an almost Hollywood, Wuthering Heights event.

Eventually, his daughters retreated to their bedroom and sought to put the day behind them. Not long after that, Bethany rose from her chair and stood next to her husband.

"I am going to bed," she softly told him. "What will you do?"

Dave feigned a deep sleep. His head was lowered and his eyes were closed. She tenderly probed his shoulder with a nudging gesture. He bounced his head and shoulders and emitted a startled, brief snore, hoping to fool his wife.

Dave often spent many nights in his wheelchair in the same spot, staring out their front living room window.

Bethany had seen her husband's health quickly spiral downward. Six years ago, he had been a vibrant young man, proud of his craft. They had talked about moving off the island, where he could start his own business. Dave understood his skills and with his optimistic, pleasing disposition they were confident he would grow his business. Then it all changed in a heartbeat. They were suddenly rushing her husband on a navy launch across choppy waters to the nearest hospital in Newport. No one knew if he would live or die. Fortunately, a competent emergency room team of doctors made saving David Brooks' life their priority, but there would no saving his lower spine: a shotgun blast had shattered three vertebrae. The nerve damage was extensive and permanent. After forty-two days in the hospital and rehabilitation, he was sadly introduced to his two-wheeled companion for a lifetime commitment.

There were a lot of brave faces displayed by doctors, therapists, and nurses. Friends and family always had words of encouragement, there were some who even offered the "it could have been worse" pearls of wisdom, but everyone knew that Dave Brooks had been sliced in half and would never live a whole life again.

Dying might have been better as far as he was concerned. Dave was completely numb from the waist down. He lay in his hospital bed for all those days, wondering how such a large portion of his body could be so alive and now so unfeeling and purposeless. He couldn't even control his bladder or bowels and only when the unpleasant odors settled in around him did he realize that he was immersed in his own filth.

He began to smoke soon after he started his rehab. One of the other patients, an ex-marine, was a smoker and offered him one of his Lucky Strikes while they sat outside on an early October day. Dave never had the urge to smoke, thought it an unhealthy and an undignified habit, but when offered the cigarette, it became the most thoughtless decision he ever made and knew it would be forever. The two men both confined to their wheelchairs for very different reasons, commiserated for the same reasons. By the time Dave left rehab, he was smoking up to a pack and half a day and it would only climb from there. In about a year he was inhaling three packs a day and every sentence out of his mouth began and ended with a lung-clearing cough. Bethany had drawn the line on three packs a day; it was becoming expensive and she had to restrict his smoking for his own sake. His cough was chronic and destructive. He struggled for the air to breathe, he became winded very easily, and seemed to sleep all the time. The last few months, he had complained of chest pains and had begun to tell stories of strangers or childhood friends stopping by to visit. His dreams were few and his nightmares frequent. His memory was failing and it confused his thought process more. He refused any visit by a doctor, nor would he change his disastrous lifestyle. Six short years had seen a man thriving in his station become a being so focused on his own destiny with death that he would use his own hatred, bitterness and self-loathing to secure that outcome.

* * *

Bethany lightly touched her husband's head. "Hope you're here in the morning," she said to herself and walked to her bedroom, expecting they would have restored electricity by the morning.

Dave raised his head and stared out the front window. They were out there waiting for him and he would go to them. No fear would intimidate, no tales of the dead stalking him would deflect him from his mission. Good men, his friends had died for reasons that made no sense. The twisted plot had gone on too long, but it would end tonight. The culprits George and Buck had visited many times, always without invitation, they had sneaked up on him when they thought he was sleeping, but he knew they were there. Their presence only reinforced his resolve. Sometimes, Bernie Casswell visited with them and they all teased him with a promised day of reckoning. He cursed them and challenged them, waving them away in frustration.

Now, they would tease him no more. He pivoted his wheelchair and headed for the back door, the same path as before and the same escape. He opened the door and the wind again tested his grip. This time he was ready and he was pulled over the threshold and out into the driveway. He forced the door closed and was again in the middle of the tempest. He pushed himself along with no panic. Destiny waited for him and he knew no hourglass would gauge its arrival.

* * *

Buffeting winds and pelting rain pushed him along as before — a lonely figure, navigating without moon or stars, no shadow, no trace of movement. Neighbors who might have been awake in the early hours would never see him. He was part of the storm, a tree limb torn free or a trash can tumbling in the wind. He moved steadily on, his propelling arms and lungs starved for oxygen and the tightness in his chest ever present. He finally made it to the entrance of the town wharf and turned into it. The winds attacked him from the side and his wheelchair was no longer a stable platform, always teetering on the edge. Horizontally-driven rain tore at his face and clouded his eyesight, but they were there, he could see them, all three of them — Bernard, George, and Buck, waiting for him at the end of the wharf. Father, son, and son of an evil bitch.

Chapter 10

They sat for hours in their quivering, fragile lodging, like victims in an air raid shelter, hoping to survive the terror from above. No conversation took place; sometimes the candle went out by a sudden and random burst of air and they would huddle in the darkness. Buck relit the candle when the gloom became too much for him. The flickering candle and his bottle were enough.

George was suddenly upright, his long shadow twitching on the walls. He turned to Buck and calmly said, "The fool is on his way, time for us to go to the town wharf. We will add another passage to our book of retribution."

Buck looked at George. "Your father has told you" — more of a statement than a question.

The simple and pointed reply: "Yes."

The rain had stopped and now only the wind challenged their movements. Walking directly into the gale, they made their way along the waterfront and onto the foremost town pier, guided only by an arbitrary flash of lightning. They stumbled to the last finger dock at the edge of the pier; it was perilously exposed and the wind and waves tore at them. They braced themselves against the pilings that supported the wooden pathway; they stood and waited.

"There is the fool now!" George shouted into the wind, and he pointed down the pier to a small figure in a wheelchair.

Making slow desperate progress against an unforgiving wind, the wheelchair and its tenant crept toward them. Buck felt sad about the scene before him. They had lowered themselves to a cowardly act. The visual reality of it all pressed in on him. A pitiful man, with most of his cerebral abilities now deserted, sat fixed in his wheelchair. His misplaced pride pushed him on toward his destiny. Dave Brooks stopped his movement forward; a flash of light revealed a glint of steel in his hand and he swung it wildly before him. He appeared to be yelling into the wind, but his voice would never find its way to them.

"What's he doing, George?" Buck asked, bewildered.

"The fool is confronting my father. How futile," George replied.

"I can only see Dave, but now you tell me your father is there mistreating him?" Buck said, now more ashamed of their actions. "What are we doing here, George? I don't want no part of this anymore."

"You don't have to be a part of this, Buck, my father and I will take it from here."

Chapter 11

Dave stopped his movements, resting his arms at the sides of his wheelchair. He gasped for air and the python that now encircled his chest squeezed even harder. His hair was soaked and his face was a sponge that could hold no more. He tried to wipe his eyes dry and held his hands to his face, trying to see through the storm. They stood there yelling at him, waving him toward them, but he could not make out what they were saying over the din. It didn't matter. They were calling him over, and that's exactly what he wanted. Dave felt for the large fishing knife hidden deep in his down vest. Oh, he would go to them, he needed no taunting, no enticement.

Arms that finally had purpose for the first time in six years propelled him on. His confronters stopped their waving and yelling. As Dave got closer, Bernie Casswell suddenly vanished and then reappeared directly in front of him floating on the winds, just out of reach.

"Your time is here, Mr. Brooks." Bernie's words were clear and crisp, as if whispered in Dave's ear. Dave had a moment to wonder about that; surely they would've been snatched away by the wind the moment they were uttered. But it made no difference. His rage and thirst for vengeance were all-consuming.

"No, it's your time, you scumbag," Dave screamed back at him. "You and your scumbag son and his scumbag friend." He reached into his vest, grabbed his knife and lashed out at his tormentor. But Bernie was gone, now standing back with the others at the end of the wharf. "Run, you coward, but it ain't going to save you tonight."

Dave cursed his wheelchair, cursed his lifeless legs; he wanted to chase the filth down. Suddenly the rain stopped and it was only the wind that challenged him. He willed and wheeled himself down the wharf and he was soon in front of them. The serpent around his chest was about to complete its death grip.

"So here are the two cowards of the island," Dave tried to yell at them, but it was only just above a whisper. "What warped little men you are! Well, I'm ready for you," and his head dropped onto his chest, his left hand instantly clutching his heart, his breath rapid and shallow.

He slowly lifted his head and challenged his assailants. "I wonder if you even have the courage to stand up to a sick man in a wheelchair?"

George reached out to grab the fool. "It's time to pay for the evil deed you did to my family many years ago," he said.

But Dave pulled a knife from his vest and slashed out at George, deeply cutting the palm of his right hand. George screamed and immediately brought the hand to his chest, cradling it. Blood flowed freely from the wound.

Buck pulled George away from the slashing knife and then a shadow or a gust of wind propelled Dave Brooks and his wheelchair face first into the turbulent water at the edge of the pier. A large splash, lost in a sea of turmoil, he bobbed there for brief seconds and then slowly rolled over. The pain was gone from his face, and a calm smile told them his pain and a lifetime of agony were no longer part of his identity. He silently slipped into the turbulence and was gone from their sight.

Reflecting on what they had just witnessed, they stood in silence with the wind buffeting them, staring into the fuming sea. Finally, Buck turned to his friend and asked, not knowing if he could even believe his own words, "Was it your father who pushed him to his death? Thought I saw something but wasn't sure."

George's answer again was simple and pointed. "Yes," he said.

Chapter 12

Brad drove up to the farm to share the news with his brother. He found Morris standing next to the backhoe with a grease gun in hand. The hurricane had come and gone and left some of the roads still muddy and impassable. They would need the backhoe to clear the runoffs in order to drain the roads of all the excess water.

Brad parked his pickup next to the backhoe and rolled down his window. "Got some disturbing news from Chief Anthony this morning," he began. "They found Dave Brooks' body floating in Bristol Harbor yesterday afternoon. Some quahogger discovered it. His wife had reported him missing yesterday and she identified his body shortly after."

Morris shrugged his shoulders and his arms hung loose and unmoving at his sides. "My damn, it's just getting crazier and crazier," he said. "Wonder how Peter Marrow is going to take it? What details did the chief give you?"

"Not many. His wife thinks he sneaked out of his home in the early morning hours when they were all asleep. Guess he had tried the same thing earlier in the day. Bethany and her daughters had to chase him down. I think Dave was real sick near the end."

"Where were the bowery boys during all of this? I guess this will get all the backyard detectives scratching their heads again. Oh boy, this is going to push Peter over the edge," said Morris.

"Guess we're going to have to rethink things. Haven't had a chance to talk with George or Buck yet, can't imagine they had anything to do with this. The ferry didn't run that day and I don't think they swam across the bay in the middle of a gale."

"Nooo! Don't think they did that," agreed Morris.

"Guess Bethany is planning a memorial service, just haven't got the details yet. Are you going to go?"

"No, not this time," said Morris. "You can do this one on your own; I don't have the stomach for it anymore."

"Too bad, you should go. But that's your decision."

"Yeah it is, ain't it."

* * *

Bethany Brooks had one evening of calling hours followed by a brief graveside service the morning after. The ferry made a special run for folks from the island who wanted to pay their respects. Brad and Milly were among the twenty-six people who made the trip.

Bethany and the two girls appeared to be holding it together. Dave had been very sick toward the end and it was no mystery to them that he was about to meet his Creator. It had been a very demanding ordeal, but it had prepared them.

Brad and Milly offered their condolences and mingled for a while with other mourners, then made their way back to the ferry for the return trip. Parked near the ferry was a Portsmouth police cruiser and standing next to it was Chief Anthony. He tipped his hat to Milly. "Hi Mildred, nice to see you." He extended his hand to Brad. "Good to see you too, Brad," he said. "I thought you might be here. Need to talk to you a bit." Again he tipped his hat to Milly.

Brad asked Milly to wait for him on the ferry, he would be there shortly. He and Chief Anthony stepped away from the gathering at the dock.

"Listen, Brad, I got some information about Dave Brooks. They recovered his wheelchair right off the edge of the pier." He pointed with his finger to a spot on the pier only about one hundred feet from where they stood. "Apparently he did some fishing there. It was just a hunch, but it paid off. Kind of amazing it didn't get pushed around considering the way the wind was blowing. We also found a good deal of blood on the pier where they think he went in. The thing is, when they recovered Dave's body, it didn't have a mark on it. So where did all that blood come from?"

Brad stared at the town wharf, trying to visualize what Dave Brooks' last moments were like. He turned back to Chief Anthony. "That is odd, Bill. How can I help?"

"I'd like you to have a conversation with Bethany Brooks. I know she'd be more comfortable with you. See if you can stumble onto anything."

"I can do that. I'll give her a couple of days to get things in order and then I'll pay a visit. We have a good relationship, she'll tell me whatever she can."

* * *

A few days later, Brad took a ride up to Crazy George's. Morris had told him about his and Fenway's bumbling attempt at playing detective. Brad was furious with Morris; his actions had been impulsive and may have caused irreparable damage.

"I may have to arrest my own brother," he told Morris. "You could do hard time over this! And why in God's name did you decide to include that buffoon Fenway in your noble plan?"

Morris could only hang his head. He offered no explanation, only a simple, defeated apology. "Sorry."

"Right you are, you are sorry," Brad said in disgust. "You better hope I can talk them out of pressing charges. You went way too far on this one."

Brad pulled into the dirt road that led to George's house. He could see George and Buck in the back yard attacking a pile of oak and maple limbs, trying to build up a sufficient stack of firewood for the winter months that lay ahead. On either end of their two-man saw, Brad saw George and Buck were a well-oiled machine, hands in leather gloves and arms covered in a lathered sweat, pumping in unison as their saw moved steadily through the maple boughs like a butcher's sharp knife through a tender steak.

"Howdy, boys," he yelled as he stepped from his pickup. "Looks like you've got this whole wood thing down to a science."

Ignoring his greeting, the two men pushed and pulled their arms in tandem until their task was complete and the log dropped to the ground.

George took the saw from Buck and nodded to Brad. Between deep breaths, he said, "Hi, Brad." Buck likewise searched for air and sputtered out his greeting. "Hey Brad, what brings you up here?"

Brad waited for them to catch their breath. "Wanted to come up here and apologize for my brother's rude behavior. It's the least I can do. I will send him up here to apologize in person if that will help."

Buck said nothing, knowing enough to defer his response to George.

"Yeah, it was real rude of Morris," George said. "And that idiot Fenway was a dumbass bully. The two of them were completely out of line with the things they said and did, especially to Buck. Assholes, both of them."

"Okay, okay, George, I came here to patch things up, but I'm not going to be a punching bag for you."

"Sorry I can't make it real easy for you." George tore off his leather gloves and pointed an angry finger at Brad. "But if I hadn't grabbed my shotgun, that clown Fenway, your brother's good buddy, would have turned Buck into his own personal punching bag."

Brad saw the bloody bandage around George's right hand. It was stained with rust-colored splotches, almost certainly dried blood, and the recent activity with the handsaw had flooded the immediate area with fresh patches of crimson. It pulled Brad in like a June bug to a campfire.

"That's a pretty nasty cut there, George," he said. "Not so
sure sawing through tough maple is the best thing for that hand right
now. How did that happen?"

George's anger vanished in seconds and his hand with it,
back into its leather wrap. "Oh, that ain't nothing," he said, suddenly
evasive. "Cut it with my fishing knife."

"Funny thing," Brad said, still analyzing George's injured
right hand. "You probably heard that they found Dave Brooks' body
floating in Bristol Harbor. Bet you're all choked up over that. But at
the town pier? Where they think he fell in? Someone left a lot of
blood. A cut like the one on your right hand could leave that much
blood. Funny, ain't it?"

"You're fishing now, Brad. What do you think, I swam
across the bay in the middle of a hurricane? Maybe the blood was
from Dave, I don't know. But Buck and I would like to get back to
sawing before we stiffen up, if you know what I mean."

"That's the other funny thing," Brad countered. "Dave didn't
have a scratch on him." He wanted to add that he remembered two
young men who challenged an angry ocean back in 1938, but he
stayed away from that for now.

"One last thing, George, you right handed?" Brad inquired.

"Yeah," George said, his impatience growing.

"And you cut your right hand with a fishing knife.
Funny!,"Okay, I'll let you gents get back to your work. Hope I
patched things up between you and Morris."

Turning his back on Brad, George walked back to the cross
braces and lifted another log into place.

"Yeah, Brad, everything is fine now, no real damage done.
Come on, Buck, let's get after this."

Brad got into his pickup and drove off, grateful for deflecting
a serious offense away from his brother and hoping the cops ran a
blood test on what they found on the pier in Bristol.

* * *

K.W. Garlick

Buck dropped his end of the saw the minute Brad's pickup was out of sight. "Oh George, he's onto us. I need my bottle," he stuttered.

George ignored Buck. He released his grip on the saw and removed the glove from his cut right hand. He examined his hand; it was still bleeding through the bandages, and he delicately removed the soiled compresses. George held his hand up to the sunlight for a better look. "I'm going to need some stitches," he said. "Was hoping I could do without them, but I was only fooling myself."

"Did you hear what I said?" Buck demanded impatiently. He raised his voice even more. "I said he's onto us!"

"He ain't onto anything, so just relax. I need you to put a few stitches in this hand and I don't welcome that if you're walking around afraid of your own shadow. Have a drink from your bottle if you want, but just calm down."

"I don't know how you can stay so calm," he said. And that was true. Buck was always amazed how George could stay so composed in the most nerve-wracking situations. "You're wrong, George, you heard him."

"You know what I heard Brad say?" George looked directly into Buck's face. "Absolutely nothing. As I told him, it was just a fishing expedition. No one will ever be able to connect the dots, ever. Now have a couple more pulls on your bottle and let's go inside and see if we can fix my butchered hand."

Things hadn't changed much over the years: George led and Buck followed. George projected confidence and Buck injected doubt into everything they did.

194

Chapter 13

Brad's instincts told him there was more to the denial of George and Buck. The serious cut on George's right hand spoke volumes, and Buck's nervous tap dance only reinforced his suspicions. But the facts simply didn't allow him any further examination of his theories. Brad was not a reporter, they never let facts get in the way of a good story. He could not afford that luxury.

The fact was that the last ferry from the island before the hurricane left Prudence with neither George nor Buck among the passengers. You can't murder someone if you can't be placed at the scene of the crime, and people had seen George and Buck on the island the next day. So, unless they mastered the skill of levitation and had walked across the bay in a hurricane, there was just nowhere to go with his hunch. Yet they had survived brief minutes in a terrible typhoon many years ago, and for some reason, that simple act of throwing themselves into a tempest gnawed at him. Would a sane man, knowing he had already cheated certain death once, pitch himself again into that same abyss? No! No rational person would do such a reckless thing. Yet his suspicions would not allow him to let it go. Simple reasoning always brought him back to George and Buck.

Perhaps a one-on-one visit to Buck's home might be productive. Buck was at a real disadvantage when his guardian friend George wasn't there to deflect or defend. Brad first needed to grease the skids; it was time to turn up the heat on Buck, rattle his cage. He started asking around — had anybody seen Buck during the day of the storm? When? Where? Anybody hear how George got the nasty cut on his hand? Brad knew if it found its way back to Buck, the cracks would appear. Sometimes he drove to where Buck was working and would sit for hours in his pickup, just watching. Buck would constantly cast a nervous look back at Brad, like a puppet on a string. He couldn't help himself.

Chapter 14

For the past two weeks, George had seen the puppeteer manipulate the strings on his marionette. Brad Wheeler's pursuit of Buck began to bear fruit. He became an agitated man. His drinking — already excessive — became extreme. With frayed nerves, Buck struggled to keep the genie in the bottle.

"Just try and calm down," George told his anxious friend. They sat at the table in George's little shanty. Once again, the Caswell family was well represented. Their pictures surrounded him with their penetrating stares, and as usual, they offered Buck little comfort. It was the end of an early fall day, and the air was cool and dry, perhaps a subtle hint to the tall oaks, maples, and sassafras that it would soon be time to show off their colors. George had built a small fire in the cooking stove. Buck was on his way home from a painting job at Henry Storey's house on the west side and had stopped off at George's to calm his nerves.

"Brad is asking everyone questions about the two of us, and they're all telling me about it. He stopped by where I was working today and just *watched* me. For hours!!!" Buck had the bottle at his mouth in an instant, choking off his last few words. He swallowed like a man whose life depended on that simple act and then pulled the bottle away from his lips. Whiskey dribbled down his chin and across a stubbly grey beard. His eyes were wide with disbelief.

"I can't calm down," he said. "He's on to something. It's all over, George."

"Ain't nothing over," George said, and grabbed him by the shoulders, forcing Buck to look directly at him. "I told you a couple of weeks ago that this was just a fishing trip. Don't you think if he had anything he'd be all over us? At least bring us to Portsmouth for questioning? No, he hasn't, 'cause he ain't got nothing. Just trying to rattle us, and he's doing that to you."

"Oh, he's got me rattled, all right. I hardly sleep at night, can't eat real well either, my stomach is all twisted up." Buck took another drink, looked vacantly at the ceiling for a few moments and then returned his eyes to his old friend. "You know, George, I've been a loyal friend to you." His voice was sad, empty, and without commitment. "I can't do this no more, I just can't. If Brad starts asking me questions, I'm scared to the bone I'll start talking."

George was about to lash out at his old friend, confront him. Tell him he had to be stronger and dig his heels in. But he stopped himself. He wanted to tell Buck that he would always be there for him. But that would be a lie; sooner or later, Brad Wheeler would orchestrate the time and place where he would bushwhack Buck and have him all to himself and George knew Buck would spill his guts. He felt overwhelmed with empathy for his old friend. The burden of saving Buck from himself was suddenly thrust upon him. It was a responsibility he had anticipated, and he recognized that he was the only one who could provide the protection and comfort that Buck had desperately sought his entire life.

"Just head on home, Buck." He reached across Buck's broad, rock-hard shoulders and pulled him gently to his side. "Give that bottle a rest, try and get some supper on a plate. I will stop by later this evening. I've got something up my sleeve, something that will make this all go away."

"Are you sure, George?" Buck asked, instantly full of anticipation. "That would be freaking great, whatta ya got, tell me."

"I'll give you all the details tonight, but it's bulletproof," George said, with confidence in his voice. "You get back to your place and dial back the whiskey, see you later on."

Puzzled by what his friend had just told him, Buck said, "Funny, you ain't never told me to lay off my bourbon." He rose from his chair, walked to the door, stopped and turned. "See you tonight, sure hope you got something good up your sleeve, just the thought of it got me feeling a little better on the inside. Maybe I can get some sleep tonight."

"Oh yeah, you're gonna love it.," said George, his voice full of optimism. "See you in a bit."

Buck opened the door and walked out. George watched him walk to his car. Buck seemed lighter on his feet and whistled a brief, happy tune. George did not like what he was about to do.

* * *

Buck's mood was lighter and he felt he should eat while his stomach was calm. Back in his own kitchen, he pulled out a can of Dinty Moore beef stew and attacked the big thumbprint on its top with a can opener. He placed the opened can directly onto his propane stove, no sense in dirtying another pan. He would have another drink while he waited for it to cook. His brighter mood welcomed that decision.

Finding a weathered glass in a cluttered sink, he poured his drink and had it at his mouth in a simple, well-rehearsed motion. He began to contemplate his new impasse. Another one of Brad Wheeler's unannounced visits, with his pointed and probing questions, had unnerved Buck. But now George had boasted that he had a plan that would throw Brad off his pursuit. He would have to wait for George to arrive to learn the details of his strategy.

Waiting and alone with his thoughts was something that Buck did not do well, especially when he thought about the way Brad Wheeler had been harassing him. "Wish George would get here," he thought and emptied his tumbler.

Chapter 15

George knew he faced another grim task, more forbidding than any before. He had seen its inception with Brad Wheeler's surprise visit. He hoped his father had not seen the birth of this ugly obligation. But George had, and he knew the clarity of the deed was too difficult, too obvious to ignore.

Buck had become the weak link in their twisted plan of retribution. Buck had been a loyal friend and had stood fast by his commitment to help his good friend complete his grim assignment, but it had begun to wear on him; participating in Carolyn Waters' death had pushed Buck closer to the edge. The first few cracks had surfaced. Forcing his participation in a suicidal trip across the bay in the middle of a tempest was exhausting; and then to bear witness as a feeble man, long absent of his faculties, was drowned in a violent ocean certainly would have tested his emotional courage. The image of the man confined to the wheelchair slashing with his fishing knife against an assailant only he could see before plunging into the depths would be lasting and traumatic. His good friend was beginning to unravel.

George's father confronted him with the obvious. His family reached out to him only hours after Brad Wheeler's impromptu visit.

Frantic callings from beyond beckoned George, crackles from the corners of his mind, dancing spots of lights, flashed across his vision, the upright hair on his arms signaling a family council was urgently required.

By the flick of a switch, George illuminated his family portraits as if he were lighting a runway, so that their wandering spirits from an alien world might safely land. Their eyes fluttered and suddenly focused, telling George their touchdown and arrival was complete. Once again, George sat before the family delegation.

"We have arrived at a critical point, one that I could never have foreseen," Bernie Caswell announced mechanically, without feeling. "I'm afraid this journey of ours has become too much for Buck. He is falling apart in front of us."

George knew where his father was headed with his words; too many discussions about how important their journey was, how no compromise or threat to its completion could be tolerated, made it clear. Obviously, his father saw Buck as a risk.

"No, Father, Buck is not the risk you think he is," said George, desperation in his voice. "We just need to remove him from any more involvement. It was never his responsibility and we dragged him into it. Release him from that burden and he will be fine. He just needs a little time."

"I wish it were that simple," replied his father, "but we both know it isn't. Buck is in a desperate place now, he is crumbling, and to pretend that he is not doesn't do him or us any good. Brad Wheeler is about to expose him and our crusade. We need to save Buck from himself."

"I know where you are going with this, Father," George said. "I will not make my good friend a casualty of our campaign. He just needs some time to gather himself. I can keep Brad Wheeler off his trail."

But George's father would not be dissuaded. He explained that they had come too far in their journey, that too many sacrifices had been offered up. Too much pain and humiliation had been cast upon them, their legacy and lineage had been forever stained. "We all agreed to follow this through to the end, regardless of the consequences of our actions. You were more committed to this expedition than any of us."

"That's because I have been left with the burden of its fruition," said George, and he reflected on his years of despair and loneliness, his family taken from him in a terrifying tick of time. A thousand times he had envisioned them huddled in their living room in terror at the hurricane that raged about them, but also comforted by countless assurances that they were safe from even the most calamitous disaster. But then windows shattered and walls collapsed and an angry sea invaded their home. They were panic-stricken as they were separated from each other, helpless to change their destiny, and then swept away by powerful waves that battered and consumed them. Reflecting on the fear they must have experienced always overwhelmed him.

Peter Marrow and his band of fools with their collective ineptness had built his family's home, only to have it become their catacomb. It had been constructed with a promise of invincibility, but then, as if his shallow vow was not harmful enough, he invaded the sanctity of his parents' marriage and brought shame to their family. Marrow's harmful actions had been broad and complete. And then George knew his father was right. There must be a complete and final retribution, but he had never envisioned that his closest friend would be a casualty of their vendetta.

"We are all tortured that it has come to this," Bernie said, but his words again seemed bare of any feeling. "Buck is a good friend to all of us. Just thinking about what we must do to our dear friend is painful. We must think this through."

"Your words seem so empty. How can you be so callous!" George yelled at his father. "We are not talking about putting down a family pet. This is my best friend!" He began to cry.

His father hung his head and softly spoke of his sorrow for his son and the task he faced and then faded back into a dimension that only the Caswell family shared.

* * *

Pacing the floor of his cottage, Buck strove to keep his uneasiness under control. Too many times he had let his nervousness dictate how far he immersed himself in his bourbon, the only elixir he had to counter the trauma his anxiety brought to him day every of his life. Tonight, his concern was escalating and so was his drinking.

Buck lit his kerosene heater to remove the chill from his cottage. The past few nights had turned cool and that night, there was an added chill. Perhaps the added warmth might temper his nervous pacing. He opened the window near his ragged bed, the sheets gray with age and neglect, an old gray woolen blanket jammed between the wall and bed.

Buck sat on the edge of his bed for a while, but became more anxious the longer he had to wait for George. His thoughts unraveled and he soon was drowning in self-doubt and paranoia. He stood on shaky legs and stumbled about his tiny home.

"Oh, God, where the hell is George?" He prayed out loud to a god that had forsaken him many years ago. He thought about saying 'amen,' but instead looked toward the heavens and toasted with his flagon. He inhaled what remained and apathetically tossed it into his untidy sink. He reached into the cabinet above the sink and retrieved his last bottle of sour mash and clumsily tore at its seal. Staggering to the front door, he opened it and stood facing out into the cool night. Nearby, male tree frogs well into their evening serenade briefly halted their performance to examine this new patron, and then began anew. Buck stared hazily into the cool darkness and once again begged for his friend's arrival. He knew George had devised a plan that would provide instant clarity to their dilemma and comfort his uneasiness. Standing in the doorway, the bright ceiling light behind him, he absently took another long drink and watched as his long shadow swayed back and forth on the dew-covered front lawn.

Seeking the comfort of his bed, he turned and stumbled back into his cottage. He lowered himself, almost falling, into his berth and banged against the back wall. It would be a bad night, and his vision deserted him. The room swirled, and strangers of bizarre shapes and colors closed in on him. Buck raised his new carafe and struggled to find his lips. He took one last long drink, rolled his eyes toward the heavens, and fell softly into his bed. It would be a long and deep sleep.

* * *

Distraught but resolved by the sad direction his family had chosen to pursue, George began the slow, painful walk to Buck's. He ambled along the back roads that connected their two homes; his was a journey that, regardless of the distance traveled or the obstacles encountered, whether physical or emotional, would have George arriving much too soon. A waning moon and overcast night hid the lonely assassin from neighbors who knew nothing of the sinful deed assigned to him, nor would they ever believe that he could exploit such a close friend. George was like a skillful surgeon contracted to remove the diseased leg of a very sick man. He and his mission would be completed only when the gruesome surgery was performed and Buck, the stricken limb, was amputated.

* * *

George tortured himself to think about how to complete the subtraction. Buck would perish by his hand and it would be an infidelity that would haunt him for eternity. There would be that moment, brief as it might be, when Buck would realize that his good friend had betrayed him. That sad look he knew would remain indelible in his memory for the remainder of his days.

George came to the hill that led down to Buck's. A lonely kitchen light cast its dim beacon outward. There was no movement within. George's thoughts raced. "Why has it come to this? Why has it come down to me? One look from me and Buck will know why I am here. I can't hide it from him. Oh, my God."

Tears followed and shortly George stood frozen at his friend's door. His movements now void of any feeling or purpose, George was compelled and he entered Buck's shack. There was no sign of Buck. It seemed no one was home, For the briefest moment, George believed he had escaped tragedy, but then he heard the grumblings of a man deep in sleep. He walked back to the tiny bedroom and found Buck curled up on his bed in a profound stupor. His jaw had relaxed and was open wide, and spittle flowed from the corners of his mouth, down his chin, wetting his dingy tee-shirt. His throat rattled with a slow and labored breath.

"Ah, Buck," he said, and tears flowed again. An old straight-back chair piled with work shirts and chinos rested in the corner. Tipping its contents to the floor, George pulled the chair next to Buck's bed and sat facing his trusted companion.

He stared at his friend now dug into a place where no one could harm him and the pain was held at bay. Buck's whole life had been like that: from a drunken conception to an abusive mother; a caring father suddenly taken from him at a vulnerable age. Unwanted and unloved, not because of any decision he made, but more the result of years of indifference and pity by those all around him. Buck was seen as comical and pitied, yet he had become invisible.

The irony of it all consumed George. He had gone to the cottage to forever remove the pain from Buck's existence by ending his life. This all to a loyal friend who had bravely saved his life many years ago.

He reached over and tenderly poked Buck's shoulder. "Hey Buck, you there?" he asked. But Buck wore his "do not disturb" disguise and there would be no retrieving him that evening. Buck had lit his kerosene heater and the room was warm and safe. George reached over and caressed Buck's hair. "This world will torture you no more, Buck," George said, and he reached over and turned the kerosene heater all the way up, then moved his hand to the partially-open window next to Buck's bed. He hesitated for a few seconds and then softly closed the window. "We will soon be challenging our own hurricanes again. We will have a grand time. Goodbye, my friend."

Leaving the cottage and gently closing the door behind him, George began his lifeless walk home. He would share the sad news with his family, but they would never understand the pain he had inflicted upon himself.

Chapter 16

Late the next afternoon, Brad pulled his pickup into George Caswell's yard. George was in his side yard, once again splitting wood for the oncoming winter. The day hadn't warmed up much from the previous night's chill. George offered Brad a quick glance and then returned to stabbing the oak before him with his ax. The dreaded moment that had kept him awake all night was finally here. He knew the disturbing news that Brad was about to share with him. The shock, tears, and sadness would not be difficult to fake. Brad shuffled up to him.

"Hey George," he said. "Looks like your hand is healing up pretty good."

"Yeah, I guess so," he returned, never stopping his chopping motions. "What can I do for you?"

"Listen George, I got some bad news for you." He hesitated while George stopped and put down his ax.

* * *

Carl Friswell had called Brad late that morning when he discovered Buck's body on his cluttered bed. Around mid-morning,

Carlt had noticed every window in Buck's cottage was covered in a heavy layer of condensation and there was no sign that Buck was up and about. Something just didn't seem right and his curiosity led to a sobering discovery.

Another death, but now someone outside the very selective and shrinking circle of candidates. Brad stood above the body of Buck. He looked asleep, as if in one of his alcohol-induced slumbers. Over the years, in his early morning rounds, Brad had found Buck passed out in his car in the usual spots. Often, he would reach in and shake Buck awake and tell him to get back home. Now he wanted to reach down and shake him one last time, but no amount of probing would bring Buck to his shack. He had moved on to another home.

Brad wondered where and when the madness would end. The news about Buck had added a new deadly breadth to his investigation. A familiar sadness surrounded him as he viewed Buck's corpse and he wondered if his harrassment of the man had brought about his death. Brad quickly dismissed the thought; he would not allow feelings of guilt to compromise his mission. Buck had begun to squirm under his close scrutiny and eventually his anxiety would have led to some guarded revelation, whether it would have been enough to unravel a deep and dark secret, only time would tell, but Buck was never despondent or suicidal. That just wasn't his chemistry. Nor was his death accidental — every fiber of his being told Brad that Buck's deranged death was the work of George. Crazy George.

He looked at George and his instinct told him he was about to share news with someone that probably was the origin of it all.

"We found Buck Taylor dead in house this morning."

George Caswell immediately took a deep breath and searched the skies above.

"Oh, my lord, what happened? I wondered why I hadn't seen him today," he said dejectedly. He lowered his eyes, never meeting Brad's examining stare, and studied the ground at his feet. "This is awful, this hurts so much. Don't imagine anyone on this pathetic island will shed a tear for him."

Removing his cap and pushing his hand back through his graying hair, Brad tried to gather his thoughts. "Sorry for your loss,

George. People will miss him. He wasn't that bad of a guy, always meant well, just seemed to have the worst luck."

"You gonna suggest that for his eulogy? Meant well but had shit for luck, real pearls those are," George said, now looking directly at Brad. "You ain't told me how he died."

"What do you want me to say, George?" said Brad, his anger increasing. "I came here to tell you your best friend died and you're all pissed off. I figured you'd be broken up when you heard the news." Then Brad noticed George's eyes were red and irritated, as if he'd been crying for most of the day.

"What's with your eyes, looks like you been crying for some time?"

"Allergies, lot of goldenrod this year, does a number on me," George said, calmer and more poised. "Brad, do you know how he died?" he asked again, trying to conceal his participation.

Brad stared at George for a moment; his instincts told him something was amiss. "I just sent his body off with the medical examiner. We'll know more when he provides his report, but if I had to guess, Buck probably had his pops of whiskey last night then lit his kerosene heater. It was a cool night. Probably laid down on his bed, forgot to open the window next to his bed, and suffocated. Carbon monoxide poisoning. Those kerosene heaters work good, but you got to keep a window open near them. Otherwise you go to sleep and never wake up. And you don't need to be so angry with me, I'm just the messenger. I didn't kill him."

"Yeah, you did, Brad," George returned, his anger restored. "You and this whole goddamn island, with your pity and indifference. It's a real shame." He returned his gaze to the ground.

"Suit yourself," Brad said, frustrated, his patience gone. He strode with purpose to his truck and left without another word.

George began to cry.

"Sleep peacefully my friend," he said aloud.

Chapter 17

George stood on the old stone wharf on the west side and tenderly offered Buck's remains to a soft breeze that lifted his spirit up the bay and into the waters that surrounded his cherished island. The setting sun marked the end of Buck's final visit to the one place he felt at peace — the sunsets were always healing and energizing for Buck. George stood alone with his friend for the last time. He allowed himself a few moments to reflect on their special friendship. His guilt would only allow fleeting moments, then a car pulled onto the dock, its headlights on, though they were of little effect in the infancy of nightfall. It was Peter Marrow, and George knew his anger would only escalate. Peter Marrow again, violating a moment that belonged to someone else.

"Couldn't you allow me this private time with my old friend?" George asked the intruder.

"I'm real sorry, George, but I thought it was time for us to talk about some things that have been misrepresented and rumored for far too long. Can't we clear the air?"

"Clear the air of what?" George demanded. "If you mean I have to pretend that you didn't have an affair with my mother that screwed up our family only months before your faulty, shoddy

209

lighthouse was washed away in a storm, despite your promises that such a thing could never happen, then no. Sorry, I can't do that."

"I don't want you to pretend anything. Pretending doesn't get us anywhere. It's time for the truth, as painful as it might be. I did have an affair with your mother, and I won't pretend anymore that I did not."

"I know now that it caused a lot of pain and I am so sorry for that," he said to George. "But you need to know it was not some cheap, seedy affair. Your mother and I were drawn to each other. She had lived many years in a loveless marriage. You need to know that, also. She was a good woman and she loved her children, just not your father. We realized it would never work; too many good people would be innocent casualties and we ended it shortly before the hurricane."

"What about the shoddy workmanship and the cheap-ass materials being used in the construction of my family's new home?" George angrily demanded.

"I have no idea where this rumor of poor workmanship and substandard material came from. That has to be the work of someone more concerned with a vendetta than with the truth, someone like your father. Your father was involved every single day in the construction of that lighthouse. He had to sign off on every piece of material brought to the job site. I took pride in what we built there and so did my workers. We all thought it could withstand the test of time, but none of us ever thought the storm of the century would test our bold predictions. You are being played, George, and by whom I'm not sure, but I am frightened by the possibilities. And to think all these good men have died because of some twisted crusade. You have no idea the price you will pay for the dirty deeds you have done. The Chinese say, 'be sure to dig two graves when you are preoccupied with revenge.' I hope you have dug that other one for yourself. You will need it."

"You say all this shit because you think there's no one to challenge your lies, but you're wrong. Despite what you think that hurricane did, my family has never left me, and we began our revenge many years ago. One by one, your crew has paid the price for their careless work. You're the only one left. Be patient, Peter, there will be another storm and your name will be all over it. But I know you ain't too good with waiting, and that just makes me all fuzzy on the inside." Mike O'Rourke then drove by in his old Buick and George made a dramatic point of waving at him. Mike waved back.

"Now I am going to drive directly to Brad Wheeler's house and tell him that you are harassing me, probably fill out a complaint against you. Mike O'Rourke will tell Brad he saw us together, gonna make life real uncomfortable for you, and then I won't have to listen to your shit anymore," George said with spite. "There were no good men here, and this talk of crusades, revenge, and crypts is getting us nowhere. I'm tired of this conversation." George got in his car and left, his rear wheels spinning wildly, throwing sand, dirt, and stones up against Peter and his car.

Peter stood with the cloud of dust distilling all about him. He shook his head in disbelief — a twisted father, a twisted son, and a twisted reality everywhere. How could it ever make sense?

Chapter 18

Crazy George filed his complaint against Peter Marrow and Brad Wheeler was obligated to follow up on it. Brad found Peter on the south end of the island; he was doing an add-on and a new kitchen at Chuck and Betty Worcester's house. Brad pulled into the driveway and Peter was nearby, off-loading framing lumber from a big flatbed with his crew. He motioned for his team to continue without him and walked over to Brad's truck. Brad stayed where he was; he would do this from the front seat, less confrontational, he thought.

"I suppose you're here because Crazy stirred up a lot of shit," Peter said. "You don't believe any of the crap he told you, I hope."

"What crap do you think he told me?"

"All that shit about me using cheap material and taking shortcuts in constructing the lighthouse. The biggest line of crap is that I supposedly told his father that nothing could harm their family as long as they stayed within its strong walls."

"Didn't mention a thing about that," Brad told him, a little uneasy. "He just complained that you were harassing him. Said he went down to the stone pier on the west side to spread Buck's ashes and you confronted him about the deaths of the people who worked for you. And I remember quite a few years ago, when you confronted me about not going after Crazy George and Buck Taylor, for the murders of Carolyn Waters, Tom Tuttle and Ted Esau. You were doing a lot of drinking back then."

"Brad, that was a dark time for me," Peter offered. "I paid a heavy price for my paranoia and alcohol abuse. I've tried to move past all that insanity. I just wanted to clear the air, put an end to the rumors."

"What about the rumors, Peter? Especially the one about you and Connie Caswell?" Brad was probing, and the expression of pain on Peter's face proved he had touched a tender nerve.

"Yeah, I had an affair with her," said Peter, his face and posture acknowledging the shame. "I ain't real proud of that, but it's not what you think and that's what I tried to tell Crazy. But he didn't want to hear that, he just went on and on about how I was next, I just had to be patient. He said I was the last one on his family's list and my time was coming. He really is crazy. Is there anything you can do?"

"I'm afraid there is very little we can do. As much as I might believe you about your conversation with George, it's your word against his, and you know how far that will get you in court. As much as we can speculate about the murders, even Buck Taylor's, there is just no way to connect any of the dots. We got nothing."

Brad paused, trying to gather his next few words, then looked up directly at Peter.

"It's good that you're talking about your affair with Mrs. Caswell. Maybe it will help you move forward in your life, maybe make things better with you and Lillian. Ain't really any of my business. But why the hell couldn't you have acknowledged it a long time ago? Might have saved you a lot of pain. And it might have helped with the investigation, too."

Peter could not look at Brad. He turned his gaze skyward and curled his lips inward. "I guess it was just too painful for me. The shame was overwhelming. But at least now you believe there was and still is a connection between all these dead people and Crazy George.

Also sounds like you're linking Buck Taylor's death to this insanity, too. Why is that?"

"Listen, Peter, believing and proving are two different animals. I shouldn't tell you this because it's pure speculation on my part, and if you let it slip to anyone else, I'll deny it, but I don't think Buck Taylor's death was an accident or a suicide. I think Crazy George had everything to do with it. It was all catching up with Buck and I think he was about to spill his guts. Crazy couldn't let that happen. But I can't prove a thing. Not just yet, anyways."

Peter stood speechless. This new information from Brad had reignited the fear and paranoia that had consumed him years ago. Finally, he looked up to Brad.

"This is all gonna start again," he said. "Hope I can stay away from the booze. And you tell me there's nothing you can do, just like before. I don't want to live like that again."

"Don't do anything stupid, Peter," Brad said, knowing he was looking at a cornered animal.

Brad saw the desperation in Peter's eyes. It signaled a man that was left with few options. Peter turned and walked back to his waiting crew without saying another word.

"Just stay away from Crazy!" Brad yelled after him. But Peter heard none of it. He was thinking only of removing the threat.

* * *

A hot cup of coffee in hand, Brad sat in his office at the farm with his feet resting on his ancient but sturdy desk. He was waiting for his 8:00 a.m. phone call from Chief Anthony. Over the years, it had become their appointed time to check in. Brad's brother was with him, peppering him with all kinds of questions about Buck's sudden death. Morris was also eager to advance his theories surrounding his untimely demise. Smoke from their Parodi cigars floated lazily in the air.

"You know, Brad, this is just another one of those freaking crazy deaths that have been going on here for the last thirty-five years," Morris said, a tattered baseball cap on his head and a gray, stubbly beard complementing his soured breath from another night of rotgut corn mash. "It's just too simple for Buck to die like that. Hell, he's been drinking and using that kerosene heater on chilly nights for the last five years. Someone stepped in and made sure they got the result they wanted. Don't you think so?"

Brad secretly wished the chief would call. Ever since Morris and his inept friend Fenway Connors had overstepped civil boundaries and decency with their untimely and vigilante-like incursion of Crazy George's household, Brad no longer shared any details of active investigations. Morris had become a liability. Brad would not leave himself that vulnerable again.

"Don't know what to think, Morris," he replied, pretending to be busy with paperwork.

Morris rose angrily from his chair and stood before his brother. He removed the soggy miniature cigar from his mouth and spit tobacco bits onto the grimy office floor.

"Hell, you ain't even listening to me. You know exactly what to think, except you ain't sharing it with me," he said, his voice escalating in volume and frustration. That was Morris, always on the edge. "You ain't been sharing much with me lately, ever since me and Fenway pulled a surprise visit on Crazy George and Buck. Nobody got hurt, and I swear Buck was about to spill his guts."

"Spill his guts about what?" Brad asked, knowing his brother's answer would not be far off from what he himself was thinking, but not willing to concede. "Going to Crazy's house like that, unannounced and invading, was against the law. You're not a cop and neither is Fenway. If Crazy had pressed charges, you could have been arrested, and there wouldn't have been a thing I could do about it."

"See, there you go again." Morris paced the office. "You know exactly what I'm talking about, how long you gonna hold that cordial calling against me? You know just as well as me that Buck Taylor was about to 'fess up about a lot of things. He was wound up tighter than a rattlesnake. And you know who else knew that?" He turned to his brother. "Crazy George, that's who! And you know it."

Morris turned and walked to the only windows in the office and stared out into the early morning sunshine as if the validation he sought was mixed in with the blueberry bushes and bull brier. "Ain't nothing crazy about him," he whispered to himself.

"What did you say?" Brad asked and then his phone rang.

Brad looked at the phone and then at his brother. Morris knew he had been invited to leave the room without being asked and stormed from the office, slamming the door on his way out. Brad was glad there was no glass panel.

He picked up the phone. Chief Anthony and he had been talking weekly, but both had been anxiously waiting over six weeks for the autopsy report on Buck. There had been no obvious reason to rush the medical examiner's report. There were no indications of foul play. Everything pointed to Buck having too much to drink and falling asleep with the kerosene heater on. But there was the remote possibility he could have been poisoned or that someone had suffocated him, and they needed the ME's report to wrap things up.

"Good morning, Chief," he said. "Any news from the ME?"

"Hey, Brad," the Chief replied. "I got the report in front of me right now. Everything seems to be in line with what we were thinking. Mr. Taylor was highly intoxicated when he fell asleep and spent the rest of the night inhaling the fumes from that kerosene heater. The autopsy showed high levels of carbon monoxide in Buck's blood, as well as an almost toxic reading of alcohol. Think you can pretty much take that to the bank."

Chief Anthony heard the sound of Brad's deep sigh, like a soft breeze across the phone's mouthpiece. "Sounds like that doesn't put a bow on it for you. What's your reservation about all of this?"

"My gut's telling me it just isn't as cut-and-dried as the coroner's report might say. The last few months, Buck was a bundle of nerves, he was drinking more than usual. The last few times I talked to him, it was like he was sitting on top of a volcano that was ready to blow. It was obvious that his good friend George Caswell was doing his best to keep a lid on it. I don't know if that was because he was trying to protect Buck or himself."

"I have been saying for many years, more than I want to say, that these are your people and you know them better than I ever will. If your gut's telling you that, it's for a reason. Do you have anything substantial to move on?"

"No, all I got is this feeling that Crazy George knows more than he's telling. It's always seemed that way. He just doesn't act like someone who lost his best friend of thirty years."

"Well, stay with it," Chief Anthony said. "God, I've been saying that for so long. Can't believe we never put it all together over there and I'm not real proud of that. Listen, Brad, you should know that I will be retiring this coming February. I don't want to walk away from all these years and all those deaths with nothing to show for our work. We don't have much, I know, but why don't you bring George in over here for some questioning. He'll be out of his element and he's never felt the kind of pressure that can get applied to someone who's in my crosshairs. Bring him in at eight Friday morning. I'll send our launch to bring you over and back."

"You really going to retire?" Brad asked, amazed. "Didn't know that much time had passed. But when you trace the years, you can't deny it."

"It'll be twenty-five years next August. I did twenty years in the navy before applying for a detective position in Portsmouth and it just fell into place from there. I think all those years in the Newport Shore Patrol greased the skids, so to speak."

"I'll make sure George Caswell will be there on Friday."

"Good, see you then. We will make this right somehow."

* * *

Knocking on the weathered oak door early the following day, Brad found George about to leave for work. "Oh, it's you," George said with apathy. "Listen, I'm on my way to work, ain't got time for you right now. Real sorry," he said sarcastically.

"Just relax, George," Brad said with irritation, "I only need a couple of minutes. You got time for that."

"Make it quick," George said, matching his visitor's prickliness. "You can talk to me on the way to my truck." He closed the door behind him and ambled toward his truck.

Brad fell in stride with his lifelong phantom nemesis. He had witnessed a lifetime of pain and heartache descend on this man and had seen him harden over the years. Brad wondered what all that pain could make a man capable of. Capable of killing five people? The thought was disturbing. He glanced at George as they walked along and wondered if he was sauntering next to a killer.

"Listen, George," Brad said bluntly. "Chief Anthony needs you to come in to the Portsmouth station to discuss a few things. Need you to make room on your schedule for Friday morning. We can take the town launch, so getting over and back won't be a big issue."

"Questions about what?" George asked, now irritated.

"We're not sure if Buck's death was accidental and we need to know about Buck's last few days. Is there anyone who might benefit from his death? You were his best friend, who would know better than you what was going on? I remember my last visit with the two of you, he was a bundle of nerves and you know it."

"You think he was murdered?" George said, sounding astounded by the news.

"We're just looking at all the possibilities," Brad said quickly, trying to keep the dialogue brief. "I'll meet you at the town dock at Sand Point this Friday morning at eight sharp."

"What if I don't want to go?" George challenged.

"Can't imagine why you wouldn't want to go. Buck was your good friend, wasn't he? I would think you'd want to help in any way you could. Though I suppose Chief Anthony could send a couple of his officers to persuade you. Do you really want to do it that way?"

"I'll see you Friday morning," said George with much reluctance.

* * *

George sat alone in a dingy gray interrogation room at the police station in Portsmouth. A rugged, simple pine table sat in the middle of the room, its once precise corners rounded over the years. Coffee and food stains were abundant. It showed all the signs of confident, over-aggressive accusations and equally-defiant denials. Parallel scratch marks and soft rounded indentations peppered the table. George wondered how many people had dragged their nails across the altar in fear of their sanity, or had pounded its surface in anger and insubordination. Brad and an officer escorted George into 'A – Room,' as the sign above the door read, and told him they would be right back with Chief Anthony and a cup of coffee. That was well over an hour ago, and a rigid straight-back chair, the sole purpose of which was to torture and harm, was beginning to do so. George stood and paced the room, pausing to look through the single grid-covered window. The door opened and Chief Anthony, carrying his own cushioned chair, strode confidently into the room. It was supremely evident to George that he was the lord of this dungeon.

"Have a seat, Mr. Caswell." Chief Anthony pointed to the chair as if George had been completely unaware of its existence.

"Where's Brad Wheeler?" George nervously asked.

"Oh, he'll be by in a bit, he had some island paperwork to finish up. For now, though, I just want you and I to talk about...well, about a whole bunch of things." He was turning up the heat right away.

"Talk about a bunch of things, like what? How long is this going to take?" He began to anxiously pace the room again.

"Could take all day. Maybe longer. If it does, we'll just have you back for another visit. That ain't too bad, is it? This place has all the creature comforts, and we aim to please all our guests. Now *sit down!*" he said in a warning voice, and Chief Anthony pointed an angry finger at the chair.

George slowly walked to the chair, lowered himself, and placed his folded hands on the table in front of him, waiting for Chief Anthony to place his chair in front of him and recline. He met the chief's challenging stare with his own confident glare.

"Ask me anything you want, it's amazing it took you thirty-two years to get to this point, which tells me a couple of things: one, you probably don't have much to go on, just a lot of speculation. Two, you're pretty goddamn stupid."

Chief Anthony placed a manila folder on the table and looked at the man in front of him, studied his eyes, and believed he saw pure evil in them — a strong, confident, and deep-rooted evil. The evil had been festering for over three decades and was terminal — no salve or antibiotic would vanquish it. Chief Anthony knew he was about to dance with the devil, and it would be a delicate dance. The eyes of a demon had shaken his confidence.

"They tell me they call you 'crazy' and I thought that was a mean thing for people to do," he said, then hesitated. "But I believe you are," he said, as if he were a physician telling his patient he only had weeks to live. "Yeah, you're crazy."

"Making you a little nervous, chief cook and bottle washer?" George sarcastically asked.

"Hell, no! Do you know how many times I've sat in this room with people a lot more disturbed than you, some at their wits' end because the horror of what they committed had finally caught up with them?" he asked, like he was reading a menu. "Those people never wanted to be sitting in that chair. Nice and comfortable, ain't it? But they had been slowly wandering toward that chair their whole lives, just never knew it. A very few people have been waiting — almost wanting — to sit in that chair, to them it's not a hard steel tool of coercion, but rather a place of prestige and honor, almost a like throne—"

"Screw you, Chief," George interjected. "I ain't in this chair to listen to you, that's for sure. You think you got me and all these murders figured out? Well you don't, you ain't even close. You're not even getting a sniff."

"Like I was saying," Chief Anthony continued, as if unaware that an exchange of thoughts would even be tolerated, much less allowed. "I got a few questions for you, first we're going to talk about Ted Esau." and he opened the folder and slid over a postmortem picture of Ted on a stainless steel slab, his eyes closed and his skin a

220

pale blue lifeless color. Then a picture of Tom Tuttle, the same stainless steel platform, the similar lifeless blue skin, but almost unrecognizable because of the beating he took while being tossed among the massive marine pilings, like a ball in a pinball machine on a Saturday night. Parts of his scalp had been torn free, and the right ear was nearly severed and hung grotesquely on the table. Both legs were broken in several places and the coroner had multiple options for how he might have laid out Tom's body on the examination table for the police photos. His limbs would have offered little resistance or objection. There were deep bruises and abrasions everywhere. The chief went to slide another photo in front of him, but George protested;

"Hey, slow down!" he said, like a young boy denied a special privilege, as if only given one whack at the large teasing piñata. "You're not giving me enough time to completely comprehend and enjoy these pictures."

George again examined the pictures. Tom Tuttle had fought an ugly engagement with the Grim Reaper. Ted Esau did not seem to suffer as much, but was just as dead.

"Oh, these warm the cockles of my heart. We can't just fly through these pictures. Bill, you're denying me my rights of life, liberty, and the pursuit of happiness." George said proudly.

"You call me *chief* or *sir!*" he yelled with rage. "We're not on a first name basis and you're not any friend of mine." With a forceful kick, he knocked the chair out from under Crazy George.

Brad Wheeler entered the room just as the chair banged off the far wall and George was trying to regain his footing. He looked to Chief Anthony for clarity.

"Oh, hi Brad, George here was about to sit down but his balance must have been a little off. Hope you didn't hurt yourself." His eyes piercing with a glint of steel. "Let's have another look at these pictures. Maybe Brad can help with your recollection."

George dusted himself off, picked up the chair, and stood before his two nemeses. "I'm okay." He looked directly at Brad. "Your chief here is a freaking bully. But you know me Brad, I ain't afraid of bullies. Especially the kind that hide behind a badge," he said in defiance.

"Put the chair down and park your ass in it!" Chief Anthony bellowed.

"Better do as he says, George," Brad injected.

"Now take a look at these pictures and start talking," the chief ordered, and he slid the folder in front of George.

Crazy George opened the folder and again began to skim through the pictures with complete detachment, as if he was looking at the parts sheet for his Briggs and Stratton lawnmower. "Sure, sure," he said. "Just give me a couple of minutes to collect my thoughts."

"Don't take too long," the chief grumbled darkly.

Crazy briefly looked at Brad and then turned back to the pleasing pictures. Oh, what a marvelous walk down memory lane this would be! Ted Esau, the first to feel the wrath of the Caswells' revenge, almost sounded like a John Wayne movie, but in the end he was the least challenging of the bunch. The fool didn't know how to swim. Imagine that! Surrounded by water, owned a boat, and couldn't swim his way out of a plastic wading pool.

George and Buck had helped him move his skiff into the lee of the island before the hurricane. He missed his old friend Buck. Buck understood their mission. Don't cry now, don't let them see that weakness, he told himself.

George advised Ted, he should move his boat when the winds changed out of the west. Like a trained seal, they knew he would do that. Just a matter of swimming out to the boat before Tom returned, lying low and ambushing him. One simple pounce and George had him in the water — a fool who could not swim would drown in minutes. By the time George made the short swim to shore, he looked back at the building surf and saw Ted slip beneath a sea of foam. George remembered thinking that Ted, in between his frantic and futile attempts to save himself, must have wondered why Crazy George had done this to him. "You'll find your answer in hell!" George had screamed into surf.

With the buffeting wind challenging his balance and rain stinging his face, the image before him became permanently sealed.

George stood on the shore, proud of his accomplishment. The first step taken, the journey begun. He was like a young shark who had tasted warm blood for the first time — he knew he wanted more.

George slid the picture to the side and picked up the mutilated image of Tom Tuttle, and turned the graphic photo to Brad and the chief. "Now that right there is the best that clown ever looked," and he laughed hysterically.

In disgust, Chief Anthony tore the photograph away from George. "Hey, moron, oh that's right, they call you Crazy; that clown was a good man, his parents and brother and sister were devastated by his death. You need to start talking."

"Let me see the picture again."

Brad took the picture from the police chief's firm grip and let it float down to the table in front of Crazy.

George stared at the image in front of him and he floated back in time to a Navy wharf battered by wind and waves. This fool's demise had been another easy one, especially with his family and Buck so committed to helping. They all knew Tom Tuttle was going to go fishing at the T-wharf during the storm; he had been boasting to all his friends about the moronic deed. Buck had even encouraged him to go. There was a big storage locker at the end of the pier and it was never hard locked. Extra life jackets, ship bumpers, rigging tools, and heavy hemp lines were stored there. Again, arriving before the storm peaked was the easiest task, concealment was effortlessly achieved, all ships and navy personnel were absent from the pier because of the impending storm. George slipped into the water and rode the tide out to the edge of the wharf, climbed the pier ladder next to the locker, quickly slipped inside, and waited for his opportunity. Waiting for hours inside the musty storage trunk, he could hear and feel as the storm grew in its intensity. Winds screeched at the openings and his hideaway vibrated in protest. In the midst of the tempest George's sudden appearance must have seemed like a preordained biblical event to Tuttle. He stood in his bright yellow downeast rain hat and slicker, his mouth open and eyes squinting in fright. Wind, rain, and salt water spray challenged his unsteady stance,

"What the...." he mumbled as George rushed him. With one forceful stiff arm, Tom Tuttle plummeted head first, fishing pole and all, into the angry bay, his screams barely heard above the fray. His body was violently smashed against a massive piling and there were no more cries. George was returned quickly to the storage locker, waiting for darkness and the storm to ebb. Hoping to hear more screams, he was disappointed that Tom had perished so quickly, but was appeased with thoughts of his body endlessly battered among the pilings.

Slipping the photo to the side as if it were a costly invoice, he reached for the next image and his hand froze — the purple swollen face of Carolyn Waters stared back at him. Now he was uncomfortable. Those memories would be difficult.

Carolyn had already paid a costly price with the loss of her husband in the Pacific in 1944. She was a good woman and was always kind to him, despite the pain she carried in her heart. He felt her death should not have been required, but his father had insisted on it and the deed was done. George and a guilt-stricken Buck completed the grim task of placing her body adrift in a hurricane, hog-tied like an animal. George had reluctantly conceded to his father's wishes, but would always be angry with him for the evil exploit. Shaking his head in abhorrence and no longer wanting to take in her painful image, he returned the picture to its folder.

A single photograph remained. Dave Brooks occupied his last act of recall. A treacherous journey across a deadly bay with his good friend and a final confrontation with the last remaining member of Peter Marrow's crew. It was a sad and almost anti-climactic ending. Dave Brooks, in his desperate, sickened state, had confronted and challenged them, although the dare was not necessary. His fate had been sealed many years ago, in 1938. He met his demise in a violent ocean much like George's family had, and George's father had escorted him in that trip to the beyond.

George put the pictures back in the folder and passed it back to Chief Anthony, but his journey down memory lane was not finished. That would only be completed when a portrait of Peter

Marrow with the same purple hue and lifeless expression as the others, was added to the folder.

The three angry men had played their cards, bluffs had been called, raises and checks positioned. But in the end, Crazy George held the winning hand and he knew it all along. He had marked the deck.

Crazy George was insane and arrogant, a bitter pill for Chief Anthony and Brad Wheeler to ingest.

Chapter 19

Morris had been anguishing over his chaotic visit to George's home with his inept friend Fenway. He could not move past it. He had compromised his brother's community and professional standing. How could a man they all called crazy have turned things around on him? It was a blow to his already fragile identity and he sought out the only recourse he knew, alcohol. Reaching out for his jug became more frequent and the consequences more severe. Sleeping and eating were no longer a priority, they actually became an irritation. Consuming food began to upset his stomach and sleep was never rewarding, it turned into short catnaps filled with disturbing images and nightmares. Always hovering on the edge, Morris's life was finally — and quickly — spiraling downward. He was oblivious to the reality that his alcoholism had entered the terminal phase of the disease.

Mary knew that her husband had abruptly crossed over into a place of no return and had no idea what had caused it. Their conversations became short, tense, and without substance. In the early hours of the morning, alone in her bed, she often heard her husband pacing the living room below, mumbling to himself things about hatred and payback. Whoever or whatever it was, it had consumed him. World War I had begun the process of adding excess ballast to a foundering ship and it only magnified his other disappointments in life: no children, no money, no sense of worth, and now this most recent incident with George and Buck Taylor had added excessive bulk. The smallest crack in his underside and he would sink violently and immediately to the bottom.

* * *

Morris knew he had to make things right. He was done with disappointing his younger brother, tired of disappointing himself. His imprudent and impulsive actions were always troubling, and carried consequences. It was time for just the two of them, Moe and Crazy George. High noon in the street, only one man would walk away. Morris left his home before sunrise, making no attempt to hide his departure. Whether Mary heard her husband leave was beyond his knowing or caring. He just got in his pickup and drove directly to Crazy George's asylum for the criminally insane.

Turning off his truck and his headlights, he coasted to a stop just a short distance from George's shack. His emotions raw, his patience gone and his desire for revenge overpowering, Morris waited for George in the early morning hours. Impatient, almost mad with the desire for his adversary to leave for work, he took comfort in his jug.

Chapter 20

I t had been another long night with his family. There had been a lot of nights like that for the past few weeks. George sensed a culminating feeling of discord among his family, and it had begun a long time ago with the death Carolyn Waters. Now it had reached a troubling point with the murder of their loyal friend Buck. In the beginning, there had been a muted acceptance of the course their father had chosen to pursue, but now a family mutiny was about to consume them.

Long ago, George was overwhelmed with despair and loneliness. They had built his little shack for him and provided furniture and knickknacks; they would leave their feel-good casseroles on the bench or by his door. But what they could never provide was the inner warmth and stability his family once offered him daily. Now there so many empty days tearing at his soul.

Then the family photographs arrived and found their way to his back wall. With a clarity only George was allowed, his family gradually returned to him. George was frustrated that he could not share them with Buck; if only Buck could have seen them or talked to them like he did, it would have helped validate what others might think bizarre. In the end, he did not care — Buck never passed judgment, and George was among his family again. It was enough for him.

The dynamics of his family had changed. Their assemblies soon became focused on a single purpose. His father had become an angry man, made bitter by his wife's affair with the man who had built their new home. He was enraged by its total destruction with the very first storm to visit the area. Only shoddy workmanship could have caused such an outcome, he insisted. He became steadfast in his demand for a complete and final reckoning.

George was confused and saddened by his mother's infidelity. He tried to understand his father's hurt, but there had to be more to the tragedy. His mother had always been the most loving and supportive person in his life, more so than his father. But George was just as incensed as his father with the destruction of their home and his family. Now they were forced to live out eternity in a bizarre dimension.

Oh, there would be an accounting, George thought, and he took pleasure in their new mission. He saw no issue with his father's constant reviews and reinforcements of their undertaking.

* * *

The unraveling of the goal had begun with the death of Carolyn Waters. His father had insisted on it and George had followed through only after his father had promised his own participation. They had done what their father had ordained, but the family had begun to question their father's motive and tactics.

His mother, shamed by her infidelity, justified as it might have been in her secret thoughts, had allowed her husband to manipulate the truth and therefore her family. George could see that now. Her children knew little of the loveless marriage she had suffered through — how could they? Their shallow father was all they knew, and as much as they loved their mother, they were all horrified by the news of her affair. There had been little time to examine her adultery all those years ago, and she had steadily withdrawn from her

family, confirming her guilt. Then a deadly storm assaulted their fractured family.

* * *

Despondent with what her husband was doing to their family, George's mother chose to be silent no more. Her guilt over the shame and pain her affair brought to her family had caused her to withdraw, but it was time to move past it, especially after her husband had judged and convicted their family friend Buck. Connie's groundless culpability prevented her from protecting her family. She had opposed the whole revenge plot from its very inception and she had made sure her son knew about her opposition soon after the widow Waters was murdered.

"This has become your father's own twisted creation. His own perverse, insecure shortcomings have pushed him down this path of revenge, and he has dragged us along with him."

She told George that his father had never once in his life been a warm or caring husband. She wondered how a man could evolve into such an empty soul. He had been a good father, had never mistreated his wife or his children, was always proud of them around people, but at home the pride never translated into nurturing.

"Your father has concern without caring, fondness without loving, and all for the benefit of strangers. It is all about how he perceives people observing him. It determines how he treats our family and what he demands of us. Your father was and still is a shallow man, in time you will see that, too."

George had listened to his mother, but little of what she said registered. Filled with the same rage as his father and only reinforced with the years of indifference from a community that acknowledged but never accepted him, he stayed his father's course. But now the irrational trip across the bay in a maddening sea, concluding with the sad end of a wretched man's empty existence and the painful death of a good friend, the only friend he ever had, provided him with the clarity and understanding his mother had predicted.

His past actions haunted him, and his killing of Buck maddened him. George lashed out at his father.

"You have taken us down this horrible road!" he said in disgust. "And we have all been fools to your twisted plot. We are all tired of this hatred and we will not be part of it anymore!"

His father was furious with the mutiny. "The journey is not done!" he screamed. "We are so close to the prize, you will not abandon me now. This is all your mother's work. She has finally twisted your thoughts. Remember what she has done to us with her whorish betrayal, remember the home we once lived in. Think about—"

No longer able to tolerate his father's venom, George shouted back at his father. "You are the one who has betrayed us! All this hatred has made you evil, although Mother thinks there was a hint of depravity even before you pushed her away. I think in time we will all understand why Mother strayed from you, and that the storm that destroyed our home and our family was no one's fault. Some say it's all part of God's plan. I'm not so sure I can believe that, but it is definitely not the work of Peter Marrow and his crew. It's insane that you could think it, and shame on you for manipulating all of us. We were all too young to know otherwise."

The hostile exchange continued into the early morning hours. There was no resolution; lines had been drawn, defensive positions were taken behind the barricades. George's father feigned deep hurt with his family's desertion from a noble cause, but with his new-found insight, George saw that his father was more upset that his twisted plan would never be seen through to its evil completion. He despised his father even more. Frustrated and exhausted by the angry dialogue with his father, George surrendered his fight. It would be the first of many angry challenges to his father's twisted scheme. His father and family retreated to their unique world.

George's real world slowly settled back in around him and he sought to reconnect with it. The darkness of a gloomy evening was now gone, replaced by the brightness of a morning well underway. Robins, sparrows, and starlings voiced their collective morning chorus. George was as alive as he had ever been. His spirit floated and his optimism soared. Confronting his father had broken the chains that had kept him a prisoner and had stunted his growth as a human being. A happiness he had never known was now filling his cup, and the dark cloud that was forever hovering over his existence had disappeared. He saw the pain that his mother had endured and he knew he would love her again. He stood before the pictures of his family and saw them all as wonderful, beautiful beings. Their images now only sought out fond and tender moments of long ago. That day, George would begin his task of making things right again. Moving to the kitchen counter, he poured himself a cup of coffee from a pot he had made during the night. Most of its flavor was gone and it was barely warm, but it tasted of a saintly brew. Nothing would temper his elated mood. He glanced up at his kitchen clock and saw that he was about to be late for work. Grabbing his hat and the lunch he had packed the night before, he opened his cabin door and stepped out into a new day—

A red-faced demon instantly stood before him on his porch and in an instant a burning pain took possession of his abdomen. With the blade of a large hunting knife planted in his belly, and dripping with blood, George stood before the figure.

In a brief moment, he felt a suffocating coldness wrap its coils around his heart. He fell to his knees. The crimson liquid leaped from his body in spurts, the knife protruding from his abdomen like a terrible new appendage.

George had been fatally stabbed. And Moe Wheeler had done it.

* * *

Moe reached down and pulled the hunting knife from George's prone form, then held the blade up to his face and turned it from side to side, like a man proud of his trophy and accomplishment. Moe's head and face were flushed red and beads of sweat were everywhere. His eyes bulged wide with rage and he snarled like cornered animal. What few teeth he had were jagged and stained an unnatural brown color from years of tobacco and bourbon.

"You're fucked now!" Morris screamed down at the bloody, unmoving body at his feet, his mouth dribbled with spit.

"You goddamn Hun."

* * *

You goddamn Hun?! What did he just say? He was light-headed and his left leg moved as if made of lead. His thoughts were now scattered. Visions of faceless, ragged soldiers wandering among the filthy trenches of a horrific wasteland floated before him. Morris shook his head violently to erase the painful images. He was instantly back in the moment. George had slumped to the floor and was clutching at his stomach with both hands, barely slowing the blood that ebbed from his body. Morris leaned over him, only inches from George's face and cursed him again.

"Oh, you're fucked real good now, Crazzzzzz…y," said Morris, dragging his name out.

Eyes focused and full of rage, George summoned what little life force he had remaining and let loose a mouth already full with his own blood. He covered Morris's face, neck, and the collar of his work shirt in blood, smiled and whispered, "Rot in hell."

"Let's go visit that special family of yours! You know, the one that only you t-t-alk t-t-o," Morris stuttered, his speech again deserting him. With his left arm now slowed with the same numbness as his leg, he latched on to the collar of George's weathered chamois shirt with his right hand and dragged George's almost lifeless body back into the shack and among the pictures of his family, his head thumping against the floor when Morris released his grip.

His body exhausted and his thoughts bedeviled, Morris released the grip on his beloved Sergeant Connelly. "You r-r-rest n-n-now, Sarge," he whispered.

* * *

233

He had taken care of Sergeant Connelly, but Private Morris Wheeler knew he must return to his position; they were about to be overrun by the Germans. There was gunfire all around him and tarnished bayonets flashed in the sunlight. His left side was now without feeling. He must have been wounded. As much as he wanted to scream in pain or warn his fellow comrades about the invading horde, his speech would not allow it. Morris crawled to his truck and, with a right hand that controlled his destiny, he lifted himself into the cab. With a series of small miracles, he started a vehicle that would bring desperately-needed reinforcements. His chest heaving with complete fatigue and his head crimson-red with anxiety and a stroke that was about to consume him, he drove his pickup straight into the nearest oak tree and he was quickly surrounded by a thousand enemy bayonets, all promising a certain death but only causing pinpricks that tortured and never terminated the delusional abyss he was in. His head trembled, his mouth hung slack and heavy, and drool dribbled from the corners of his mouth. Nothing seemed familiar to him and everywhere he looked, demons moved in on him. Everything and anything terrified him and he was unable to close his eye nor reason that he should. Morris had finally arrived in hell.

* * *

George lay among his family, all but his father gathered at his side. Tenderly stroking her oldest son's hair, his mother told him his time was at hand and they would be together for eternity. They were no longer a fractured family; together they would find peace with God. George's father would never find that peace and had removed himself from his family. There is no place in heaven for a man who endorses hell on earth.

George squeezed his mother's hand and felt her tender kisses on his cheeks. A deep sleep took control of his body and he was now at peace. He would be Crazy no more.

* * *

Mary had heard her husband leave in the early morning after torturous hours of his anxious pacing and loud vocal threats of revenge. Morris had been drinking heavily the whole day and into that evening. Slamming the door behind him, he announced his departure. Every fiber in her body told her that Moe had begun a journey that would reap only ugly consequences.

Dressed in her nightgown and housecoat, Mary sat at her kitchen table for hours, pondering what to do next. The caffeine in her multiple cups of coffee had only stoked her anxiety. Gut instinct told her to go to Brad and Milly's home and she was quickly out the front door and running across the long connecting fields that separated their homes. Her bathrobe and the hem of her nightgown became wet with the cool morning dew.

Now bent over at the waist and with her hands on her knees, she stood at her brother-in-law's front door, out of breath and profoundly frightened. Brad and Milly were early risers and Mary desperately hoped they had already started their day.

She pounded on the entry, she would break the glass pane if she had to. But Milly was soon at the front door. A look of alarm was on her face as she tried to unlock their front door and gather her housecoat at the same time.

"Mary, what's going on?" she anxiously asked. One look at her sister-in-law's face told her that something terrible had happened.

"Oh Milly, where is your husband? I think Moe has done something very bad," she said in between frantic breaths. "Brad needs to stop him right now."

Milly stood stunned with her fingertips to her lips. She was about to say her husband was in the bathroom, but then Brad was in the room with them and was steering Mary toward a living room chair.

"Mary, try to catch your breath, calm down," he said in a rehearsed voice. "Where's Morris?"

"He left in the middle of the night, he was mean drunk, I've seen him like this before, nothing ever good comes of it." She was crying and alarmed. "Oh Milly, I've dragged mud all through your house." Mary looked back at the murky tracks.

"Don't worry about that," Brad said. "Did Moe say where he was going, did he take any weapons with him?"

"I don't know, the .45, if that's what you mean. I hid it away months ago, maybe his hunting knife. I just don't know." She sobbed.

"I think I know where he is. You stay here with Milly for now, just stay away from your house until we know where Morris is."

Brad walked to his bedroom and emerged with his .38 strapped to his waist. Milly was directly by his side and walked her husband to the door. He leaned close to her ear and whispered. "Keep a close ear to the police radio, my gut tells me I will have some disturbing news for Mary and for Chief Anthony." He softly kissed her lips.

* * *

The drive to Crazy George's home seemed to take forever. It was the destination Brad was sure of and he knew tragedy was waiting for him there. Odd how hindsight improves with age. He looked back on it all and the horrible outcome he was about to walk into might have been predicted years ago, certain ingredients, when mixed together, have a secured outcome.

Turning the corner down to George's shack, Brad saw his brother's pickup at an odd angle to the narrow road. Steam rose from under the hood. With his senses now raised to a new level, Brad stopped his truck and chose to walk the rest of the way. Removing his revolver from its holster seemed the prudent thing to do, and as Brad moved closer he could see the left front fender crushed against a sturdy oak, and the back of Moe's head visible through the rear window, unmoving. The engine was still running but struggling with its radiator destroyed.

Brad turned to face his brother and the sight before him took his breath away.

"Oh, Moe," he whispered. "What have you done to yourself?"

Morris sat slouched in his seat, his head still upright. Lifeless, bloodshot eyes stared through a crimson mask of dried blood. With his lower jaw limp, he had drooled down his chin and soaked his tee-shirt at the collar. His chest rose and retreated in short quick movements, the air in his throat gurgled with phlegm and emitted a soft whistling sound with each shortened exhalation. There was no other measure that would have told Brad his brother might be alive. He moved his left hand back and forth in front his brother's eyes. They never blinked, never moved, only stared straight ahead.

"I hope you're finally at peace, wherever you are, my brother," Brad whispered again. He reached over and turned the key. The engine coughed and shuttered to an abrupt stop. The sound of a hissing radiator and the crackle of a motor about to seize were all that remained to validate a dying man's last moments. As if waiting for the quiet peacefulness of the island to wrap him in its arms, Morris took his last breath and softly exhaled. His journey was over. Brad reached in and folded his brother's hands in his lap and tenderly patted them. He turned and walked to the cabin, knowing full well another gruesome discovery awaited him. His gait was slow and measured; he felt like a country doctor about to enter a home festering with smallpox.

* * *

Like a bright red welcome mat, a large swath of blood greeted his first step onto the splintered front porch, and two prominent trails directed him farther into the house. It was obvious a body had been dragged through the blood and into the shack. No blessing would be at the end of this dark trail. Gun raised, Brad tiptoed his way around the cherry-red stain. Off to his left, lying in a pool of blood, was the body of George Caswell. A deep wound was in the middle of his stomach and it was clear that George's life had streamed from it.

Standing over George's body, he re-holstered his .38. Brad knew the final sad event would be the closing chapter of a terrible narrative years in the making. The memories came flooding back and

Brad sought to hold them at bay. He tried to study the crime scene as a detective should. The trail of blood, where the body had been dragged, the bloody footprints, probably his brother's. The blood dried in several spots, maybe a time of death could be determined, but the memories began to overpower him and Brad knew he must surrender to them.

* * *

A frightened teenage boy, suddenly stripped of his family in a devastating hurricane, flashed before him. Long ago, sitting in his living room, wet, shivering, wrapped in a blanket. His eyes red from the endless tears he had shed for his lost family. Brad's wife next to the young man, trying desperately to comfort him, and his good friend Buck standing next to him, also trying his best to console. A sad event and even bitter now. The hastily-constructed shack in a place where George was banished for the simple act of surviving, and then the cruelest treatment of all. They began to call him crazy. At first as a collective diagnosis and then sadly as part of his surname.

All the nutrients for a bitter teenage boy to grow into an angry man were placed around his footing. No one should have been surprised by the path he took and the outcome now visited on them. Hindsight was again providing its usual clarity and Brad despised it. He should have done more for the poor boy, they all should have.

The images of the victims of the twisted plot, one that Brad would never really understand, floated before him. Ted Esau, Tom Tuttle, Carolyn Waters, Dave Brooks, and now, mixed in, the cruel bloody images of George Caswell and Morris Wheeler.

The scene was consuming, and Brad took a slow small step back, removed his hat, and offered a deep sigh. He turned and looked at the Caswell family, all attached to their spots on their shared intimate wall. They all looked down on him. He wondered if they had witnessed the horrific scene.

"Oh my lord, how did it come to this?" he asked them.

The damaged frame that held the picture of George's mother precipitously rocked on its hinge and then crashed to the floor, shattering its wooden frame and scattering glass across the room. Brad twitched in his stance, as if jabbed with a pin, his eyes focusing on the tattered image of Connie Caswell as it floated to the side of her murdered son's body.

"Take him home, Mrs. Caswell," Brad said, as he stood numb with disbelief. He knew it was time to contact Portsmouth, time to treat this like the crime scene it was. He slowly walked to the door, once more steering clear of the blood evidence. Stopping at the door and turning to face the Caswell family, he said quietly, "I'll leave you for now, but I'll have to come back pretty quick."

And then, "I'm so sorry for the way we treated George, he was never Crazy."

Chapter 21

Morris was buried in a small grove of white pine trees. Mary wanted a place where his grave was always sheltered from the sun year-round. Daylight was the most trying time for her husband. Each day he would venture out, shaking and screaming on the inside from a wound that would never heal and few could ever comprehend. Sadly, the only relief was his sour mash, and he struggled daily against its control over him.

Brad had pleaded with Mary for a simple granite marker for his brother's grave. He would pay for it, it was the least he could do. In the end, she gave in to his demands, but insisted he be buried where that headstone was never visible. She would not live the rest of her live having to look at his gravestone daily. There were too many painful memories, too close to the surface. She could visit him when she felt the need. She rarely did.

* * *

The island had once again come together for a Caswell funeral. It would be their last. A service was held at the Union Church on Pier Road and the pews were full. They asked Brad to give a small eulogy; no one else wanted that uncomfortable task. Brad gave in to their pleading and, standing before a gathering of hypocrites, he wanted to tell them that they had all contributed to George's death with their indifference, but instead asked them to think fondly of George and to embrace his legacy, simple as it might have been. No one shed a tear. On a chilly evening in late October, Brad scattered George's ashes to the wind at the stone wharf on the west side. It was the one place where George had always found peace.

The acts of revenge and retribution were completed, lives had been taken and others severely damaged. A dark history had been written and mysteries with no real answers had been planted. There would be those who, throughout the ages, would have their theories and philosophies on why there had been those tragic deaths, and whose hand had brought about their demise. Chief Anthony from Portsmouth, with assistance from the Rhode Island State Police crime lab, had done due diligence and had offered an official report with no concrete finding, just more theory, but with a town and state seal to make it look more plausible. Even Peter Marrow had finally escaped a death he seemed convinced of. Dodging a curse that many thought was inevitable had allowed him to thrive again. Peter and Lillian's marriage slowly began to heal itself.

Officially and privately, they all believed that George Caswell and Buck Taylor had orchestrated the long, drawn-out, twisted plot. But they couldn't prove a thing. Perhaps somewhere, George and Buck were smiling.

Epilogue

rad Wheeler retired in the fall of 1970. His beloved Milly suffered a fatal heart attack three years later and left him all alone. Complaining for several weeks of shortness of breath and a nagging sporadic tingling feeling in her left arm, Milly had ignored her husband's urging to see a doctor and refused to alter her lifestyle. She had been weeding her garden most of that morning and it had been an unusually warm day. Lying on the ground with her straw sunhat on and its yellow ribbon still tied beneath her chin, Brad discovered her body when he returned home from a morning fishing trip. She appeared to be napping. A bouquet of yellowr snapdragons laid only inches from her right hand. Terrified to touch his bride, fearing but knowing the outcome, he tenderly nudged her shoulder. "Milly," he said softly, hoping she heard him in another plane. She was only 66, much too early for the both of them. With a simple funeral and a private burial, in a field spotted with wild honeysuckle, Brad said goodbye to his soul mate.

With his brother dead, his sister-in-law returned to her native Attleboro, and his beautiful Milly now absent from his life, Brad Wheeler was alone and lonely. His days were empty, and he ventured out less and less. Brad and Mildred had walked through life together and now there would be no one to share a stunning sunset with, no one's cold feet in the night, none of the little things that validate a close marriage. Brad no longer wanted to suffer in silence and isolation. His roots severed and atrophying, he knew it was time to leave. He said goodbye to those he had friendships with, sold their home, tied up the loose ends and moved into the Red Maples Retirement Home in Newport, Rhode Island.

He was in the wine room, that's what that they called the game room at the Red Maples retirement center. It was a perfect day in early September, and a cool breeze out of the northwest had chased away the heavy tropical air. It had been oppressive those past few days. But that's how a hurricane functions, pushing the hot steamy air well ahead of its course. Hurricane Belle had rampaged up the eastern shoreline. Every community ahead of its projected path had hunkered down and was as ready as they could be, but the storm fell apart as it approached Long Island and lost most of its tenacity when it moved across that narrow isthmus.

A few boats had been torn away from their moorings, there was high water in all the low places, and numerous trees, probably old or weakened with disease, had sacrificed themselves to the cause that folks would have an event to connect to that storm for the rest of their lives. But there had been few minor injuries and no deaths. Brad was grateful for that; hurricanes had always meant death in his world.

He sat among his retirees, reading the morning paper, a soft smile on his face the only indication of the appreciative relief he was feeling on the inside.

He looked out onto the rear patio; some of the folks had taken their coffee with them and sat in the warm morning sun. Japanese maples offered their imported shade and a morning dew still sparkled in the sunlight.

A stranger stepped in the path of his pleasing grandeur.

"Hello, Brad, it's been a while. I wonder if you remember me? It's Bill Anthony, Portsmouth Police," said the large stranger. He extended his hand.

Hesitating only seconds, Brad finally recognized the man before him, "Well, I sure do, Bill, didn't recognize you for a couple of seconds, not seeing you in your uniform threw me off a bit. How are you?"

"I'm doing just fine. I retired about twelve years ago, haven't worn the uniform in a long time. How you doing? How do you like living here?"

"I'm doing fine. I like it here, they take good care of me. Food's pretty good, they make the bed every day and I get clean sheets once a week. You know, three hots and a cot. I come and go as I please."

"Sounds good. The wife and I should check this place out, maybe it's something that'll work for us. Mind if I sit down?" He pulled a nearby chair alongside Brad's. He removed his Portsmouth Auxiliary Police cap from his head. What little hair remained had turned a soft gray. His once broad, barreled chest had migrated south to his mid-section.

"Need to talk to you about something that has us all scratching our heads at the station. Normally I don't get involved with the day to day, but the new chief asked me to pay you a visit, since we had worked together a lot in the past."

"Figured this had something to do with the business of being a cop."

"Listen, Brad. Hurricane Agnes has come and gone as you already know, really wasn't much of a thing. But a body did wash up in Potter's Cove on Prudence yesterday morning and it was—" he hesitated, looked directly at Brad, "it was Peter Marrow."

Time suddenly stopped. A hurricane, a dead body washed ashore, and now it was Peter Marrow. Brad Wheeler was numb. How many times had this scenario played itself out? He sucked in a long breath through puckered lips. He twisted his head and looked at Chief Anthony from the corners of his eyes. His voice low and lifeless.

"Suicide?" he asked.

"Don't think so, Brad." He hesitated again. "Had his hands tied behind his back."

About the Author

orn in Providence, Rhode Island, and a lifelong summer resident of Prudence Island, K. W. Garlick is the beneficiary of a rich and varied professional background, from marine tradesman to educator to commercial contractor.

Ken finally realized his enduring passion for writing and recently published his nationally recognized and locally acclaimed *Call Me Madame Alice.*

He, his wife, and two sons currently live in North Attleboro, Massachusetts

Member: Association of Rhode Island Authors

Other novels by
KW Garlick

CALL ME MADAME ALICE

"CALL ME MADAME ALICE is a tale told on a perfectly etched landscape featuring a wondrous mix of tones both dark and vibrant. K.W. Garlick serves up a beautifully balanced meshing of the normal and paranormal in fashioning a tale epic-like in its sprawl and deeply disciplined in its conviction. Think Caleb Carr or E.L. Doctorow ably mixed with Stephen King at his most subtle. Both historical and prescient, timely and traditional, *Call Me Madame Alice* is a 20-carat gem of a book, the value of which increases with the turn of every single page."

~Jon Land, USA Today bestselling author

Made in the USA
Columbia, SC
19 November 2017